THURSDAY'S STORM

THURSDAY'S STORM

THE AUGUST GALE OF 1927

DARRELL DUKE

FLANKER PRESS LIMITED

ST. JOHN'S

Library and Archives Canada Cataloguing in Publication

Duke, Darrell, 1970-, author
    Thursday's storm : the August gale of 1927 / Darrell
Duke.

Issued in print and electronic formats.
ISBN 978-1-77117-274-5 (pbk.).--ISBN 978-1-77117-275-2
(epub).--ISBN 978-1-77117-276-9 (kindle).--ISBN 978-1-77117-277-6
(pdf)

    1. Windstorms--Newfoundland and Labrador--Placentia
Bay--History--20th century. 2. Shipwrecks--Newfoundland and
Labrador--Placentia Bay--History--20th century. 3. Placentia
Bay (N.L.)--History--20th century. I. Title.

FC2199.P53Z64 2013   971.8'02   C2013-904655-0
                                                C2013-904656-9

© 2013 by Darrell Duke

PRINTED IN CANADA

MIX
Paper from
responsible sources
FSC® C103567

This paper has been certified to meet the environmental and social standards of the Forest Stewardship Council® (FSC®) and comes from responsibly managed forests, and verified recycled sources.

Cover design by Adam Freake   Edited by Paul Butler

FLANKER PRESS LTD. PO BOX 2522, STATION C ST. JOHN'S, NL CANADA
TELEPHONE: (709) 739-4477   FAX: (709) 739-4420   TOLL-FREE: 1-866-739-4420
WWW.FLANKERPRESS.COM

9 8 7 6 5 4 3 2

Canada

Canada Council   Conseil des Arts
for the Arts   du Canada

Newfoundland
Labrador

We acknowledge the financial support of the Government of Canada through the Book Publishing Industry Development Program (BPIDP) for our publishing activities; the Canada Council for the Arts, which last year invested $157 million to bring the arts to Canadians throughout the country; the Government of Newfoundland and Labrador, Department of Tourism, Culture and Recreation.

This book is dedicated to the men who lost their lives with the fishing schooner *Annie Healy*, and their families who carried on in the hardest of times.

CONTENTS

Preface ix

PART I

Chapter One *The Foleys* 1

Chapter Two *Annie Healy* 18

Chapter Three *The Healys* 31

Chapter Four *The Mullins Family* 48

Chapter Five *The Bruces* 64

Chapter Six *Liz Bruce's Living Nightmare* 77

Chapter Seven *The Kellys* 88

Chapter Eight *The Midwife and Bridge King* 98

Chapter Nine *The Sampsons* 104

Chapter Ten *Uncle Watt* 117

Photos 131

PART II

Chapter Eleven *Leaving Home* 147

Chapter Twelve *At Sea* 154

Chapter Thirteen *August 25, 1927 Thursday's Storm* 166

Chapter Fourteen *The Storm At Home* 178

Chapter Fifteen *Southeast of Merasheen Bank*
     11:00 a.m., August 25, 1927 184

Chapter Sixteen *Argentia, 2:00 p.m.* 187

Chapter Seventeen *The Bad News* 191

Chapter Eighteen *Friday, August 26, 1927*
     From the Crow Hill 202

Chapter Nineteen *Friday, August 26, 1927*
     More News—Better off Buried—Letters 212

Chapter Twenty *Sunday, August 28, 1927*
     Poor Hearts Broken 226

Epilogue 239

Acknowledgements 245

PREFACE

Twenty years ago, in August 1993, I was standing in the seldom-used front room of my great-aunt Bernadette Murray's home in Fox Harbour, Placentia Bay, Newfoundland. Aunt Nettin, she was known to us. I remember days and nights, years before, when she smiled more, especially in the company of her sister and best friend, Laura, my grandmother. Nanny, we called her.

Aunt Nettin and Nanny were seven years apart in age but shared the same birthday, August 23. Other anniversaries fell in the wake of their special day. Their only brother, Gus, died on August 25, 1924. Aunt Nettin was just seven, and Nanny, fourteen. Both were grown women in those times, sharing endless chores under their mother's care.

Their father, John Foley, was known as Jack Fowlou in Fox Harbour; Fowlou was the English bastardization of the Gaelic surname *Ó Foghladha*, "descendant of *Foghlaidh*," meaning marauder, or someone engaged in banditry, but I imagine that such a family occupation ended many years before, in Ireland, as Jack was laid-back, seldom expressing his opinion, if he bothered to have one at all. Like most men and women, he was tired, old before his time, and, like every man, had to fish for a living. The chores once shared with his only son were now his own. He had nothing and owed everything. He was no different than any other man in Newfoundland—save many merchants, perhaps, and priests furnished and fattened by the Vatican.

Jack worked for a local merchant family, the Healys, from a schooner named *Annie Healy*, also known as the *Big Annie*. Three of his cousins—Charlie Sampson, and stepbrothers John and Patrick Mullins—were fellow crew members on the *Big Annie*. In a small town and on a big sea, all crew members were close, out of necessity, if nothing else. So, being a relative afforded no special considerations for the other. They needed one another to make it to the next day. If only one man had a stick of tobacco, he shared with the rest. The same went for a drink of moonshine or the rare bottle of smuggled rum. All were sons or grandsons of Irish immigrants who found their way to Fox Harbour, mostly by way of "Yankee Bankers"—ships sent to Newfoundland by fishing merchants from the eastern seaboard of the United States, Massachusetts, mostly to collect herring, squid, and mackerel for bait. Others had relatives already settled in the area, who came as servants and fishermen of English merchants and planters.

The quaintness of Fox Harbour—which had originally been named Little Gloucester by those first settlers in the late 1700s—The Sound, nearby Marquise, and Little Placentia (renamed Argentia), made never returning to the overcrowded shores of "The States" an easy decision. But the life of fishing and farming in those times of rampant and then-incurable diseases such as tuberculosis (consumption), diphtheria, pleurisy, and the common cold, among others, took its toll on every family until well into the mid-twentieth century. They all had harsh stories to tell, and the sharing of those and other tales was an anticipated art form and entertainment in the absence of radio, television, and the variations of computer-based technology available today.

The schooner *Annie Healy* gained the title *Big Annie* after record numbers of fish caught in 1909, and while she had little to boast about, before or since, the prestigious designation remained. But the *Big Annie* was no match for a hurricane that struck Placentia Bay on the morning of Thursday, August 25, 1927.

While I'd noticed the framed photo of a sad-looking man on Aunt Nettin's front room wall most of my life, I'd never asked about it until that lovely summer's day in 1993. With much hesitation, accompanied by red, welling eyes, Aunt Nettin said, "That was my father." Without her dear sister, Laura, by her side to share the heavy details of a buried past, she told her version of the tale.

It was too much to digest at once. A week later I moved to Manitoba. There I wrote "The Annie Healy," a song largely based on Aunt Nettin's account. But rather than leave it at that, I went on a quest which lasted almost two decades: writing, calling, meeting, getting to know, and doing my best to non-invasively pry lips that had been pressed together tightly for sixty-six years. The unearthing of these and related memories and subsequent feelings inevitably unleashed torrents of tears (from both parties), along with questions they were never allowed to ask as curious but hushed, heartbroken children.

It was heavy stuff: sitting across tables from gigantic men whose hands were like catcher's mitts, whose shoulders had borne three-

and four-hundred-pound barrels; watching them bawl like babies as they peered right through me. Sometimes those big mitts clasped over my weak artist's hands as I kept one eye on the nearest exit. But I never attempted to leave. Friendships spawned that lasted till these old men and women died. Others couldn't have cared less if they ever laid eyes on me again, I'd upset them that much.

A son of a lost *Annie Healy* crew member used to appear in my driveway, blowing the horn of his truck. I'd go out, get in, and he'd hand me papers he'd dug up, or tell me other memories he'd forgotten, saying how he hadn't been able to rest much since I last visited him.

Unknowingly I searched not only for information but also for love, the kind of love only an old person could give, the kind of love I lost when my grandparents died almost twenty years before. I found beauty seemingly lost on my generation and, in return, received silent love and respect in their nods, smiles, even their unsettled tears. A void had been filled. Now I had a book to write.

The song had won first-place nods in myriad insignificant competitions across the country. In the summer of 1997, it made its way to a recording studio as part of an audio cassette designed by a cousin, John Whiffen, to help raise money to restore the facade of the church at Fox Harbour. The song's original lyrics contained a misnaming of one of the crew members; this information was provided before I had the opportunity to sit with a daughter of the man, who quite promptly and nicely corrected my mistake. In 2001 the song was transcribed to musical notation by a good friend, Darryl Collins, and then performed by twelve-year-old Amy Wilson, backed on guitar by her uncle, Chris Newhook, in a Kiwanis

Festival where the song placed first, defeating the usual catalogue of traditional Newfoundland and Irish music entries.

After a few months spent talking with some children of the lost crew, there was too much good information to wait for a book, so I spent eight months writing a play and called it *Thursday's Storm—The Annie Healy Story*. I was fortunate enough. The timing was just right to inspire enough volunteers to fill the roles of characters for the stage. At the time, I operated a former movie theatre on the old base at Argentia that once entertained American service people and their families and friends with movies shipped from New York. It had a big stage and the room was completely acoustic-tiled, ceiling and all, and was perfect for re-enacting events of the past through live theatre. I'd also been privileged to be interviewed by CBC Radio One, Toronto, for their series the Great Canadian Story Engine and wasted no time spewing details I'd learned of the schooner and her crew's tale, and the great impact it had not only upon the immediate families but the entire community. So, by the time the play was ready for production and its fitting debut at the old hall at Fox Harbour, I'd done radio interviews with CBC, both locally and nationally, plus received good coverage from the local newspaper, the *Charter*. More than 160 people squeezed into the small hall to see amateur but highly enthused actors (including myself) take the stage by storm. The play ended with the very pregnant wife of lost crew member Jim King, Bridget (Bridge), performed by Amy Smith, rocking in her chair, in candlelight, having just made a monumental pact with the local priest regarding her children in the wake of her husband's death. A ship's bell rang once after each of the crew's names was called, while Stan Rogers's heart-rending version of Otto Kelland's

"Let Me Fish Off Cape St. Mary's" provided an audio background to the roll call. Surviving children of the lost crew sitting in the front row, including Aunt Nettin, did little to hide their tears, and they quickly exited the building when the show ended. Back to their old homes they went to digest the fact they'd just been portrayed by strangers and in an event that until that evening had been among the most privately guarded occurrences of their long lives.

Several generations of the crew's relatives expressed their gratefulness for learning of the individual stories, character traits, and events that, in ways, may have shaped their own lives.

Following the tragedy in 1927, the collective grief of the community was so intense it became something not to be talked about in the presence of children. This silencing inevitably led to many assumptions discussed in private that eventually made their way to local legend. But, according to the children of the lost men, no one really knew what happened. And because no one really knew, perhaps it wasn't worth discussing. All of these things make up the story of the *Annie Healy*, and all we, the readers, can do is accept what these unearthed memories have to offer.

A lady, in the middle of a complete breakdown of sobbing tears, whose father was lost with my great-grandfather, thanked me for bringing those memories back. She felt better, she said, after having them locked away since the age of eleven. And there she was, almost ninety. I wrote down or audio-recorded every memory and the lines spoken between her parents the last time they talked to one another. Those words, and the words and memories of other children of the lost crew, are written here to the letter. Sadly, critics have shunned those words and phrases as "parodies of Newfoundland speech." However, there is neither room nor call for embellishment when what is important is that the vernacular of our ancestors be presented as they spoke it. These efforts are paramount in helping preserve yet another disappearing aspect of the Newfoundland people: our language. We should embrace these words and sayings with all their original wit and pass them on to our children with pride. We should do so without the mysterious shame so prevalent today.

That same lady reluctantly came to see the play. Sitting in the front row, armed with tissues galore, she watched a young girl onstage portray her as she was when her daddy was lost—the part where she overheard men talking about the storm and the ship with her daddy aboard. According to audience members, one of the most moving moments of the play was when her great-uncle brought news of the schooner's demise to the kitchen of her parents' home. The collective display of shock and grief led by her mother's pleas for a better ending to her husband's life immediately followed. It was too much, and at that moment I fretted; what had I done? I stood to the side of the stage, watching my new, old friend doubled over in her seat, her son comforting her. Her own nightmare was replaying, and she pleaded, "No!" through frantic cries, as if she were that little girl all over again. I wanted to end the show, but having learned it was always hardest to do the right thing, I reluctantly let it end naturally. When the play finished she clapped, smiling through tears. She hugged me like I was one of her own and thanked me again. She meant it. The cast and crew soon surrounded her, offering their appreciation for her open heart—for having the courage to sit through the performance.

It was the men, mostly, who didn't go to the play's debut in the old Fox Harbour hall. One called later to say he was on his way and got sick. I wasn't surprised. The others simply didn't want to relive it. Who could blame them?

Following the national exposure provided by CBC Radio's the Great Canadian Story Engine, CBC Radio One, Toronto, picked up the story, integrating it with a program feature on "Perfect Storms," coupling it with details and imagery from the then-new Hollywood movie *The Perfect Storm*. CBC Radio NL also attended the debut and interviewed some of the surviving children on their way out the door, along with offspring of Annie Healy herself. From a tale of much death, the story now had new life. And some of those silent, sad folks were now celebrities, whether they liked it or not.

The following year the play was awarded the annual Cultural Heritage Award from the Placentia Historical Society for the preserving of local history. Board members of the Argentia Management Authority, responsible for a newly created walking trail in the area, decided it was important to have an Annie Healy Lookout, a peaceful spot overlooking the sea surrounding Fox Harbour and Argentia where the *Big Annie* last sailed. Citizens of Fox Harbour, too, made sure the schooner and her lost crew wouldn't be forgotten, erecting a storyboard monument and holding a special ceremony in honour of the lost men at the water's edge, as well as collecting memorabilia from the crew's families for display at their quaint museum.

Like their parents before them, the busy adult lives of the lost crew's children didn't offer enough "spare" time to try and piece it all together. Now they were old, exhausted, and, mostly, without the ability to express themselves—not to mention a bit cynical and weary of a nervous young man asking too many questions. And he not even from Fox Harbour! The latter fact alone was obstacle enough.

Luckily or not, my grandfather, (Poppy) Jimmy Houlihan, taught school there for fourteen years, and he lived there a further twenty-five years while working across The Reach at Argentia. He met Laura just after her Dad, Jack Foley, was lost with the *Big Annie* and crew. Jimmy's father was a well-respected, well-to-do businessman, fisherman (he was really a rum-runner), and politician who afforded Jimmy a college education *and* a radio—something no one else in Fox Harbour owned at the time. Awaiting word of the missing crew and other news of the storm consumed all ears in the company of Jimmy and his radio, then boarding at the home of Dan and Agnes McCue. His introduction to the community was a good one, and he soon won Laura's heart. His love of song, poetry, and storytelling would do wonders in mending her hurt then and in the hard years yet to come.

While some of my interviewees hated his strict way of running the one-room school, others thought Poppy was the best thing they ever had. Some of the undecided folks he'd eventually win over with his passion for sports, introducing basketball, softball, and soccer, and forming teams whose roots and some then-future players, and their children, are now embedded in Newfoundland sports history. He was also instrumental in helping form the town's co-op store. These and other examples of Poppy's devotion to his new community did wonders in getting me, the writer, inside doors to ask questions about the *Annie Healy* tragedy, while others had little time for a big shot, or "educated person." I, too, received my official designation as a big shot when I called and asked for "Mister" So-and-So, complete with a please and thank you. "Who is it?" he called out from the background. "I don't know," she said, disgusted. "Some big shot!"

Furthermore, Jimmy Houlihan's ties to this Fox Harbour tragedy went beyond his radio and marriage to a lost crew member's daughter. During teacher training at St. Bon's College, St. John's, in the 1920s, he was good friends and teammates with Tom Furlong, a son of the to-be-lost schooner's namesake, Annie Healy Furlong. She was childhood friends with most of the schooner's crew, and while she'd been living in the city for eighteen years prior to the schooner's end in 1927, she visited Fox Harbour with her children as often as time permitted. It was still home. Her life, too, would never be the same. All in all, the fact Jimmy Houlihan and Tom Furlong were buddies in the 1920s was a shoo-in to that side of the family. Without that connection, obtaining the information I did from that vital side of the story may never have happened.

So, that covered the land side of the story. Now, in order to properly recreate the storm-at-sea portion of the tale, I needed at least one person with such experience. Luckily for the story's sake, I had the great fortune of meeting and befriending Captain John Russell, formerly of Tickle Cove, Bonavista Bay South, and lastly of Bonavista proper. Captain Russell spent most of his long life at sea, and he had experienced all elements of that great force of nature, coupled with wind, rain, sleet, and snow. Like the crew of the *Annie Healy*, Captain Russell had experienced a hurricane while fishing off Cape St. Mary's. But unlike the *Annie Healy* crew, he and his crew survived, albeit not until after a long, hard, two-day battle, where his schooner was left almost derelict and was carried sixty or more miles away by heavy currents and gale-force winds. The storm scene depicted in this story was co-written by Captain Russell, and the acute attention to detail came only from his experiences and sharp memory. He'd been there, and without him this story would lack the action and probable traumatic familiarity the crew endured during the storm. Captain Russell remained my best friend until his death in 2012. He was 105 years and five months old.

This is not a history of Fox Harbour. It is the story of the lost crew of the fishing schooner *Annie Healy*, as told to me by some of the children and grandchildren of the crew, along with others associated with Fox Harbour, Placentia Bay, in the summer of 1927.

PART I

FOX HARBOUR, PLACENTIA BAY,
NEWFOUNDLAND

TUESDAY, AUGUST 16, 1927

CHAPTER ONE

The Foleys

Last week Jack Foley said he's never going handy to a boat again. He's scarcely stopped saying it since. He'd been fishing for the Healy merchants of Fox Harbour since he was a boy. First for old Richard. Now for Jim and Mike, Richard's sons.

"Enough of the sea," he says, his voice hardly ever rising above a whisper. "What do I ever get out of it, anyway? Poor knees an' a bad back."

"And don't forget the list of things we owes the Healys for," says Lize, Jack's wife, her usual response to the same old complaints she's been putting up with for the past six days. "And it gettin' neither bit smaller, either, that list."

"'Tis not enough fish left in Placentia Bay to pay for it all. 'Tis not like I'm able to go off to the States like the young crowd 'round here. What odds about it now," he grumbles, banging his pipe hard on the table.

The sound always grates on Lize's nerves.

"Saints preserve us," she says, facing the stove and rolling her eyes.

She flips the flattened dough frying on the stovetop. "Ah, Jack, b'y, keep your gob shut, will ya? You have me all sharoused!"

"And what in the name of God is an old man like me still doing out in a boat, anyway?" he starts again, paying no heed. "I'm not able to work till all hours of the night, like I could one time. Ah, the company I'm liable to miss. But never the cursed sea."

"Mind your mouth, b'y!" she scorns. "You're neither a hurt nor a service to them men, I know."

Lize waits in aggravation for a wisecrack or at least for the clumping of Jack's big boots traipsing across the floor and out the door. But she doesn't get either. She sits back in her rocker and picks up her knitting.

"At least Gus never died at sea," Jack moans like it's the first time he's said it today.

Lize agrees with a nod of her head, quickly forgetting the argument. She leans out from her rocker and stretches her long neck to see in around the doorway of the hall, where Gus's picture hangs. Too disarmed for the moment to offer a brazen remark, she closes her eyes and mumbles a quick prayer for their dead son.

"You're good for nothing, Jack!" she mutters under her breath at last, eyes still closed, sick of looking at him.

She's trying again to have the kitchen to herself, but her words aren't loud enough for Jack to hear over the swiping of the axe blade. He's making shavings from the handful of splits he's thrown on the floor alongside the stove.

"Spare them 'long now, Lize," he says of the kindling.

"Yeah!" she says sarcastically, as if she's witnessing his saving the world from eternal damnation. "Don't know what we'd do wit'out ya," she slurs.

Her lips pressed tightly together, she says nothing else, only "mmm," allowing her attention to fall peacefully into each stitch of the sock half made in her bony hands.

Jack pays little mind to Lize's insults. He knows he'll never be the man he once was. She has a right to complain when he's laid up with his bad back on the daybed half the time and she with so much to do. At the best of times, though, Lize doesn't need much of an excuse to call Jack good for nothing. It's as if she's practising for the times ahead when she won't be in a good way and there'll be no one around to take the brunt of her frustrations.

Jack is an easy target for his wife, hardly ever responding to her attempts to get him going. This makes her worse. Although this badness of hers never makes its way into the confession box, part of her daily prayers include little requests for forgiveness. Silently, she acknowledges how hard life might be without him. But she's hardly going to say the like of that to him, afraid he might get above himself.

Jack sees Lize's mad face—the eyebrows drawn tightly together and the pursed lips. He holds his breath and reaches past her to the long sideboard, the one from Lize's father's house, here for the past twenty years since the old man died. Jack grabs his pipe and tobacco, doing his best to avoid the look of the devil in his wife's eyes, as she temporarily halts her knitting. He prepares for a long afternoon out of the house.

Out in the shed Jack turns sideways to get through the mess of wood and tools and junk he's brought home over the years, mostly things off wrecked schooners for which he may never have any use.

He gets somewhat comfortable on his cot made of brin bags and last year's hay. Every so often he gets up and stands to the bench, knowing Lize is making frequent trips to the kitchen window ensuring he's busy at something, mending this or that.

Most of Jack's fifty-seven years have been used up at sea. The time between trips to sea and in over the hills for wood have been spent here in Fox Harbour, where he and Lize were born, and the only place they've ever lived. Little mind is paid to what goes on outside their lives locally, much less to the outside world. They hear bits and pieces of news from their daughters in the States, but that's it. The big story these days, according to their girls, is the airplane *Pride of Detroit*, scheduled to be the first to take flight from the new airstrip in Harbour Grace, Newfoundland, on the twenty-seventh of August.

Every family in Fox Harbour has at least one good story, their own, the one that's better than anyone else's. And all are far superior to some foolish tale of machinery traversing the skies like a bird.

"How in the name of God do a piece of metal fly in the sky when an anchor that two men are able to handle can keep a forty-ton boat in the one place? That's what I'd like to know. All foolishness, if ya ask me," Jack says to himself, glad Lize isn't there to say no one asked for his opinion.

He thinks back to the spring, that time out in the boat when they saw the red light in the sky and the sound of a thousand make-and-break engines filled the air and all around the water. Like the rest of the crew there that night, he's content to believe, yes, indeed, it was the Devil himself. What else could it have been?

Neither Jack nor Lize could care less about an airplane, but they suppose it's all right to mention it to a few people when they ask how their daughters are getting on, living away and taking the time to write of it in their letters.

"Everyone from here has someone in the States, don't they," Lize says, paying no mind to the airplane story.

Jack appears from behind the *Daily News* at the kitchen table, nodding in agreement. He's glad to be in out of the shed.

Lize's face relaxes again, and Jack sees vague traces of the fine-looking woman she once was. They hate bickering over foolishness, things that seem to take up so much of their time, and the things they always end up agreeing they have no control over.

"Yes, girl. God knows we're not the only ones left here to fend for ourselves, Lize, girl," Jack says, grabbing her from her rocker and dancing her around three times while humming a made-up tune.

"Go on, b'y, will ya, ya auld fool," she says, pretending to want to get clear of him.

"'Twill soon be time to have a crowd over again for a time, to put a few more scuff marks on me floor," she says, out of breath and back in her chair.

A meek smile skims the deep lines around her mouth.

"Perhaps next week, when I gets . . ." Jack stops and rattles the paper.

"When ya gets back from fishin', 'tis what I knows you were gonna say, Jack Fowlou!" Lize is satisfied. "Coddin' me barefaced, now, is all you're at all week."

Jack says nothing. He's surprised to see an article about the many Newfoundlanders who've taken up residence in the States.

"Would ya listen to this?" he says, ignoring her taunting at the truth.

> *Young men and women alike from all ends of the island have been taking the train to St. John's and catching passage on steamships traversing the eastern seaboard to Ellis Island and Boston, mainly, in a mad exodus for the past ten years. There, men continue to fish, and for the first time in their lives have the option to seek a berth on more than one or two vessels, and a chance to make money. Others work for the railroad while some climb hundreds of feet into the sky early every morning to put up high-rise buildings, held by nothing more than the pledge of another day's work tomorrow, and better yet one they don't have to do on weekends.*

"A steel beam, now, on a concrete foundation—not much contest for a swaying schooner mast on a bottomless movin' sea," Jack reassures Lize. He tosses and shakes his head, wondering what will ever become of the world; it's all changing so fast.

He thinks back to when he was eighteen, when the railway finally made its way in from Whitbourne to the Jersey side of Placentia; no longer did they have to spend weeks scrounging passage on a ship bound for St. John's to see if supplies could be had any cheaper. But it was never the case, anyway, cheaper prices, and he supposes much of his life was a waste of time. No sense in looking back, he always says. He's about to bring up the stupidity of the men flying the airplane again, but he can't be bothered.

"Lot of young girls from here finds work as maids. Domestic servants, they calls themselves," Lize says, again staying clear of Jack's most recent ramble.

"Yes, an' some gets married and does the same work for free," he laughs.

"Don't be talkin'!" Lize mutters, turning over a big flapjack on top of the stove. "Anyhow, Jack, b'y, everyone knows ya got to fish to keep alive."

Jack sits quietly at the table, waiting for his share of the fried dough. Quitting fishing only exists in theory, but he feels he has a right to complain, with the way the poor fishery has been the past number of years.

Lize, too, knows this fancy will soon pass. She can handle the bit of complaining, no problem. She's not bad at it herself, according to Jack.

They're no different than any other couple around, clinging to the good times and fighting to scrape away the bad. As Catholics, Jack says God is responsible for the works, so what's the use in worrying? But he only says that.

Each year's seasons are mindlessly depicted by the chores defining their lives. In late summer and fall, the women pick berries while the men cut logs and continue fishing. Jack's cords of wood are cut and piled in over the hill, on The Barrens, and will grow throughout the fall months, once the fishing dies down. If it ever picks up.

The coming winter, like all the rest, will be passed with song and gossip, with men knitting traps and nets, playing tricks on one another for a laugh, and sawing, splitting, and piling their wood. They will go to the wakes of neighbours, inevitable with the winter's chills, with all the wood and coal going to fight off the consumption.

The women never stop: knitting and darning underwear, socks, caps, and cuffs, hooking mats and rugs, and sewing heavy quilts out of scraps of old clothes. Not to mention making sails for schooners and skiffs, rearing housefuls of young ones, and tending to their men who are perpetually hungry and worked half to death.

"'Twould be cheaper to have a horse again than to feed you, Jack," Lize says with a little smile, although she knows he knows she's serious.

Logs and longers will be hauled out of the woods over paths through the snow and used throughout the spring to build sheds and flakes and boats, and to replace palings on garden fences and sticks on animal pens.

Lize scrubs Jack's other shirt against the glass washboard in a big black pot. She hangs the worn garment to dry on the line, which stretches the length of the kitchen ceiling beams to catch the heat of the stove. Then she cleans vegetables from the garden to be stowed away in the cellar up behind the house. The kettle hardly takes a breath all day, boiling water for the loose tea keeping them going.

Jack says he'd like to afford enough paint to finish the house next spring. What paint he did have went on and washed off the exposed studs during the typical cold spring, when it rained night and day.

"'Twould be some good to afford boards to cover the house, too," Lize says, looking out the window and pointing her head toward a clapboarded home farther up the road.

"Perhaps there'll be enough fish this time 'round for that," Jack says.

Lize smirks. "I thought ya said you were stayin' home out if it"

"I am," he says dryly.

Caulking hammers echo through the air as men make away with the leaks in their boat hulls. The big, strong arms of men push heavy wooden planers over rough lumber and haul spoke shaves as they clean longers of their sticky bark. Youngsters catch conners, flatfish, and sculpins and relentlessly swear, screech, and shout.

"I stepped on a fookin' whore's egg," one young girl cries, hopping around on one bare foot, holding the other bleeding one.

Lize tut-tuts and bangs the window down.

"I s'pose we can spare a bit of wood for the church," she says warily.

"Mind, now! All ya does is fret over the priest and never havin' enough wood in the church when we hardly ever sees 'im," Jack grumbles.

"We can't well turn our backs on 'im, either, now, can we, Jack?" She's fretting more than usual.

The complaints and the swearing will be taken care of in the confession box, but how can she keep bringing a scattered yaffle of wood for the priest when they have a job to keep themselves warm half the time? Jack's back is bad a lot, and with everyone else in Fox Harbour living the same way, they can hardly ask for a bit of wood.

"I must be out of me mind, Jack," Lize says. "Remember years ago when the priest hit Harb?" she says to change the subject.

Jack's half-hearted grunt of acknowledgement is interrupted by a noise—someone in the porch.

"Need a hand with anyt'ing, Jack?" the visitor asks. "Oh, hello, Mrs. Lize."

"Come in, Charlie, b'y. How're ya gettin' on?" Lize asks. "How's Mary Jane?"

"The best kind, me dear, the best kind," Charlie says.

"How's the *Annie Healy* comin' 'long, Charlie?" Jack asks.

"The best kind, Jack, the best kind. Ya never guess what they hauled out of 'er last week."

"Besides n'er fish?" Jack laughs.

"A gun!" Charlie says, excited. "A real old cannon. 'Twas down amongst the beach rocks in the ballast."

"Go on, b'y! I wonder where that come from?" Jack asks.

"I don't know, b'y, but perhaps our luck'll change this time 'round, now that 'tis offa the boat," Charlie says in an attempt to sound optimistic. "Jim Healy said the French likely used it when they were here two or three hundred year ago."

"Talkin' 'bout Annie Healy," Lize butts in, "Mrs. So-and-So said they see her down be the big flakes t'day."

Charlie smiles. "I had a fine chat with her just now. She's out from S'n John's with her young ones for a day'r two. Were ya about t' tell a story when I come in, Mrs. Lize?"

"Oh, yes, b'y, 'bout the time the priest hit poor Harb," she says.

"Always time for a quick story, Charlie, b'y," Jack says, pretending to be interested in a tale he could deliver word for word himself, if only he was allowed.

"'Twas after school one day," Lize begins, "when meself and me sister, Kate, were walkin', linked into Harb, see, an' we met the priest comin' up the road. We laughed an' carried on, with Harb makin' fun of this wan an' that wan. When he neared us, the priest, see, he struck poor Harb right in the face . . ."

"Go on, girl," Charlie says with a face to match his disgust.

"Yes," says Lize, "for havin' the cheek to show such disrespect in public; an unmarried man carryin' on in such reckless fashion in the company of two unmarried women, he said. He let on he didn't know we were the wan family, mind, so he said by 'n by."

"What became of it, Mrs. Lize?" Charlie asks.

"Well, b'y, poor Harb wrote the archbishop, tellin' 'bout what the priest was after doin', and Harb was satisfied when the archbishop wrote back sayin' Harb had like to hit 'im back. At least that's what Harb always said," Lize laughs.

"'Magine!" Charlie says, shaking his head.

"Yes, 'magine," Jack mocks. "And Lize, Charlie, b'y, she frets over keepin' a bit of wood in the church for the like of them."

"Now, Jack, b'y, be quiet, will ya? 'Tis not like 'twas Fadder Dee," Lize says, shaking her head.

Everyone in Fox Harbour has an obligation to God, and the closest thing to God in Fox Harbour is the priest when he visits twice a year.

"We can like it or lump it, as poor auld Mother used to say," Lize says.

Father Dee, the priest, lives in Argentia, his precious time divided among the many communities scattered from hell to high water this end of Placentia Bay. Once in summer and again in winter he makes his way to Fox Harbour, and it will soon be time for him to be making his rounds again.

Not much can be done in winter to boost the visual appreciation of the priest's coming, but now that it's August month, when everything is in bloom, the offerings in honour of his arrival come in a variety of natural colours for decoration. Fresh flowers picked from gardens, marshes, and the roadside sit in vases and jugs adorning the best tablecloths on kitchen tables and in parlours, reserved for important events, like the priest's visit, and wakes. The flowers send lovely fragrances throughout every home. Some have even gone as far as to make up wild bouquets and hang them on fences. Youngsters will soon be groomed half to death, scrubbed red raw, and told to stay clean because you never know what time Father will be by.

"God help 'im this time if he comes out of the room after his nap an' complains 'bout the bit of lint on his pants," Lize says, rolling her eyes.

Because she still feels compelled to lug wood to the church to keep the damp and mustiness at bay, Jack says it's the pure heights of foolishness.

"Not like they can get cauld in them long getups they wears," Jack mocks. "Not to mention they can afford a drop of the good stuff to keep warm."

"Ah, Jack, b'y, mind yer mout," Lize says. She tosses her head, looks at Charlie, and rolls her eyes toward Jack.

Charlie's too quiet to say what might be on his mind.

Most women and men of the harbour are busy recounting their sins since the priest's visit last Christmas. In the back of their minds, their young ones keep a sufficient list of familiar lies, memorized to spit out in order in the confession box.

Father Dee, with his lean figure and the redness of high blood pressure dancing about his face, is their conduit to the Almighty. He'll soon be dishing out the familiar host of beatings to those whose names the teacher has written down for defiance of both the Lord and the law during school last year. The fear of God will be smeared across the faces of the young ones, and after a few "Sorry Fadders" and a handful of Hail Marys they'll be right back outdoors resuming their chores and games of summer sport. With sore arses and boxed ears right full of all the reasons blasphemers like them will never see heaven, they'll pick up where they left off and never mention it again. Until the next time.

But the priest's visit is a week away and there's lots else for Lize to worry about now. She's busy with her housework and outside tasks that have no end. Not unlike most married women in the harbour, she carries a bundle of mental burdens, and afternoon conversation with neighbours and company between things to do is liable to go in either direction, good or bad. She only tells the one about the priest and Herb out of boredom, when there's no news. And no news is often good news around here.

"I got a good wan for ya, Charlie," Lize says, sitting in her rocker, waiting for the potatoes to boil. "More tea, Charlie?"

"Just as well, me dear," Charlie says, standing bent over and leaning toward her with his empty cup.

"'Tis just like yesterday we sailed over to Li'l Placentia," she begins. "Get out of that, Jack! You'll ruin me bread!" she says, waving the dishrag to shoo him away from peeking under the quilt at the dough in rise.

Bernadette, Jack and Lize's youngest child, comes into the kitchen and sits on the dark brown wooden chair by the stove, waiting to hear the story she, too, could tell herself, if only she was allowed to open her mouth.

"'Twas a munt before Christmas, eighteen ninety-five. Jack just straightened up the bill wit' H'aly's. We could hardly afford a weddin', but everyone else managed, and so could we. We never figured we'd have much, but wit' family and friends, sure, we'd get by, same as the rest."

On account of the parish covering most of this side of Placentia Bay, with just one priest serving all the communities, it was suitable for the priest and anyone getting married to have a ceremony in Little Placentia.

"Usually people from here went by dory, but a load of new rope an' twine arrived at Keats's Wharf, and Healys were sendin' their big schooner over, the *Queen of Providence*. I thought 'twas something shockin' havin' to cross the water in a big auld dirty divil of a boat on our weddin' day, but 'twas easy passage for us. Sure, me own mother, she said a spinster like me had no ch'ice but to accept whatever came me way and I was lucky to be gettin' married at all at twenty-four years of age. 'Magine, now!"

Small growlers drifted in and out the bay, scraping the mouth of the harbour, but they were no match for the *Queen of Providence*.

"Jack'd just as soon have waited a couple of more munts, but no way was I helpin' to lug a dory over ice pans, 'fraid I'd fall in an' catch me death.

"Kate, and Martin, Jack's best man, see, went wit' us. And Skipper Bill King was at the wheel."

"Yes, b'y, she was a dandy sight, the auld *Queen*, anchored in the lee of Little Placentia harbour, hove to in the light wind," Jack recalls, anxious to have a little part in the telling of the story.

"Keats's Wharf was big an' dirty, see, much worse than it is now," Jack goes on, "an' Lize dreaded every step it took t' get clear of it. Barrels of mackerel lined the walkway headin' off the wharf and ya wouldn't know if they were gonna come alive and jump out at her, the way she was gettin' on."

"I remember that auld wharf, Jack, 'deed I do," Charlie adds. "The old fellas with the big beards and worn woollen sweaters coilin' stiff manila around their great big hands an' arms. I used to be frightened t' death to look at 'em when I was a young fella. But they were the best kind. Come straight from Ireland, most of them, when they were lads, escapin' the Famine."

"Yes, b'y, men don't come like they did one time, big like that," Jack says.

"No, I tell ya," Charlie agrees.

"No, and women mustn't have come like us, neither, the way they were gawkin' at us," Lize laughs.

"Now, Mrs. Lize, everyone knows there's no beauties like Fox Harbour beauties," Charlie says shyly.

"'Twas enough to skin ya," Lize remembers, wrapping her arms around herself as if she were still cold, not reacting to Charlie's sweetness, and anxious to take back the part of storyteller.

"I carried me dress folded in half over one arm," she says, "an' balanced me step with the other."

"The horse and cart tracks in the road, see, were after hardenin' on account of the frost," Jack interrupts, "but there was still 'nough dirt to spile her dress, see, if she had to slip an' fall."

Lize shoots Jack a dirty look, as if to say shut up, while Jack eyes the pipe and tobacco he put back on the sideboard should another quick escape to the shed be required.

"Meself, Kate, and Cousin Mary Anne Meade from Little Placentia were right giddy wit' excitement, and headed upstairs to get me into me cauld dress and veil. To be sure, be the time we got downstairs, Jack, Martin, and Uncle John were well on 'er to the kitchen table, nippin' at Uncle John's moonshine. I remember the church . . . 'twas no warmer than out be the door," Lize says, hugging herself again. "An' the crowd blowin' their bret on their hands an' stirrin' to keep warm."

"Yes," Jack interrupts again, "Fadder S'n John was to a christenin' on Red Island an' wasn't long back, see, an' he askin' the biverin' crowd what they were all carryin' on about, see."

"Yes," Lize says, slying her eyes at Jack again. "And everyone knew he'd been in the cuddy of H'aly's boat, *Revels*, wit' a lovely heat from the Queenie stove." She goes on, tossing her head back in disgust, "The smell of whisky from his breath cut through the cauld like, like I don't know what. An' he lettin' on he was cauld himself, but he never codded us, no sir, 'deed he never."

"The potatoes are b'ilin', Lize, girl," Jack interrupts.

"'Twas a grand story, Mrs. Lize," Charlie says, laying his empty cup on the table next to Jack. "I must go over and get me barrel of cods heads from the *Annie Healy*."

Lize is glad to have a story or two from their past. Now, almost thirty-two years later, so much has changed. That day will always be a nice time to consider, something she and Jack bring up when there's little else to say, or to help dim their worst memories when they come to light.

Mostly, after all these years, Jack has been fishing from the schooner *Annie Healy,* and for the longest time now he's been the eldest of the crew. John Mullins, the captain, didn't say much last week when Jack told him he wouldn't be going back to sea. Jack has been saying that for ages, and the fact he hasn't missed hardly an hour helping out around the boat since hasn't gone unnoticed, either. Jim King and Mon McCue from the crew told Jack he was off his head and asked what do he think he'll do without fishing. His willingness to help make the schooner ready for leaving is respected, whether he stays or goes.

CHAPTER TWO

Annie Healy

Anne Healy Furlong stands in the front garden of the house where she grew up, breathing air familiar to her lungs. Her eyes take in the load of activities embracing Fox Harbour this morning. The sun, hot on her face, and the air, fresher than she's used to in the city, is soothing to her soul. Shadows of clouds cross the sun and distract her momentarily, revealing distressed faces in the craggy rock walls of the Crow Hill.

Looking back to the scene below, she can't help but smile. Provisions for a fishing trip are carried by pairs of men using handcarts usually reserved for transporting fish to and from the flakes and capelin and kelp to vegetable gardens in once-rocky meadows above the road. Now and then, men stop to guzzle bottles of homemade beer to ward off the thirst. Other supplies brought to Healy's Wharf by horse and cart are checked by knowing, accountable hands and sent to their appropriate destinations. Some materials are loaded into trap skiffs and dories tied up to bigger boats around the wharf. They are brought out to two big schooners anchored farther out in the harbour, in deeper water. Empty barrels for bait are rolled up splintery wooden planks and onto the deck of the *Annie Healy*, the only schooner small enough to haul up alongside the wharf at high tide.

Murray's Island looks smaller than ever, wrapped in dark blue salt water. Gulls of every size and variety cover the handful of rocks left above the sea. Smooth waves wash past the gulls and the water sweeps quickly, almost silently, along the thick grass of the banks. Long, black rats scurry through the wet grass to higher ground.

Before Anne's eyes meet the crowd at the wharf, they are drawn to the potpourri of colours adorning the plant life rimming the sea. She loves flowers. Daisies are smiling at the sun. Clover, some still purple and some dying and brown, lie about in clustered beauty. Buttercups glow. Yellow hawkweed in great bunches, and others standing alone, are surrounded by small rocks. Deadman's daisies are backed by the flowing sea while timothy hay, used for feeding cows and horses, reaches tall and bends charmingly with the gentle wind.

The sea stops for nothing. It moves along heavily, washing the big rocks of the shore until reaching beneath the wooden bridge that joins both sides of the harbour where the ocean meets the brook.

Men are busy coming and going to the wharf. Some roll barrels. Others carry them in their arms or on their shoulders. Some of the containers have flour or sugar while others hold mended trawl lines and hooks. The barrels are placed on the *Annie*'s deck and secured around the mainmast with half-inch rope. Wheelbarrows of salt for preserving fish make their way onto the boat. The salt is lowered in buckets to below deck, where it is dumped and shovelled into two temporary pounds built in the centre of the ship's hull. A two-foot cast iron auger used in the drilling of new holes during last winter's restoration is tossed up out of the hole. Michael Mullins picks it up off the deck and brings it down to the wharf, where Henry Healy snatches it from his hand and hurries off the wharf.

The air is full of grunts and panting, cursing and swearing, singing and talking, friendly insults, and laughter. Fishing gear, tools, clothes, food, and water are passed over the heads of the crowd in barrels, puncheon tubs, wooden trunks, and brin bags. No pair of useful hands dares escaping the work necessary to help guarantee a good voyage.

Anne admires the strong sense of spirit and pride in young and old alike. The weather-beaten faces sweat, squint, blink, and smile. They know that each trip to sea is a chance at a better tomorrow for all. And with no signs of bad weather ahead, the old fellows say this next trip to Golden Bay will be a successful one.

The air is much the same as that of downtown St. John's. The foulness of fresh fish guts and raw sewage from the landwash mixes with drying cod on the tall flakes hovering over the land around her. The aroma of baking bread and buns drifting beneath raised kitchen windows manages to find a place of its own in the warming air.

The hundreds of split fish giving up their moisture to the sun on the flakes are part of a long chain of commerce. Most of the fish has been caught by crews from outside Fox Harbour. From here it will be shipped to St. John's, sold again, and redistributed to foreign-going vessels. In Spain, Portugal, and the West Indies it will be traded for rum, molasses, and spices unavailable in Newfoundland. The foreign commodities are brought back and tagged with high prices by big city mercantile firms for outport merchants like Jim and Mike Healy, who will jack the prices themselves for local fishermen like Jack Foley and Charlie Sampson, who, like their fathers before them, will never live free of debt.

Anne's brothers, the proprietors of M & J Healy Ltd., once called Richard K. Healy & Sons Ltd., will get a morsel of the profits. When all is said and done, they'll be no better off than anyone else at the end of the season. No matter what some say. Working together Monday to Saturday, getting drunk Saturday night, telling stories, singing and dancing arm in arm will carry on as it always did.

The Healy brothers, Jim, Mike, and Henry, have made this miserable trade their life's work. Just as their father showed them. Jim and Mike skippered their father's vessels for ages, but in the past few years they preferred to stay ashore. With trustworthy skippers like John Mullins, the Healys have little to worry about.

The vegetable drills on either side of Anne are not unlike her own on Allandale Road in St. John's. She's glad she's not responsible for these crops today. A couple of her boys and girls play over around the store while her oldest child, Tom, helps his Uncle Mike. They're out at the end of the wharf, coiling large spools of trawl line into tubs to go aboard the *Annie Healy*.

Anne and her children came on the train yesterday. The trip

from Placentia Sound in her father's boat, *Tojori*, revealed little change since she was a young girl. *Tojori* is special to the Furlongs, named by their grandfather Healy for Anne's first three children, Tom, Joan, and Richard.

The Furlongs are staying until tomorrow, to see the *Annie Healy* leave. The next morning they'll part on the train. The young ones have a couple of days to explore the woods, ponds, rivers, hills, and behind old barns and under stores. Little treasures are always waiting to be found. The trip back will be just as exciting. They'll soak up the sun and the salt spray coming in over *Tojori* as she makes her way out around Connor Cove and into The Sound. The twenty-minute walk from the water's edge to Ville Marie Station will give their legs a good stretch. They plan to spend Saturday afternoon at Bally Haly Golf Course outside the city. "And God help you," Anne said to her young ones before they left home, "if you use them clubs in the yard and break a window, the clubs will go in the corner and that's where they'll stay."

Taking in her surroundings, the days and nights of Anne's youth flood her mind. Feelings of innocence and freedom. Playing with her friends, Kate Whiffen, Sarah Reilly, and John Mullins. She smiles even more and wonders where the time has gone.

John Mullins, her old friend, yells orders to the crew of the boat named for her. She's proud of him. The hard work of the crew goes far beyond wrestling a living from the sea; she knows that well. It's for their wives and children and neighbours. Even for strangers, should they show up at doorsteps having survived schooners wrecked on the shoals of the harbour's entrance. Especially in November and December storms, when the place is often mistaken as a safe haven.

"It's good to be home, Jim," Anne calls out to her oldest brother. He's standing with a tally sheet, counting fish on the flakes.

"No place like home, Annie, girl," Jim replies with a little laugh.

He makes his way out of the yard and under the flakes toward the wharf.

Jim is like their father. At fifty-five, Jim is big and tall, tough and strapping. He's carrying a large killick with one hand, with a ten-foot plank on the other shoulder.

Anne laughs to herself, remembering the time Edward came home with an amusing tale of her daddy's strength. Edward, Anne's husband, is a manager with T & M Winter Ltd. He was travelling around the city drumming up business while Richard, his father-in-law, tagged along for company. Finished business and leaving the office of a gymnasium, Edward noticed the old man hanging and spinning on a pair of gymnast's hoops. The best part, Edward told her, was Richard still had on his winter coat and boots.

Anne walks out of the garden and turns onto the road. She's to meet someone who's not so busy and perhaps has time for a chat. Alongside the lane past Jack and Lize Foley's, she says hello to little girls playing among the big rocks. The white glare of the sun across part of the harbour's surface takes her back to winters long ago. She and her friends would jump from one drifting ice pan to another, often falling into the water near shore, where the ice was not as thick and less stable. Then came the chastising from the parents, who later admitted they had been punished for the same reasons, in the same places, when they were young. Anne smiles again. She knows if she visited Fox Harbour in winter, her own young ones would want to jump ice pans, too, and her nerves would be gone.

Open areas where houses once stood are grown in with alders and grass. Pink rockets, normally shooting straight for the sky, are a little bent in the light breeze. Goldenrod stands tall, catching all the wonder of the sun.

Anne remembers old people who lived here and there. And the songs they used to sing. An old wood-horse, nearly chopped to bits, peeks through the high grass in search of a bucksaw blade to pierce its weather-worn, dull, grey, termite-ridden surfaces, to bleed its dust to the wind. At one time it held little children who swung their legs in time to made-up nursery rhymes. Later it was known to generations of young lovers—a fearless girl standing in her homemade summer dress leaning into a shy boy in his dungarees and clean white singlet, resting on the wood-horse in the gripping marvel of that first kiss. A seat for minds of all states to sit and contemplate what it's all about, to feel, to dream, to fall off with too much moonshine aboard, to watch the shooting stars of the Perseid fall behind The Isaacs or over the Crow Hill. To be. A simple sawhorse and all those thoughts.

The haunted houses long abandoned are all gone now, but several incumbents stand by. They're leaning into the wind, foundations not what they used to be, sure to take the place of their predecessors in years to come. People have died in every home in Fox Harbour. But from some, once they're abandoned, come noises late at night. It's not safe to walk by alone, night or day. Evil curses, for some reason left behind.

She wonders if angry fairies still hide in the woods and meadows, and if they're still responsible for the loss of those two little brothers who went sliding and never came back.

The wind stirs Anne's long, greying hair. She's pleased to find herself so much a child again. Rekindling her youth, she remembers the games of truth or dare, where stubborn tongues and weakened nerves often resulted in having to kiss on the cheek boys she wouldn't have otherwise chosen over a sculpin.

Had she been anywhere but Fox Harbour, she might have been the quintessential spoiled merchant's daughter. But not here. Children know better than to talk back to their elders, and a clout in the gob for being brazen might be expected from anyone, anytime. Unlike St. John's, where several small towns lay scattered about, most here take on the responsibility of the community, youngsters and all. Girls follow their mother's apron strings, learning how to keep a man fed, clothed, and looked after in general. Chores have their place morning, noon, and night. Between chores, people visit where they like and don't have to knock. Anne finds inviting people to her home in the city a little strange. And that's only on Sundays.

When she was young, feeling she'd witnessed more refined people and things on trips to the city, Anne thought nothing of leaving Fox Harbour behind. Now, these people, her people, so full of character and life, never fail to beckon her. She's glad to be home. And no time could be better than now, with community spirit on bust in support of the schooners preparing to leave for another spell of fishing.

From her handbag she takes a small ledger. She found it in a musty box in her father's old office this morning. The ledger is green with a concoction of black and cream lines resembling the remnants of a rotten curtain, not unlike ones she noticed in the abandoned houses. Just above the centre of the book's cover, running diagonally from left to right is carved, *Mr. RICHD. HALEY*. Holding the book, Anne traces each letter with her index finger, trying to imagine her father inscribing his name there. Was it day or night? Night, most likely. Not enough time in the day. What did he use to carve each letter so straight? A blade? What was he thinking at the time? Was he happy? Was his business worth the hassle of all those days and nights spent in St. John's bartering and trying to secure deals to outfit his shop? Where did the book come from?

When she opens the cover, her eyes are drawn to a dark brown stain from a kerosene lantern, its light having guided her father's eyes over his pen's light soaks in the ink bottle. No breaks in the writing tell of uninterrupted thoughts, as his business thoughts fill the pages. The eloquently written date, *Nov. 2, 1883*, tells the book's age. A faint trace of the stink of kerosene remains after forty-five years. At the top of the page in neat handwriting reads: *Mr. Richd. Haley in a/c with Job Brothers.*

The first entry in the little log is *40 hhds Salt*, and Anne wishes, for her brothers' sake, it was still only eighteen pounds. And *1 Puncheon Molasses*: eighty-four gallons, just eleven pounds and eighteen shillings. Not that anyone here goes by that currency anymore. But Anne remembers it well, as it was used outside St. John's, in places like Fox Harbour, for years after it was replaced by dollars and cents.

She sees the names of men, mostly long gone. Their own sons, now grown men, still carry their fathers' and grandfathers' names and debts. Their sons to follow are sure to remain in books like this one forever. They'll all die owing something to someone. They have that in common.

On other pages, *Mr. Richd. Haley in a/c with Job Brothers* appears again. Pride is evident in the easy-flowing loops of her father's penmanship.

Page to page, no kerosene stain is the same. A few people's names appear, showing what they borrowed from the store and how much they owed. Anne knows some of the poor souls never lived to pay off their debts, and she wonders how her father ever explained to the Jobs those instances when he hadn't enough money to cover what he, himself, borrowed to lend out to poor fishermen in the first place.

The dates on the surprisingly white pages make it to 1884. On the top of a couple of pages dated that same year in lead reads *Anny*. Anne thinks of her mother and longs for her. The long nights, years ago by the stove, in lantern light when she was about three and a half. Mother's warm hand lay over her own little hand, tracing over the letters of the alphabet. Her first attempts at spelling her own name. "Now, Annie, only black Protestants spells their name with a 'y,'" Mother would say. The lowering of her voice suggested she knew it wasn't proper to say such a thing, even when no one was around to hear. A little rectangular sticker on the inside back cover reveals where the book was made: *C. & H. Ratcliffe, 4 Rumford Street, Liverpool.* Anne imagines the little book being assembled in some brick building on a bustling street like those described on the pages of Dickens's *David Copperfield.* Then packed in a crate and floated across the Atlantic in tall ships in wild gales where men prayed for death and on calm evenings where silence beckoned them to never go home, or anywhere—to drift forever. The little book. All the way from England to St. John's and then here, by boat.

On an unused page and, at the risk of soiling her good dress with black ink, she dares to reflect. She's inspired by what her brothers, Jim and Mike, were saying this morning over tea about last Saturday's time at their house:

Each person here contemplates life in his or her own way, never without the wit, marinated handsomely in the well-timed sauce of our Irish ancestors. All ages are glad to shed tears for ballads, and still, through good seasons and bad on the water, on Saturday nights, circles of friends, linked arm and arm, sway too close to the stove, rattling dishes in sideboards from their boots pounding kitchen floors like tomorrow will never come. Fox Harbour. Home. Of course, they didn't say it quite like that.

"Hello, Annie H'aly!"

"Oh, hello, Mart," Anne says, startled out of her daydreaming. "Still delivering babies, I s'pose?"

"Never stops, me dear, never stops," Mart says. "I'm on the lookout now for Mag Whiffen. She's ready t' go any day now."

"Well, I better not keep you, then."

"Don't be so foolish, girl. I've lots o' time t' talk wit' an auld friend," Mart laughs, perching upon a big rock alongside the road.

"Ah, what would Fox Harbour do without good women like you, and your mother and your sister, God rest their souls?" Anne says.

"There'd be no wan here, I s'pose," Mart says, laughing, "'cause they wouldn't be born."

Anne lets out a laugh and slides over alongside Mart. "You're liable to be right, girl." She laughs again.

"Ya know," Mart says, "Mother often told 'bout all the babies yer own mother lost, the poor t'ing. The consumption, me dear, 'twas much worse than 'tis now, b'lieve it or not. You were lucky, I dare say, t' muster 'nough strengt' t' fend off the cursed TB. Mother said ya never knew what was lingering in the damp recesses of every corner o' this place, the way the youngsters were dyin'. 'Tis not half so bad now, Annie, girl, as bad as 'tis. Poor Lize Foley's daughter, Jane, in the States lost her little fella just last year. He was only two. Poor Lize isn't over it yet."

"The Lord works in mysterious ways," Anne says.

"'Deed He do, me dear, 'deed He do," Mart says. Both women lower their heads and make the sign of the Cross over their chests.

The women silently explore their lives. The moist salt air sinks into their sunburned faces while the breeze dries the sweat on their foreheads. Each woman sighs at the beauty of the harbour. The dark green hills, silhouettes in the bright day, rolling back from The Isaacs are woven into the haven of big hills behind that seem to go on forever.

"Well, dear, I must be goin'. Too much work t' be done this lovely day. 'Twas lovely talkin' to ya, Annie. How long ya out for?"

"The day after tomorrow. I'm sure we'll run into one another again before then."

Is letting Mart go away this soon wrong? Anne wonders. *Perhaps she mistakes my silence for arrogance. After all, this is a little holiday for me and the children, and what right do I have to let go of a chance to have a good yarn with an old friend?*

"Mart!" Anne gets up from the big rock and dusts the back of her long cotton skirt. "I know you're on your way someplace, but I'm heading up the lane to the old meadow, not far. Want to come along for a spell? Just a while."

They stroll up the lane and on to the meadow they both knew well from childhood. It was so much bigger one time, they agree, having grown in lots the past forty years. The delicate scent of alders and their shiny green leaves soothe their senses. A big rock beckons them. They enjoy the rugged beauty of the harbour. Anne begins talking about her family. Their life. A symphony of hard work in the background breaches the air. Through the glare of the sun, The Isaacs and the Neck are lovely silhouettes against the emerald sea.

CHAPTER THREE

The Healys

Richard K. Healy was born at Fox Harbour in 1840. He had been a merchant and general dealer there since 1882, when Annie was less than four. He married Johanna Whiffin of Long Harbour, a small community just north of Fox Harbour.

Richard bought and sold fish, and he got supplies for his store on trips to St. John's. *Bought* in this case meant he took the majority of fish brought in to his premises by fishermen with berths on his schooners in exchange for supplies they had borrowed from his store throughout the year. Supplies weren't especially those required for going to sea. They also included basic possessions such as oleo; molasses used for baking and in tea in the absence of sugar; flour; raisins; sewing and knitting needles; thread; and material for both the making and mending of clothes. Most clothes, however, were made by wives and daughters from used sacks in which food items were shipped. The fish he took in was brought or shipped to St. John's, where the process started over. Seldom did money exchange hands, especially between fishermen and Richard.

Before the twenty-six miles of railway track was completed from Whitbourne to Placentia in 1888, Richard and his hired captains sailed his schooners the lengthy trip out of Placentia Bay, around Cape St. Mary's, Cape Race, and Cape Spear and into St. John's.

Also acting as the culler, Richard decided the grade of fish brought to him. This decided its worth. His family wanted for little. Johanna looked after the children, Jim, Mike, Mary, Annie, and Henry, while servant girls were hired and did what was expected of most wives. They cooked and cleaned, washed clothes and diapers, sewed and harvested vegetables, and tended to fish on the flakes and hens and livestock in the family's gardens.

But regardless of the presence of servant girls and shore boys, and due to the endless amount of work required to operate such a business, the Healy young ones were little different than other children in the town. They did their share of work. Curing fish. Mending twine. Hooking mats. Growing vegetables. Shoeing horses. Minding sheep and cows. Carding and spinning wool. And cleaving and lugging wood. Girls made the boys' and men's clothes, and hated it, especially Sunday jackets and suits kept for weddings and wakes.

As a planter, Richard owned boats and hired other men to use them. Since the early 1880s, he chartered two big schooners, *Hope* and *Queen of Providence*, from Job Brothers Ltd., an elite mercantile firm in St. John's. They'd been around since 1750, with irons in fires all over the island of Newfoundland. Richard's store carried all available makes of fishing gear. Trips to the city weren't always necessary. Job's had an outpost in Placentia, where Richard bought portions of his store's supplies, and sold fish there, too, if the timing was right and boats were heading to St. John's.

At the turn of the century, when Job Brothers had stakes in the short-lived silver mines at Broad Creek Canyon near Little Placentia, Richard acted as an agent, supplying local workers for the mine.

He also had two schooners made for himself: the *Mary H.* in the 1880s and the *Annie Healy* in 1900. The four schooners of Richard K. Healy & Sons Ltd. provided fishing berths to men from all over Placentia Bay.

From spring until the middle of November, men in boats left Fox Harbour to fish Golden Bay, near Cape St. Mary's. The old saying, *Cape St. Mary's pays for all*, was little more than a saying a lot of the time. The waters off and around Cape St. Mary's have been a forest of schooner masts since the mid-1850s.

Some years the nearly fifty-mile sail from Fox Harbour proved fruitful, while, following other fishing seasons, both Richard and the fishermen were left in the worst kind of plight. Shortages of fish brought no end to debt, and the inevitable lack of food brought a want of energy. And if lack of fish wasn't enough, young and old alike were regularly dragged down the suffocating halls of consumption. People also felt the deadly pangs of dropsy or the incurable chills of the common cold. This, along with a lack of medicine and no doctor to be found, at least on time, made winters longer and harder. Community spirit and an unrestricted devotion to prayer kept them going a lot of the time.

Healy's home is a large whitewashed two-storey in The Bottom, looking straight out to the harbour's entrance. On the right of the harbour is the biggest of The Isaacs: two great hills of granite protecting the town from the impulsive tides of Placentia Bay. The closest hill climbs almost 350 feet while the other is about half its height. The Point on the other side of the harbour is clothed in evergreens rolling off Sampson's Hill. A small grassy meadow at the base of the hill has a handful of boulders gnawed off the cliff by wind and wave over the years. This point of land stretches out across a fair bit of the entrance, making the harbour shallow and tricky to navigate. Hundreds of years ago, French soldiers called it a "faux" harbour on their maps, but no one seems to know or care where the name came from. Not even the Church had the power to rename it for a saint in 1918.

A widow's walk running the length of the roof of Healy's home once gave the place an air of importance—this, and the rarity of a front step. Everyone still thinks the step foolish. A waste of wood, only used by the priest when he visits. Why can't he use the side door like everyone else? He'll stand there on the step, people say, straight as a whip, looking back to the water, right proud of the big operation in front of his eyes, like he had a hand in it himself. As if the women and children hobbling around, bent over with perpetual bad backs, laying out and picking up fish on the flakes, enjoy their work. As if they wouldn't drop it all in a second if opportunity to make a different living presented itself. As if they're not sneaking a peek his way now and then, cursing and swearing on account of his clean clothes and the two hands never known to a callus.

A large saltwater-stained transom over the facing entrance once allowed bright shafts of sunlight to breathe life into the house. Now, a murky glow falls on the hallway and half the stairs. A cobwebbed kerosene lantern perched on a fancy cast iron bracket swings from the wall.

Looking at it, the home still might give off a mild glow of old fortune, but that's only compared to the roughly hewn dwellings of most of the town. The picket fence, distressed with grey and black lines of age, runs alongside the road to keep in the sheep.

Upstairs in the store, a rectangular, two-levelled affair about forty feet from the side of the house, is where Richard sat in his solid oak chair and kept his office—a large room, with boxes of account books, deferred invoices, and stock, where no one has bothered the dankness and dirt since he left Fox Harbour. Anne found that out foraging around up there earlier this morning. Tonight she will take the young ones up there, show them why their grandfather's work was often interrupted by skies of vivid oranges, reds, pinks, greens, purples, and blues. Not to mention the impressive, calming shadows of The Isaacs and The Neck at sunset.

From the bottom half of the building, people continue to take supplies and borrow tools and fishing gear on the awkward promise of catching enough fish to repay it all.

Telling someone their dead mother or father still owes for this or that hasn't gotten any easier, according to the number of empty liquor bottles strewn about the big room partitioned by forty-odd years of bills in boxes, old tools, more dust, and more dirt.

Running out from an unpainted, heavily built barn in the far corner of the yard, the flakes span over the road, right past the water's edge. A series of walking planks run through hundreds or thousands, depending on the situation, of split and salted fish drying on the longer-topped platform when the rain bothers to stay away. Otherwise they wait out the weather in round piles, covered in tree rinds weighed down with big rocks.

Jim, Mike, and Henry always did shore work, fished, and handled their father's schooners while Annie and her sister, Mary, helped keep the store's records in order. They sometimes accompanied their father on business trips to St. John's, giving him time to socialize with the powerful merchants of Water Street and Duckworth Street.

As a young woman, during the busy fishing season, Annie, as she was called, went with her father more so than the others, who couldn't spare the time.

On the long train ride from Ville Marie Station to the bustling city, Richard smoked his pipe and rarely spoke, while young Annie dreamt of St. John's and how its people might one day admire her as they seemed to respect her father. She loved not feeling out of place in her good dress, learning to stroll with purpose along the busy sidewalks of the city. There were big shots everywhere. And she loved the way the young men dressed in their Sunday best, even when it was the middle of the week. They were a far cry from the boys in Fox Harbour.

Corner boys gawked at her while other lads, dressed in felt hats and jackets of tweed, tried selling her newspapers. The attention she often received brought a lovely red glow to her face now and then.

Anne loved looking at fancy clothes in big store windows, and not having to walk under shady fish flakes where, at home, she was sure to be pinched by dirty old men and curious young boys alike.

In the big mercantile shops, Annie smiled shyly at the fine-looking businessmen in tailored suits running on her father like he was a king. She even made eyes at clerks, although they weren't nearly as important as the sons and nephews of rich, powerful merchants.

When she was nineteen, in a city studio, Annie had a portrait taken of herself in a fancy dress. Her staunch Catholic upbringing wouldn't allow her to go out of her way to show the photograph to many, in case they'd think she was getting above herself. But she was proud of it. It was no secret the girls of Fox Harbour were rare beauties, but all weren't so fortunate as to be brought up like Annie. It wasn't always easy for her to blend in at home where women were expected to marry the next available man, get pregnant one year after the next, and, wrapped in a dirty apron, tend to a husband the rest of their lives. One day, she always said, she'd have a job of her own, in the city, and a clean, handsome man with money, who didn't smell like fish.

In 1904, while accompanying her father on a business trip to T & M Winter Ltd., Annie sat on a wooden bench, waiting for the clerk. She read the *Evening Telegram*, and had enjoyed that newspaper for as long as she could remember. Richard always had copies sent or brought from the city. She especially loved reading the section on world news and sharing stories with people in Fox Harbour who couldn't read or afford the paper. In later years, Richard had taken her to see a few moving pictures at the Nickel Theatre, too, and she had no trouble drawing an audience at home with her recounts of the stories she'd seen on the big screen.

"Buffalo Bill Cody," she read audibly. "Did you know he helped build a town in the States three years ago and they named it *Cody* after him? Just imagine. And, he named a hotel after his daughter just two years ago?"

Annie glanced over the paper at the clerk for a reaction, but got none. She thought how nice it was for Buffalo Bill, such a famous man, to think so much of his daughter.

The clerk cleared his throat and Annie neatly folded the paper, setting it on the low table next to the bench. She stood in front of the large oak desk full of papers stacked tidily.

"Your purchase order, miss," said the clerk, looking up and handing it to Annie.

He's some polite, she thought. She couldn't get over how good he looked in his suit of clothes. Pocket watch and all.

The clerk wished he'd gotten his work done sooner. Perhaps he did look up once or twice, only to see the back of the newspaper.

"Thank you," Annie said, sitting back down to examine the order.

The courteous clerk started another order while lifting his eyes often to take in the warm presence of the beautiful young lady carefully looking over the bill. Her lips scarcely moved as she quietly made sure they had all they needed for the family store.

"Twelve barrels of flour, Lakewood's, $6.10 a barrel; two hams, butt pork, $25.00 apiece; 10 tubs of butter . . ." her voice faded. She gently cleared her throat before continuing. "Twenty-two cents apiece; one barrel of seeded raisins, fancy, $4.00 . . ." She stopped murmuring and read the other five items in silence, having noticed the handsome clerk watching her.

For two or three seconds she dropped her head and raised the corners of her mouth, never taking her eyes off of his. He couldn't get over how beautiful she was, and they both blushed and laughed quietly at their awkwardness. It seemed to last an eternity.

"It's the best kind," she said.

"Good, then."

Annie watched him initial the bill.

"E.T.F. What does that stand for?"

"Edward Thomas Furlong, miss," he answered, handing her a receipt. "And you're Richard K. Healy," he joked, pointing to the signature on the dotted line.

"That's what I have to write," she said. "My father's name, I mean, the business bein' in his name."

"I know," he smiled. "I was just . . ."

"It's Anne," she said under her breath.

The clerk's penmanship was sort of eloquent, like hers, she mused. She blushed again when his hand accidentally touched hers.

"So, Anne, you live in Fox Harbour."

"Yes," she answered. "Placentia Bay. Not Labrador," she said quickly.

"It's you," the clerk said excitedly.

"I was gonna say," Anne said, a smile spanning the width of her face. "I knew it. I should've said right away that you looked familiar . . . the dance."

"Yes! The dance before Christmas three years ago," he said, as if he'd had the line rehearsed ever since, waiting for this moment. "And you had to . . ."

"I had to go. Tell me about it!" Anne said, rolling her eyes.

"Do you still work there?" he asked.

"The Royal Stores? No. I got sick, rheumatic fever, and had to leave. I went back home to help with the family store, after I got better."

"You're all right now?"

"I'm fine, except I'd rather be in here."

"Not too much in the way of excitement out your way, I suppose."

"Very little. I mean . . . it's home and everything, but . . ."

"I know," Edward laughed softly. "It's not St. John's."

"No, it's definitely not St. John's," Anne said with a little chuckle, relieved by not having to give a detailed description of her life in Fox Harbour.

Richard K. Healy and Marmaduke Winter clinked glasses and bid goodbyes in a room across the hall, and Anne stepped back.

Edward smiled. "You'll probably be in here again, then."

"I dare say," Anne said.

Anne and Richard walked from Duckworth Street, down over the hill toward Water Street. Tall wood-and-brick buildings held back in reserve. The sun dropped and horses snorted while their weary masters steered cartloads of everything imaginable along the lively corridors of prosperity. Barking dogs chased flapping miniature Union Jacks on carts while dignified women proudly shoved prams of babies over the streetcar tracks and up the steepest roads, even steeper than the one leading to the graveyard in Fox Harbour. Ornately trimmed dormer windows pouted boastfully from mansard roofs. Clad in shingles of black, red, or green, attached homes leaned on one another, for fear of falling down the sheer hills, reminding her of the men staggering home early on Sunday mornings at home; only the houses were silent, singing no songs of Irish rebellion and freedom. There was peace in that, but silence, she knew, was never an option for drunken Irish mouths sworn to keep true to the promises and memories of their forefathers.

The stench drifting up from wharves and schooners behind the buildings rivalled tantalizing smells of supper escaping through open windows where mothers and wives beckoned all hands home to eat. Less lively women, cloaked in black from head to toe, stared blankly from half-open doorways, calling no one, just like the widows in Fox Harbour.

A dishevelled specimen of what might have been a handsome bachelor begged for a few coppers for a bite to eat, and Anne wondered to her father why the man didn't just go into someone's house for food like they would at home.

Colourful row houses, no older than the twelve years since the Great Fire, lent warmth to the cooling twilight as Anne wrapped her shoulders in her mother's black woolsquare. Perched upon iron posts letting go of the sun's warmth, gas lamps hissed at the oncoming night while manikins in the front windows of the Arcade Store masqueraded heaps of the latest fashions to the emptying cobblestone street.

The jarring streetcar rattled its way to the enormous train station at the end of Water Street. Though her eyes scanned her physical surroundings, Anne's thoughts looked only into her heart for something she'd scarcely, if ever, felt before. She couldn't think past Edward—his handsome face, his polite manner, and the lovely suit of clothes with the pocket watch on a silver chain. And the fancy initials, *E.T.F.* How she wished her time longer with him that night of the dance, and back there today, in the city, how she was dying to find out if he was courting anyone, but she could hardly be so bold. He was awfully nice to her, but perhaps he was like that with everyone. Would seeing him again put her right back where she was after they first met—home? Would she soon be sick to her stomach, with little to do but think about him, wondering if she'd ever lay eyes on him again? How unwanted doubt and spells of pessimism had replaced her dreams of waltzing him again, of having a sensible conversation, the way she couldn't with the young, single men at home.

Rarely has a child of a Roman Catholic family been spared the encouragement to become a priest or nun. In keeping with pure Irish Catholic tradition, every parent knows having a child wear a habit or a collar in a world where only Roman Catholics are entitled to God's forgiveness will automatically place them higher on the social scale.

Anne's intentions, however, didn't involve entering a convent. Instead, she chose to go to Littledale College and boarding house in the city to further her education.

On the train ride back to Ville Marie Station, Anne dreamt of her time in St. John's six years ago when she went to Littledale. Then, the enjoyable days at work, and walking the streets in the evenings, watching people and going to the moving picture shows with her new friends.

Littledale, the post-secondary school run by the Sisters of Mercy, was also a place for young ladies training to become nuns in the convent located on the same grounds. While praying in the chapel for the souls of her five siblings, and walking the long hallways between classes, Anne witnessed young girls, no older than herself and some much younger, wholeheartedly giving themselves to Jesus in musty pews and damp, gloomy vestibules. Echoes of whispers of novenas to the saints, litanies of the dead, and acts of contrition, faith, hope, and charity that seemed to hold the walls together, sometimes left her to wonder if her plan to work and raise a family and simply go to Mass and to eat no meat on Fridays was good enough.

On sunny afternoons in the usual late Newfoundland spring, Anne spent most of her time studying outdoors. Upon the ancient grounds, young nuns-to-be strolled, stopping from time to time to rest on cool, elaborate cast iron benches in the shade of old tree branches and new leaves. Clothed in summertime white from head to toe, the nuns hovered over the manicured grass like mislaid ghosts in grave contemplation. They'd appear and disappear behind big, straight, knotty pines and gigantic Carolina poplar, and rose bushes adorning the air with thick scents worthy of heaven itself.

With her new schooling behind her, Anne went back home to Fox Harbour. She terribly missed the many forms of excitement so bountiful in the city.

Richard said she could move to the city again, but only if she had a job. So, it wasn't long before she was hired to work in the hat department of the Royal Stores. There, her employers and co-workers treated her with kindness and respect. Life was good, both at work and at her new home staying with her sister, Mini, and brother-in-law, Jim Davis, at their Duckworth Street home. When rheumatic fever brought a hurried end to Anne's working life, she was lost.

Before she knew it, Richard was waking her up at Ville Marie station, between Dunville and Fox Harbour. During the four-mile jaunt home, Anne paid little mind to the words spoken between her brother, Jim, and their father about low fish prices, and their fearful talks of a big union in the near future.

The supplies he'd ordered in St. John's would arrive in two days' time, Richard said. His sons would retrieve them in their longboat, *Revels,* at the railway terminus on the Jersey side of Placentia. Their moving lips and eyes were revealed now and then by the light of two square kerosene lanterns swaying and rattling on brackets fastened to either side of the rickety cart. At times, silhouettes of the horse's head and treetops covering Birchy Hill appeared when the clouds made way for the big, bright moon.

After another handful of visits to T & M Winter, the awkwardness Anne and Edward once felt was no more. They hurried through routine business dealings, making time for uncomplicated banter.

Anne agreed it was okay for Edward to send a postcard or two to keep in touch, as telephones outside the city were scarce.

As time passed, the emptying of inkwells spelled out their budding mutual affection, and soon the whole of Fox Harbour knew the couple's affairs. The postmistress, taking it upon herself to dish out the latest news of their relationship, met terrible dismay one day when Edward's latest card arrived. He'd invented a code of words and phrases only he and Anne could understand.

Alone in her room, rereading the handful of postcards, Anne wished she'd stayed in the city and had reunited with Edward much sooner.

The next year, 1905, Anne's mother died. When the fishing season ended that same year, Jim Healy married Kate Davis. Their daughter, Johanna, named for Jim's mother, was born two years later. Shortly after the baby was christened, Kate came down with the consumption. Keeping up with the demands of an infant was tough for the young mother and, although Jim would never let on, he'd seen too much of the disease to believe his Kate would last the winter.

"I can't stand the thought of her endin' up in that cursed hole," he'd say to Mike every morning in the fall while they cut wood for the winter.

Without her knowing, Jim had dug Kate's grave long before the frost set in. Storing her corpse in the shed, covered in salt and sawdust until the spring thaw, like some had had to do, was never an option. Kate died the day after Christmas in 1908.

After his father and his brothers helped him lower his dead sweetheart into the cold ground in the box he'd made, Jim rarely spoke. Only words related to business matters and the weather crossed his lips. The latter was an easy topic to discuss, living on an inhospitable island in the North Atlantic.

"The little one's not even a year an' a half old," and, "He can hardly rear her on his own," everyone said.

Having neither the skill nor the time to take care of a child, Jim allowed his sister, Mini, to take the baby to live with her and her husband in St. John's.

For nearly thirty years, Fox Harbour fishermen had been going to sea in Richard Healy's *Queen of Providence* until early in the fall of 1912. While all other schooners fishing around Cape St. Mary's abandoned the area on account of a scarcity of fish, the *Queen of Providence* lingered behind, ending up with a full load.

On the way home to Fox Harbour, a gale blew, nearly capsizing the boat on occasion and almost swamping her other times. But the crew managed to get her in, barely scraping past the harbour's shoals and sunkers. There she was anchored.

"Leave 'er be till the marnin'," Jim told the crew, his big arms and long frame reaching down to help swing each man to safety from the dory being battered alongside the shrinking wharf.

From their big catch, the sharemen of the *Queen of Providence*, among them Jack Foley and Charlie Sampson, were delighted with the fact they'd be able to spare a bit of sugar, molasses, and salt pork for worse-off families not so fortunate fishing from other schooners. But all hands of the crew, and the community, too, were set in deep despair the next morning. When they looked out their windows, they saw nothing but two masts of the 102-foot-long schooner reaching skyward from beneath the cold, murky water.

Among the Healys' losses that year was the death of Mike's wife, Maggie, at Christmastime. She—like Jim's wife, Kate—had been smothering with consumption for almost a year. With a busy fall fishery and the sunken schooner to fret over, Mike never had time to have a grave ready in the cemetery. Maggie's coffin was shoved and shimmied into the frozen ground next to their infant son, Richard, dead just a year himself from the same dreaded disease.

In the spring of 1913, when young ones' shoes were put away and spared for the coldest months ahead, the *Queen of Providence* was refloated and cleaned up. Many quintals of ruined salt fish were removed and discarded.

Impressed with their efforts to tidy the boat, the Healys renamed the risen schooner *Spotless Queen* and sold her back to Job Brothers. The *Annie Healy* was then the merchant family's only schooner, and their best hope of keeping the store and, in turn, part of the community afloat. The *Hope* had been lost in a gale years before, the crew having made it safely to shore in a dory. After running her course for almost forty years, the *Mary H.* was put ashore and left to rot on the rocks in The Sound.

Still holding on to the 600 postcards she'd received from Edward in the five years since they met again on that cheerful day at T & M Winter, the feelings of loneliness Anne once carried were long gone. Edward had become one of the most popular outside salesmen in the city. He was also a lieutenant of the Catholic Cadet Corps, which was quite appealing to the father of the young woman he loved. In late summer, 1909, Anne and Edward were married.

Now, twenty-two years later, Anne says it is remarkable how sitting so close to the earth where she first entered this world, in the town she couldn't wait to leave, can allow such a clear window to her past. It's the most she's reflected on her life since Richard died several years ago. And although he's buried in the city, she has no trouble sensing her daddy's presence around here today. Here he pounded the dirt beneath her feet and sailed and rowed the water in front of her eyes for so many years to stay alive, to keep his family in want of nothing. She's grateful, maybe even a little guilty, that she never thought it necessary to tell him while he was alive.

"Thanks for the lovely stories, Annie, girl," Mart says, jumping up. "I have t' visit Bridge King, too. She'll have her baby soon, ya know."

"Oh, it was nice to see you again. Say hello to Bridget and tell her good luck," Anne says.

They smile at one another and dust their skirts before heading back down the path and onto the lane to meet the road.

CHAPTER FOUR

The Mullins Family

Bridget Mullins is sitting to the kitchen table. Her eyes are half shut when Liz Bruce walks in.

"Hello, Mrs. Bruce," says Mary Ann, the Mullinses' youngest child, on her way out the door with a straw broom to beat the dust out of a couple of mats she's just flung atop the fence.

"Workin' hard, child, that's good. You'll make a fine wife someday," Liz says, patting the little girl on the head.

On the stove a round, cast iron pot shivers, its cover clanking like mad from a fit of dancing hot water inside. The pot looks primal, with strips of plated metal covering holes around the rounded edges of its bottom.

In the frying pan on the damper closest to the old pot, scruncheons hop and tumble and roll in their scalding, juicy fat. Spattering grease flies in every direction. Tiny plumes of smoke from the grease shoot off quickly from the top of the stove, lending a burnt tang to the air already thick with the smell of cooked salt fish and heated sap from the spruce junks behind the stove.

A dark fog clings to the flue of the unlit lantern. The picture of the Blessed Virgin tacked into the floral-papered wallboard folds in the damp air. Like the sound of sheets of cold spring rain hitting a tin roof, the sizzle of the frying fat allows the tired women a bit of comfort while the invisible gas of the frying onions stings the eyes out of their heads. Bridget gets up and goes to the stove to put aside two plain fish cakes she's made for herself. Then she carries the heavy pot out by the door to drain the water off the potatoes.

"'Tis 'nough t' kill ya here wit' the heat, girl," Liz says with a big heave of her chest, following Bridget outdoors.

They both agree the breath of fresh air is nice.

"Don't be talkin', Liz, girl," Bridget says, wiping the sweat from her brow and neck.

Making their way back into the house, their eyes dry quickly but are soon stinging again with the pungent smell of onions.

The steam is gone from the lantern's glass, and Liz notices the Blessed Virgin and Her sorrowful eyes peeking up at the ceiling from behind the curled edges of paper. Liz has never seen Her any other way in this house. Only first thing in the morning, before the cooking begins, and late at night, can Her full face be seen, Her halo and hands covering Her chest.

"Ya wants a frame for that picture, Bridget, girl. Give Her a good look at the place," Liz says, laughing. "Hard for Her t' keep an eye out for ya if She can't see ya."

"'Tis there a long time now like that, Liz, me dear, and we haven't had any bad luck since we come to Fox Harbour."

"I s'pose, girl," Liz says.

"Annie H'aly will be here by 'n by," Bridget says eagerly.

"Yes, Mrs. Mart said she was with her a while ago, and I saw a couple of Annie's young ones out playin' with yours o'er be the flakes. The b'ys were chasin' the girls with the sculpins," Liz laughs.

"The brazen divils," Bridget says, tut-tutting loudly. "Do ya want a fish cake?"

"No. Not hungry. Thanks. Just over here now t' get outta me own kitchen for a spell. Meself and Johnny have berries galore t' clean."

"I know," Bridget says, setting the heavy black pot back on the Waterloo. She eyes several gallons of her own berries on the floor in buckets of water waiting to be cleaned.

"We lugged this auld stove from Crawley's Island," Bridget says, lifting a damper and sliding the kettle over the open fire for a quick boil—Bridget's invitation to stay a little longer.

Liz knows a story is to follow, and she pretty much knows which one. She looks down to the daybed and thinks about sitting again.

Bridget pours tea into two orange and black Alfred Meakin cups sitting on matching saucers, ignoring Liz's intentions to get home.

"The berries aren't goin' anyplace, Liz. Here!" Bridget beckons Liz to join her at the table.

"Lovely cups, Bridget."

"I got them off the packman last month," Bridget says, adding a drop of molasses to her tea and stirring vigorously. "He said that's real gold 'round the edges."

"Imagine," Liz says, resisting the urge to make a crack about the unlikelihood of the packman selling things made of gold, let alone gold at a bargain.

The clinking of Bridget's spoon gets on Liz's nerves, and she can't help making a crack.

"Ya might want t' use that lovely cup again, Bridget, girl," Liz laughs.

"Yes, girl, John says the same t'ing to me. 'Twas almost ten year ago . . ." Bridget begins her story.

The Waterloo stove weighs a ton, and when it slipped from the grip of men lowering it with ropes from the wharf into Peter Murphy's skiff, Bridget's heart nearly broke. The stove landed front legs first, striking the gunwale. Into the water it went, shoving the boat off the length of her ropes. One of the stove's front legs was the only part that managed to stay out of the water.

A while later, four men had the stove back on shore, out to the end of the wharf, and in the boat this time. All of it. John was sure the salt water had ruined it, saying the cast iron would one day split.

"Woulda been a good time t' have Mick Fowlou 'round," Liz says.

"Yes, I often heared Poppy Mullins talk 'bout Mick Fowlou," Bridget says.

Mick Fowlou was a legendary name in Fox Harbour; he was a man known for incredible strength. Even stronger than the Healy brothers, who people can see on any given evening dragging a stubborn bull by the horns into their barn.

Around 1865, before the days of tracks and trains in Newfoundland, Mick Fowlou walked from Fox Harbour to St. John's, all 120 miles of it, to get whatever he needed to keep his family comfortable during the winter months ahead. Mick bought a new stove and had it shipped home, along with himself, on a local boat. When he got home he realized he had the wrong oven for the stove. The next morning, after learning another man from Fox Harbour was in St. John's in *his* boat and heading home in the evening, Mick threw the stove's oven on his back and walked back to the city, exchanged the oven, and sailed home with the new one.

"Yes, girl, I'll never forget the day we left Long Harbour for here," Bridget bursts back in, eager to get on with her story.

Bridget was pregnant, feeling miserable, and had to sit so long in an open boat in the middle of a not-so-warm summer.

"I shivered the whole way," she says, shaking her head and holding her arms as if it wasn't a hundred degrees in the kitchen.

The pain of leaving little Jimmy behind in his cold grave was something she tried hard to quell, but she'd never get over it as long as she lived.

The northeast wind was more than enough to fill the sail, helping drag the four-oared skiff over the sea, past the many points of land, southward toward Fox Harbour. The chill of the wind slithered around their necks and down their collars, into their bones, which felt as one with the hard boat beneath them. The steady rhythm of the dancing of their legs to keep warm made the child in Bridget's womb kick like a savage. Along with each rise and fall of the sea, the keel sliced through the lops while the boat bobbed back and forth and side to side, sometimes with sudden jerks. The whitecaps were plentiful and water on the wind splashed their faces now and then.

"Me nerves were nearly gone, Liz, girl," Bridget huffs. "I was right ready t' haul the head clean offa John."

Bridget rubbed her swollen belly beneath the heavy patched quilt John put over her before they left. Most of the time was spent gathering the blanket always slipping off her shoulders. Gripping the top of a grapnel in front of her, it felt like the cold of the rusty iron would carve a hole in the palm of her hand. But it was better than having to bend over farther to rest anyplace else.

"I'll never forgit the pain shootin' up me tired arm," Bridget says. She makes a face to try and match the soreness she remembers.

"And the youngsters, then, wit' their teeth chatterin' from beneat' the tarp."

Now and then the young ones would come out and take a few rocks from their pockets. They'd fling them at hovering gulls with slingshots their father made.

The fluttering sail and the wind in his ears didn't bother John. He was used to it. His big hand was locked hard around the skull oar as the cold and the salt spray streamed across his plump face.

He was content, somehow. Glad to be leaving it all behind. There was peace in knowing his son wasn't suffering anymore. The last four months of Jimmy Mullins's life were pure torture for John and Bridget. And all the family. The child was five and had meningitis. He was confused more and more each day and sore as a boil all over. Everyone stared at him helplessly until the headaches finally killed him.

Liz grabs the kettle, shakes her head, and shows her most pitiful face. Knowing there's a ways to go before Bridget finishes, she tops up their cups once more with tea.

"'Twasn't long before that that John taught poor Jimmy how t' skip rocks on the water from the beach below our house," Bridget goes on.

When the time came to leave Crawley's Island, only a few months had passed since little Jimmy finally gave up. They'd laid him out in his Sunday best in the front room. It wasn't the first body they'd said the rosary around in that old house. But it would be their last. Enough was enough, and they would go back every couple of years to make sure his headstone was okay, cut the grass, and say a few prayers for little Jimmy's soul. They were sick of fighting and blaming and, after all, it was no one's fault.

"'Twas God's will, we agreed, and 'tis all it ever would be," Bridget says firmly, banging her fist on the table. "By the time we left Crawley's Island, John was after fishin' and sailin' for old Richard Healy for years. My God, sure, we were married eighteen years by then. John was still fishin' from Red Island a couple of years by the time we left Crawley's Island. After the weddin', he wanted t' move back to Fox Harbour. But I wanted to stay there, ya know, close to Long Harbour, where Mom and Dad an' all me crowd were, see?"

"Like ya would," Liz agrees.

"But after so long, the thought of comin' here was invitin'. Closer to John's heart, ya know. Home. And I was happy so long as he was happy, too."

In the open boat John savoured the smoke from his pipe. He let it out slowly through his nose, as his thoughts of little Jimmy muffled in the ripples of the boat's wake. John's stare was no longer vacant but filled with pleasant thoughts of earlier evenings at home with his family, especially with the new baby, Mary Ann, due that September. He longed for the change. The newness. The past three years of winter with longer days in the woods cutting the right sticks for the house would be worth it all one day.

"He must've spent half of that last year here at the house, till 'twas done."

Crawley's Island was too open to the wind and sea, and no place to stay any longer. The bit of shelter sometimes offered here, below the Crow Hill, is considered a blessing compared to the place they'd left behind.

"He thought he'd have this place ready in time for poor Jimmy to get his strengt' back, and the change might bring him around. But the winter was milder than usual. The fish come early. And the house stood unfinished.

"We've been contented here, Liz, girl. Wit' good people like yerself an' Pad, it'd be somet'ing awful if we weren't happy." Bridget heaves a big sigh and smiles alongside Liz making her way out the door.

"See ya later on. Thanks for the mug-up."

"Don't mention it, Liz, girl."

On her way back from checking the clothes on her line, Bridget stops to watch a group of men going around the turn. It's up the other side, by Mon McCue's. John and some of the *Annie Healy*'s crew are on their way back from John Kelly's, most likely. Mon is right sick, everyone knows, and he won't be going to sea tomorrow.

Bridget is having a little rock in her chair, nodding in and out of sleep, when Michael drops an armload of spruce junks next to the stove and goes back to close the porch door.

"God, b'y! Ya give me a fright," Bridget says.

The aroma of fresh splits meanders through the strong smell of salt fish buried beneath a mound of potatoes, oleo, and a couple of gulps of milk from the goat.

"These rabbits will do yer father," Bridget says, mashing the pot of potatoes.

"He's all right so long's he have his tea an' bread an' molasses, Mudder," Michael laughs.

"Yes, but he needs more than that, out there for a week," she says.

Michael goes back to the porch and splashes water from the barrel over his face and head.

"We're goin' swimmin' into The Falls by 'n by," he says. ". . . when we're done on the flake."

"Who's *we*?" Liz teases.

"Meself, and Katie . . . and a few of the b'ys."

"A few of the b'ys, me arse," Bridget mocks.

"Now, Mudder. I'm sure you an' Fadder did stuff like that when ye were courtin.'"

"Yes, now, like we had time for the like of that." She laughs, stirring the fatback in the pan.

Bridget often peeked out the window to watch Michael's girlfriend, Katie, standing shyly at the bottom of the lane, waiting for Michael to finish his chores. Bridget never missed the lightness in her boy's step, jumping over fences and anything else he could leap over, after walking his girl home.

"Oh, my. Where do the time go at all?" Bridget wonders aloud. "Poppy will be dead three months next week. Nan seems to be gettin' her strengt' back, though. He ran on her hand and foot, didn't he, Michael? He had her ways down pat, too, I tell ya. When she was able t' get around, before her legs give out, she was awful picky, ya know. Sure, did ya know she used to spread the capelin in her garden head to tail, hundreds of them, in perfect rows? Precise! 'Twas enough to drive ya. The space between every one of them capelin the same. And none out of place. 'Magine, now! Yer grandfather loved her somet'ing shockin.' 'Tis a sin to say, I s'pose, but she's able to do a bit for herself now that he's gone. Love can make you as weak as it can make you strong, Michael. Sometimes people depends on each other too much, never thinking that there'll come the day when one or the other will be gone. Auld age can be awful sad, so . . ."

"Mudder, girl! We're only goin' swimmin'," Michael says, his big laugh tearing his fretful mother away from her thoughts and what he sees as her foolish fears.

Bridget admires her son's handsome face with her hand and then tousles his unruly head of black curls.

"Go on, girl, leave me 'lone," he jokes.

"You'll know what I means someday, me child. Now, here! Eat this an' have a nice time with the *b'ys* into The Falls *after* yer work."

Michael makes a face at her, shakes his head, and rolls his eyes. They both laugh, and Bridget pours the last drop of grease and onions over six big fish cakes. Mary Ann comes into the kitchen. She adores Michael and sits on his lap. Michael eats to his heart's content, feeding his little sister a bite whenever she asks for more with an open mouth.

"I hears yer father's big feet comin' 'round the house," Bridget says vibrantly. "Who's that with him, I wonder?"

John Mullins comes into the kitchen in a hurry. The brisk mid-August wind is at his back. He's stocky, wider than the door frame, and the benefactor of his son's good looks, according to Bridget. Little Mary Ann gets up and goes to her daddy's side.

"Michael, you're goin' out wit' us t'morrow. We haven't enough men t' make the run," John tells his son.

Michael shoots a swift, frantic look for help in his mother's direction but knows better than to protest. The look on his father's face offers no incentive for appeal. Mary Ann also looks to her mother for help. Michael always makes time for his little sister, and she adores him for it. Especially when he sings to her.

"Never ya mind lookin' at yer mudder, now, Michael," the captain says. "Make ready for a week and be down t' the stagehead in no more than an hour t' help make the boat ready for leavin' tomorrow!"

Michael is upset, having thought about swimming with Katie as often as possible for the rest of the summer. That amounts to the rest of this week, with September already sending scattered days of chilly winds from the northeast. Not that The Falls is ever that warm. The running water and shade from the trees on either side of the swimming hole keep it good and cold. But being close to Katie will take care of that, though. Michael is engulfed in thoughts of her, the prettiest thing he's ever seen. He thinks of her working a flake, or just standing there, waiting by the front gate. He sometimes makes her wait on purpose so he can watch her from the window of his room. He can see more from a distance. Close up just gets him lost. Katie is so beautiful with her big brown eyes to match her thick, long hair. And that smile that couldn't get any bigger or better. When they're alone, Michael tells her nothing else matters in this world but right now. Every time.

In Poppy's twine loft, and by the woodpile in the cold rain in front of her father's house, they kissed their way through the bitter winter and its leftovers—spring in Newfoundland. Hardly a day passes without one or the other making a crack about doing something more serious when they're alone. "We'd have t' be married, or Mudder would have me head," Katie always says. "And me fadder would have yours." When she pretends to be his bride-to-be at the altar, with the priest all the one time, Michael likes to play along as the patient groom and would love to know if she's really serious. But he's scared to ask, for fear of scaring her away. He thinks of ways to convince her they can pretend to be married and do what they like and no one will be any wiser. When she gulps at the onset of his advances, he senses she's serious, maybe even a little afraid of what might become of their desires, and he backs off, saying he's only letting on. "I know, b'y," she always lies. He prays for every drop of strength to keep from being knocked over by the pounding of his heart, his legs right weak.

At these times, more frequent these days, Katie's head falls slowly to one side, and her full lips press tightly together while her stare drains him of all energy. Then he doesn't have the guts to hold her the way he wants to, the way she might like him to. The look in her eyes forces him to run from his thoughts, to laugh awkwardly, to say stupid things he knows she won't recall the next day because each night apart—the waiting, the dreaming, and more waiting until those few short hours each evening bring them together again—allows their minds plenty of rest from the night before.

He was deflated at the thought of not seeing Katie for a week or so. But something enlivens him again, something he's not sure he's ever felt. Pride, perhaps. *Did Daddy just call me a man?* Michael wonders, smiling, and looking back toward the kitchen, afraid his mother might see him and wonder what's the matter with him, smiling to himself. He's close to running out through the house, to asking his father. But a conversation about life, they both know, isn't about to happen now, if ever.

"What about your dream, Michael?" Mary Ann sings out in an anxious voice.

"What dream is that, dear?" Bridget asks her little girl.

"I can't say. Michael said not to say it to anyone."

"It's just a dream, sweetheart," Michaels sings out from his room.

"But you . . ." Mary Ann is interrupted when her father comes back in from outdoors.

"Go out and beat the mats some more, Mary Ann, darlin'," John tells his daughter.

Up in his room, Michael's thoughts are consumed with Katie and his plans for the future. At least he'll get to spend this evening with Katie, and there'll be plenty of time to long for her at sea. Maybe even make up a poem or song to surprise her when he returns. In another couple of years at the most, he knows, they'll be married. Michael plans to go to school, to get away from this life of uncertainty, and to sing wherever and whenever he can. But there will be plenty of time at sea to go over all of this in his head.

Now he's consumed with Mary Ann's reminder of the awful dream he's been having lately. There's no thunder. Nor lightning. The sun is even shining. But he's floating, more like fumbling, above a raging sea, crashing through walls of spray and foam. He's hurting. Buckled over in pain. But he's singing. It's a sad song. Mary Ann is there, too, but not in danger, just smiling, listening to her favourite person singing. All of a sudden, a schooner rises in front of him and crashes down upon him. He's sent to the ocean floor, where he gets caught up in seaweed and old nets. He hears his father's voice yelling orders to hoist the mains'l, with an old man trying to help. He's relieved to be back on board the boat, but they can never get the sail to budge. The old man isn't trying hard enough. "Pull! Pull!" Michael screams at the old man. The old man doesn't respond, but his head turns slowly toward Michael. Beneath his torn sou'wester there is no face. Just blackness. Space. Staring into the old man's head, the wind swings the mains'l's boom and strikes Michael in the guts. He's carried over the side and into the boiling sea again. That's when he always wakes up. He's had the same dream for the past week or more, and shared it with Mary Ann and Katie one evening out walking around the harbour.

Down in the kitchen, Bridget serves John his fish cakes and sits at the table at the opposite end to eat her own.

"Who's out to the shed at the wood, John?" she asks.

"The youngf'las from H'aly's Wharf. They're luggin' a few junks from the store for the trip. There's plenty left t' do you till we gets back. When I'm done eatin', I'm goin' over t' tell Mother we'll be leavin' in the mornin.'"

Through the window Bridget watches Healy's shore boys lug the handcart piled high with wood down the rocky lane. They turn left onto the road leading past Murray's flakes to Healy's Wharf. She turns her head back to stir John's tea and lays his mug on the oven door to keep it warm.

In fifteen or twenty minutes, John is back from his mother's. Bridget has his food packed away in a brin bag and is back in her chair for another rock.

"How long will ye be gone this time?" She hates asking the same old questions.

"A week at the most. As long as it takes t' make up for the last trip, I s'pose, Bridget, girl. Mon's right sick . . ."

"Yes, I heard."

". . . and John Kelly, too, but he says he'll come out and do what he's able. Ellen was fit to be tied."

"I s'pose she was. I wouldn't want you goin' out, either, if you were sick," Bridget assures.

"And brudder, Pad," John goes on. "Pad's liable t' be lyin' down for another week after fallin' off the roof."

Besides the familiar low key in the house when it's time for John to head back to sea, there is something else. Looking up from the floor where he's knelt by the stove to poke at the fire, he sees Bridget's eyes are glassy, like they've been polished, and darting around the room. She rarely stops to focus on anything while her hands find their way in and out of her apron pocket. Her fingers fiddle through her hair, unguided, without purpose. She knows he knows she's been talking about little Jimmy again.

"Where do the time go at all, John? Where do it go?"

John heads to the porch for more splits. He doubts sailing away from little Jimmy ever took away the hurt. Bridget retelling that story will never make the next day any easier. He bangs the palms of his big hands hard off the woodbox.

"'Twas God's will, Bridget. 'Twas God's will. That's what we agreed."

"I know, John, b'y. I know. I'm sorry. I'm sorry." Bridget sobs from her place at the table.

"'Tis not yer fault, girl. 'Tis not our fault," he says.

Michael comes down over the stairs and quickly stops singing when he sees his mother crying at the table. He pretends not to notice, keeps going again, and does the same when he sees his father hove over the woodbox. Michael heads out the porch door. The enthusiasm he'd been feeling is banished again by the talk of his dead little brother. He was only seven when his little brother died, but it seems like yesterday, they were that close.

"What about your dream, Michael?" Mary Ann's voice breaks into Michael's thoughts.

"Who knows what dreams are all about, sweetheart," he says, kneeling and pulling her close to him. "It's just a dream. I just told you and Katie for something to do, that's all. I didn't mean to scare ya."

"Will ya take me into The Falls with ya as soon as ya gets home again?" she asks, reluctant to accept his explanation and his having to go away.

"Of course I will, sweetheart," Michael says softly. "Of course I will." He kisses her on the head and takes off down the lane toward the schooner, where his father told him to go and see if the men need any help. He joins Kate at the end of the lane and they both walk to the *Annie Healy*.

CHAPTER FIVE

The Bruces

The wind from the northwest is strong. Sporadic gusts swoop past The Isaacs, stirring the grassy meadow and the long, wide expanse of black spruce, fir, and juniper of The Neck. A schooner hove to in the cove bobs gracefully. Cool salt water hisses and sighs over the lines anchoring the large boat to its rest. Great white sheets of reddish canvas fastened by rope to the tall masts of the boat have been hoisted to dry. Swift blows from the passing wind echo throughout the vast hills of scantily clad rock strewn along the coastline, all the way to Ship Harbour.

Two young boys skip rocks across the top of the small whitecaps, trying to hit the wooden nameplate, *Pauline*, on the bow of the schooner. Lunging mischievously in their bare feet, the lads taunt the ebb tide. They slip now and then on the green, slime-covered rocks. Their shouts and laughter get carried away on the breeze.

The pushing and dragging of beach rocks by the open sea on the other side of The Neck is eerie, as if the boys might be crushed and swept away any minute. But the heavy action of the sea is far enough away, and the creepiness only adds to their excitement.

Old schooners lay abandoned, rotting in varying degrees around the whole of the harbour. They're wonderful playgrounds for curious children in their spare time. In the little cove below King's Meadow, a pair of young teenage girls plays, posing for each other on the mainmast of a beached schooner.

"Luh, I'm Greta Garbo," one shouts over the rustling of the trees.

The girls love pretending to be famous people. They hear about them from newspaper theatre ads. It makes them feel as though it will help fulfill their dreams of one day getting to St. John's to see a real moving picture. They'd do anything in the world to get a train ride to the city.

"Lots of people from Fox Harbour lives in New York where the stars are, makes the movin' pictures," one says, continuing to strike poses for an audience of birds. Crooked crows scowl at full-bellied kingfishers fluttering to dry themselves on dead, grey tree branches.

"I know. Sure, one of the H'alys lives in California, where Hollyrood is," the other says, certain she's outdone her friend.

A little farther up the beach from the pair of daydreaming starlets, four or five other girls, younger ones, collect chainies for their cubby. Huddled behind a big rock, in the shade of an old tree, they count their little treasures. The little pieces of old cups, saucers, and plates, their once-jagged edges smoothed by years of tumbling in the sea, are the real thing for playing house. Homemade rag dolls with woolly hair and mismatched buttons for eyes rest on the big rock. They gaze through the yellow grass, partially hiding the girls meticulously sifting through the black muck filling the spaces between their toes.

Goose grass appears in places, tall and waving in the breeze. A swampy floor reveals itself. Juicy mussels hide in their shells, but not well enough to escape the flocks of hungry seabirds constantly circling the earth for food.

The girls are too busy playing to bother chasing off the noisy gulls stealing from their collection of mussels promised to their parents in exchange for time to play.

The gusts of wind leaping over The Green cause crisp white sheets on clotheslines to snap sharply. Tiny twisters of dust leaving the road spin to their death at the water's edge.

By the time it reaches The Bottom, the big gust of wind fades considerably. It slightly rattles the half-raised, single-paned glass in Bruce's front kitchen window.

Liz is busy darning her husband's sweater. It wasn't all that long ago she'd mended it, and here she is wasting precious time at it again. It's a lovely summer's day with no end to work in sight.

Earlier this morning, before the sun lent its warmth to the misty air, Pad was down to the landwash lending a hand to Mike and Henry Healy. They were tanning nets for the *Annie Healy*. The sails were done last week. The heat from the big fire warming the copper tanning pot was too much for Pad, so he took off his sweater and laid it on a rock.

Nearby, a few young boys were rubbing the belly of a sculpin they'd just caught, causing the fish to inflate to a good-sized ball. A handful of palm-size rocks tossed into the ugly, bony lips and the wide-open mouth of the fish gave it a bit of weight.

A flanker from the tanning pot fire landed on Pad's sweater, quickly etching a hole in the wool.

Just as he was about to give the fish the first kick, six-year-old Arthur Sampson buckled in fits of laughter at the sight of big Pad Bruce cursing and stomping up out of the landwash and onto the road.

"Jaysus! Jaysus! Jaysus!" Pad shouted, dancing across the coral- and conch-covered beach in his rubber boots. "Liz'll have me fookin' head," he said, shaking and swinging his sweater over his head, each curse delivered with a passion deeper than the one before.

The group of young fellas, along with Healy's shore boys, laughed at the top of their lungs.

"Get back t' work, ye!" roared Mike Healy.

Henry Healy snickered loudly through his nose, rooting up more laughter from the boys on the wharf now intensely involved in a game of soccer with the ill-fated fish.

Walking toward home, Pad waved his sweater to Liz as she edged along Murray's high flakes with an armload of salt fish. Laying them side by each, she was careful not to let them overlap. It was her second time this morning laying the same pile of fish out.

"Put it on the table next t' the rockin' chair where me needles are," she said.

The look on Pad's face told a familiar tale, and he knew he didn't have to say a word. Liz turned away and smiled, careful not to let Pad see.

It's no secret she loves him to pieces. No matter the time or day, or what they're at, together or alone, she always feels that strong surge of adrenalin in her chest, as he's constantly in her thoughts.

Pad is funny. Perhaps too funny at times. But she'd choose no world other than the one he's in, if she was ever made to decide. She takes his temper tantrums lightly, knowing he's liable to be making a wisecrack a minute later. "Pretty bad if ya can't have a laugh," he always says. "An' he's right," Liz told Bridget Mullins earlier. "Ya never know what's goin' to come out of his mout' next," she said. "But he's as good as gold an' would give ya the last bite out of his mouth if he t'ought ya really needed it."

Bridget didn't disagree. All the men were the same. They had to be. But Pad *was* really funny.

Liz thinks back to last year, in May month, when she sheared the sheep by herself. It's usually a job for two women, but there was no one else around that day. The sheep were good and round, and one at a time, the fidgety, smelly brutes were held down with one arm while, with her free hand, she forced the wool off. The old scissors she used wouldn't cut butter. Carrying a load of freshly cut wool in her apron with the illusive feeling of more fish and a brighter tomorrow always brought a smile to Liz's pretty, round face. Her long ponytail of dark brown hair swung side to side over her back as she waded through the tall grass behind their house. She'd washed the wool once or twice in Billy's Brook and would do so again before carding it. Throughout that summer she and Ellen, her daughter, picked at the wool stored out in the shed, removing twigs and other dirt. Later on in the fall, she carded and spun the wool. Over the winter, while Pad wore out his old sweater, Liz knit a new one. She often wonders what all the hard work is for.

After working on the flake since daylight this morning, Liz made her way home.

"There's no end to it," she bawled out to Lize Foley.

Lize was coming out the side door of the church, brushing dirt and sawdust from her apron.

"Tell me about it," Lize muttered. "That bit of wood should keep Fadder Dee from complainin' 'bout the musty smell next time he comes. I s'pose we'll be let into heaven for keepin' him warm."

She tut-tutted and tossed her head, then rounded the corner of the church and disappeared from sight before Liz could finish her next sentence.

"One of these days the fish'll be so big an' plentiful we'll be able to buy sweaters in St. John's an' I won't have to be mendin' Pad's all the time," Liz said, not caring if anyone could hear her or not.

"One of these days the men might learn t' make their own," said Bridget Mullins, shouting over the flapping of her sheets next door.

"Ha! Mind, now. Make their own, me arse," Liz said.

Both women laughed, knowing full well there'd be little chance of that ever happening. Winter was the time for that stuff. Mending sweaters and traps. There was too much else to be done before and after.

With their husbands, fathers, and sons fishing together, most of the women in Fox Harbour get along well. A cup of flour here, a few potatoes there, and a bit of this and a bit of that to get them by is part of their lives. All ages share a special sense of the Irish humour. Like their ancestors, much of the time it's all they have to get them through.

Liz can't believe the sweater is nearly a year old already. It seems like just yesterday she made it. She had mended it at least half a dozen times since. When she thinks about it, she supposes he hasn't done too badly with it, considering what a man goes through in a year. Not to mention the poor sweater. Pad loves it, and anything else his dear wife makes with her own hands. The sweater slows the etching of raw rope burns into his forearms. It helps numb the chill on dreary days at sea when the bitter black fog creeps through the dyed stitches, into his skin, gnawing at his tired bones.

Liz was up before daylight this morning, like every morning, and had taken the fish from the round pile, carefully laying them out side by side on the bough-covered flake above the salt water in time to catch the early breezes mid-August dawns are sure to send. At first she thought she'd pack them up for Pad and Uncle Watt to lug up to Healy's, but then she decided it was best to give them an extra day in the gentle wind. The sun had appeared in places, eventually burning off the fog. There'll be no worry of ending up with number-two fish when the time comes to trade them in. It will never see the West Indies. Not if she has her way. If she can make it merchantable, and once the score is just about settled on fishing supplies and food, her well-made fish might mean she can have that new shawl she's been wanting for ages. She thought she'd have it last year, but what a terrible year it had been for the whole community. And with the extra costs associated with fixing up the *Annie Healy* this past winter and spring, the Healys are not likely to do favours for anyone. Hanging on a wooden hanger in Healy's store window for the past two years, the shawl has been the envy of most women in Fox Harbour.

There'd be some talk if they ever see me wit' that on me back, she thinks. But it will hardly stop her from buying it, if she can. She wonders when the shawl draped around her tired shoulders will fall apart for good. Lize Foley has a lovely soft, black shawl sent home from one of her girls in the States but won't dare wear it, afraid people will say she's grand.

Down by the water the contents of last night's slop pails entertain ugly sculpins, tough conners, and flatfish alike. Saddleback gulls, their voices like angry men, banish smaller gulls with quick swipes of their great, wide wings. The regal kingfishers mind their own business and dive for fish small enough to fit their bills.

Pad and Mike talk about what a fine day it is after all the rain last night.

"These nets should do the *Annie*'s traps for all next year."

"'Deed they will, Pad," Mike says with little expression.

Henry grabs the handle of a galvanized pail and dips cod-liver oil from a nearby vat. His nose twitches uncontrollably and his stomach convulses beneath his soiled overalls. He pours the reeking liquid into the blackened tanning pot bubbling with water, tallow, and ochre. With a homemade wooden ladle, Mike and Pad take turns carefully removing large amounts of the scalding liquid from the pot. Their birch brooms have seen better days. They've been soaked in tanning oil and used to smack the sails laid out on the bawn. The mixture will stick and sink in.

After scraping dried seaweed and other dirt from a seine, Cyril Leary, one of the shore boys, painstakingly gathers the net. He soaks it in the gigantic copper pot filled with tanning oil. His eyes water and squint constantly while his nose and upper lip lift to one side from the merciless stink.

With soot-soiled faces, the men agree they'd rather be at anything else on such a lovely day. The shore boys say the same thing, but only where the men can't hear. The oozing, awful reek is a familiar one around the town. So is the sound of crackling, burning sticks and boughs under half a dozen or so similar black pots spread along the shoreline on both sides of the harbour. Erratic breezes off the putrid water suck fire through last year's blasty boughs. Thousands of rust-coloured spruce needles burst and pop in all directions.

Cyril Leary's eyes are still watering as he keeps the fire going. Billy Penny spreads the freshly tanned nets and helps the big men roll the extra sails spread along the shore.

Yesterday Billy painted the three dories aboard the *Annie Healy*. He's done that for the past four years.

"This fresh coat will do 'em till this time next year," he tells Cyril.

It might also be this time next year, Billy jokes, before he gets the yellow oil paint off his hands, neck, and face from scratching fly bites. His mother will surely make him scrub the skin clean before he hits the hay tonight. They both laugh, although they say there's nothing funny about it.

Billy's real last name is Murray, but, with several William Murrays in Fox Harbour, they call him after his mother's maiden name. Billy went to work for the Healys when he was ten. Cyril started last summer. Billy torments Cyril about Nellie Reilly, Billy's cousin, but gets little reaction, as they're already considered an item. The boys' afternoon will be spent turning over hay they'd cut a few days earlier. "If it don't cloud over," Billy says, "it should dry 'nough to store 'way in the loft 'fore dark."

No job is more disgusting than that of the shore boys. Constantly covered in fish guts and blood, their skin absorbs the stink and keeps it for a long time. Cuts never seem to heal because of the continuous exposure to salt. Mothers and grandmothers apply poultices of bread and Vaseline to draw infection from red-raw waterpups on hands and wrists. The roar of greedy gulls, along with the stench of liver oil vats, is a constant, too.

The boys are good workers. They're proud to have a credit at Healy's store to help their families along in the hard, bitterly cold months of winter, when fish are safe from men and most men safe from the sea. Boats are hauled up, turned over or covered, made better, and given a rest until spring.

The hiss of steam from the heavy black kettle anchored on the stove takes Liz from her thoughts. She grabs the bottle of Sloan's Liniment from the windowsill, knocking over the plastic Blessed Virgin she bought from the packman last month. She's glad *her* Mary, Mother of God, is able to keep watch over the house, unlike the wrinkled picture tacked up in Mullins's kitchen next door.

With the palms of her hands, Liz gives the window a bang. She puts the medicinal bottle back under the frame of the raised pane.

Pad's sweater is mended and laid over the back of the chair, and the darning needles tucked safely away behind the dishes in the sideboard. A bowl filled to the brim with plump blueberries is off balance. It teeters between the smooth, rounded indents in the seat of the chocolate-coloured wooden chair from her Grandmother Duke's on The Rams. Uncle Watt never fails to say where it came from before anyone sits on it. Liz grasps the sides of the table with her hands to quicken her trip to the stove. The metal bowl clinks with a dull softness when her bare knee strikes the chair.

After his work with the Healys, Pad goes to John Kelly's to get Uncle Watt.

Liz changes half the water on the salt fish in soak since last night and throws in the potatoes, carrots, and turnips. She then tops the boiler off with fresh water from the brook, lays more dry wood into the fire, and waits for the pot to boil.

The rest of the morning is spent cleaning berries to be used in pies and jam later in the fall. She hopes Pad will remember to cut the rhubarb tonight. She's anxious to make her second batch and to have the pantry shelves full of jam for the winter, until next summer.

Scratching the bites on the back of her neck, Liz tut-tuts at the thought of the nippers and blackflies she'll have to face for the next two weeks of evenings berry picking on The Barrens. The rust of the pail's wire handle, colouring the deep cracks in her callused hands, allows a bit of grip until the sweat begins. She's spent more time this year telling Johnny to stop eating berries than she did picking.

It's not much odds to her, though, remembering the excitement berry picking brought her as a child. Although, there were times she had like to let Johnny eat until he was blue in the face, like her mother did with her. But berries were more plentiful back then, it seemed.

Dabbing the dried-in rust spots with a damp rag, Liz watches Johnny play with the cat's kittens under the raised window from where she told him not to stir. She has enough to worry about.

Johnny's not half as much trouble as Ellen, who's eight and liable to be anywhere, anytime, at anything. She was no better, herself, when she was young. Ellen is tough as a gad. She brings water from the brook and wood from the shed every day without being reminded. Johnny is only five and not strong enough to do that yet. But he's a fine hand at cleaning berries and carrying shavings from the damp porch for someone else to light the stove with in the morning.

The moment Liz thinks to tell the King boys to go home and for Johnny to get in the house, she sees their mother waddling her way up the lane.

"Get home t' the house, ye little shaggers."

Bridge King's voice is muffled by the closing window.

Johnny bolts past the tied-back storm door and into the kitchen with an armload of dangling, mewing kittens. The harsh bawl of the scolding mother cat isn't far behind.

"Put them cats in wit' their mother before she scratches the face off ya again," Liz says.

She expects Bridge King to drop in but sees her heading off down the lane again. Her boys criss-cross each other's path just out of the reach of their mother's hand.

Johnny lays two kittens in the wooden box and two more in the iron washtub. He watches them skid down the smooth side of the glass washboard and fumble into the waiting mother cat, who grabs them by the scruff of the neck. One by one, she lugs them across the floor and drops them into the box with the others fast asleep on the bloodstained patchwork quilt.

"Can we clean the berries now, Mam?"

"Take this rag first an' wash yer hands out in the porch."

"Yeah."

"Did you an' the b'ys have fun wit' the kittens?" Liz asks softly.

"Yeah." Johnny's voice is raspy and tired from a long morning in the fresh air.

"Can we keep one, Mam?" Johnny pleads, catching a blueberry stem between the nails of his thumb and forefinger.

"Ya better not let yer father hear ya say that. One cat is able t' catch mice an' rats as well as two," she warns. "Ya better enjoy yer time wit' 'em before they goes to the harbour."

The kitchen is quiet, and they go about their work.

CHAPTER SIX

Liz Bruce's Living Nightmare

The sun no longer lingers behind the Crow Hill. It's flooding Liz Bruce's kitchen with wide bands of light, drawing attention to the air full of dust from the floor just swept.

Squinting past the glare coming through the front window, Liz sees two young boys running past the house. Their bodies twist and turn as they throw pine cones at one another. They jump, push, trip, and fall into the grass off the side of the path where they rampse and spar. Their playful squeals rob the house of its stillness.

Mindlessly putting her fingers into the bowl, Liz takes out a few blueberries and begins cleaning them. She drops them into the dented aluminum boiler quarter-full of fresh water. The sounds from the boys outside drag her back to a time she'd sooner forget, but her Catholic guilt will hardly allow her mind to stand for such inactivity.

Through a film of familiar tears, the bright sheen of the wet berries dims. Liz is mindful not to catch Johnny's attention. She dabs her eyes with her apron, and realizes little is likely to distract her son from his work and eagerness to have blueberry jam and cow's cream on fresh bread. His favourite.

She sometimes craves to revisit the same old sad excuse for a break against this life of repetitiveness. There are happier stories in her family, but this one always manages to make itself welcome while Pad's not around.

In their nine years of marriage, little has gone on in Liz's heart without Pad's knowing. In or out of his company, thoughts of her dead brothers often make away with her time. In the grip of old torment, she shuts her eyes and fights to turn her head from the window. By the time she looks back, the boys are gone, but their untroubled voices are heard above a gust of wind fresh off the water. She begins to hum a song, but no tune can keep the memories away.

Liz supposes if she hadn't heard Mammy retelling her own version of the story so often, she'd have little or no account of it at all. But Mammy always included her in what is now another hushed legend in Fox Harbour—one so dreadful her own brothers' ghosts have appeared to generations of Fox Harbour children listening to one too many stories at night, the horror on their faces when they died, however they died, etched forever in the colossal rocks of the Crow Hill. Liz has her own version of the tragedy, and none can top this one. She'd like to be able to tell it to others. Perhaps then there'd be a chance of the nightmare going away. But the nerve for that will never come.

Liz's brothers, Ben and Mike Sampson, got a sleigh for Christmas. Liz was only four and too young, Mammy said, to go galleying with them in the meadow alongside the path leading to The Sound. Instead, Liz spent the cold, clear morning watching a snowball fight between a crowd of older boys and girls on the frozen harbour. It was Christmas, and there was so much to do. There would be plenty of time for her to play with Ben and Mike, Mammy said.

After an hour or more of whizzing down the frozen tracks of the path below The Barrens, tipping over, rolling, tumbling, swallowing mouthfuls of snow, and tackling the steep climb back to the top again, the excited brothers took turns dragging one another on the sleigh through paths cut for hauling wood. They might even find a rabbit or two to take home to Mammy for cleaning. A drop of rabbit soup would be nice after such a long day in the cold. And Mammy made the best drop of rabbit soup in the harbour.

It was only early, and, if they liked, they could go all the way to The Sound—a long, deep arm of the sea reaching in past Little Placentia and Fundy Hill. It's accessible by land through paths in over the hill behind Fox Harbour. A few people still lived there, planting gardens and setting nets.

When dinnertime passed without the boys' return, no one paid much mind. "They'll be home when they're good 'n hungry," Daddy said, tipping back the first of many drinks he would have that day. No one worried. After all, they were just two young lads with a new sleigh. Christmastime, and what else could you expect?

About four thirty that evening, the winter sun set on the harbour's smooth surfaces. Rough patches of ice near The Bottom glistened.

Liz, alongside Mammy and some other women, went around to every house in the harbour. The boys were likely caught up in some foolish games only boys could make up. In their minds, each of the searchers had the answer, knowing the boys would show up sooner or later. Perhaps they were long back from sliding and, in their excitement, decided to offer rides to other boys brave enough to hold on for dear life, the brothers pulling with all their might. "P'raps they're off on other paths. There's t'ousands of 'em 'round here," one woman exaggerated. "What if they went out on the sea ice an' went too far where the water don't freeze like it do in here?" one woman whispered, thinking Mammy couldn't hear. "Nah," a whisper returned, "someone would've seen 'em."

Liz and Mammy headed for home, alone with inconsistent pangs of gathering panic. The road was blanketed with fresh, thick snow that scrunched and squeaked beneath their boots. The snowflakes were big. Perfect for catching on your tongue. But there was no time for that. The increasing wind kept the ice-covered potholes clear of snow, providing little glimpses of light whenever snow clouds parted for the light of the moon. Slushy tears climbed clumsily across Liz's numb, red cheeks, under the band of her wet woollen cap, and into her frozen ears ringing from the last words she heard her brothers speak:

"C'mon, Mammy, let Lizzie come wit' us. We'll mind her."

The hurt was made stronger when Liz and Mammy entered their kitchen stuffed with tall, silent men ready to take to the woods for the night in search of the boys. Liz's tears merged with Mammy's as the pair fell into each other's embrace alongside the wood stove.

The smell of alcohol was sharp and strong in the heat of the small room, as each man downed several swallows of moonshine to fend off the cold, uncertain hours ahead. Daddy made sure every man had enough shot for his gun to last the better part of the night.

"We should've went wit' Ben an' Mike, Mammy," Liz sobbed.

Her hot tears plopped to the floor, mixing with the melting, dripping snow from her cap and mitts hung on the drooping line above the stove. Other drops of water danced and sizzled audibly on the stovetop, melting snow from Liz's sodden coat. She was too distracted to take it off. Mammy was too preoccupied to notice. A brew of melting snow and relentless tears trickled into the dirt-filled cracks of the uneven floorboards.

"I wants t' go find 'em, Daddy," Liz cried.

Daddy didn't have to speak for Liz to know she was too small to leave Mammy's side.

With oil lamps, and torches made from sticks and rags soaked in kerosene, men and older boys from the harbour took to the woods. The scene was like an ancient ritual march, without the chanting, without even a word. Prayers were said in silence and all ears listened vigilantly for any sign of Ben and Mike. Two wood sleds with heavy quilts were towed along in case the boys had frostbite or were hurt and unable to walk. Some carried axes, others bucksaws, to clear windfalls from the paths. Each man had a flask of moonshine or rum. A speckled trail of black spit ran alongside the men's tracks from the strong plugs of Jumbo and Beaver carefully savoured in the corners of their blackened mouths. Others nursed pipes, while a few smoked cigarettes. Tobacco smoke whipped around and over the road behind them, mixing with the coal- and woodsmoke sucked from chimneys by the rising wintry wind.

Having to use precious oil to light the way was an awful expense, and what an arse-trimming the boys would get once they were brought home, Daddy said, breaking the stillness of the journey. Gunshot blasts, along with the boys' names called out, echoed all through the hills of Fox Harbour and around The Sound. This continued until daylight. The noises stirred only the attention of resting gulls, nervous hare, and crows that never seemed to sleep at all. Other than Daddy's words, sounds occupying the air consisted only of wood and iron sleigh runners on snow, boots scuffing, mouths spitting, and a growing chorus of huffs and puffs. The trudging through heavy snow began to take its toll.

At different times of the decaying night and budding morning, men were heard coming under Healy's flakes, in front of where the Sampsons lived. Liz hadn't stirred from Mammy's arms in the front kitchen window since the men left last night. The kettle boiled steadily, and Mammy passed around cups of tea to the women who came and went all night. The mark from the little girl's nose and forehead stayed on the windowpane full of condensation.

Mammy paid little mind to the fretful company and their theories of where the boys might be. The snow had stopped about six hours ago, around ten o'clock. Only a couple of torches remained lit, as the moon's reflection on the snow and harbour ice was plenty to guide the tired men home. Their collective laboured breath created a thick fog that hovered over their slouched backs. The air turned more bitter with each step taken.

In a mad tear to greet her brothers, Liz slipped on the hooked mat in front of the porch door. She grabbed hold of the bucksaw's handle where it hung on the wall alongside the woodbox. Dangling by one arm, she reached for the latch of the door and pushed it open. She was like something wild. Would she scold her brothers or would she be happy, saying how she can't wait to go galleying tomorrow? Daddy must be awfully vexed, as no talking could be heard. They must have each gotten a good clout and there'd be no more galleying for the rest of the winter, Liz fretted. Perhaps she wouldn't get to go at all. And like Mammy said to the women earlier, it would be more Ben's fault than Mike's because Ben was older and he should have better sense.

But Daddy was the only one coming in the lane past Healy's. The heavy quilts he carried in his arms looked no different than when he had left—no signs of tired or sleeping boys beneath—and she could see no smaller legs scuffing behind as Daddy trudged through the slush. A trail of smoke from his pipe lingered behind him. At the best of times he was quiet. Now he was quieter than ever, not even humming. That couldn't be good.

"Where are the b'ys, Daddy?" Liz asked.

"Get in the house before ya catches yer death!" he snapped. "What are ya doin' up at this hour?"

Daddy was rarely any other way than cheerful, and it hurt her to hear him this way.

Liz had slept in Mammy's arms in the rocking chair since just after midnight. With an emptiness she'd never known, she made her way to her room. The steps of the stairs creaked under her woolly socks. Guided by the light of the tall, white Lent candle in Mammy's hand, Liz crawled into her bed. Except for down at the foot where Mammy placed a hot beach rock wrapped in brin from the oven, the bedclothes were icy. Mammy flicked the usual douse of holy water in the sign of the Cross over the bed, but Liz still couldn't relax. She thought only of Ben and Mike. In the middle of Mammy's prayers, Liz drifted off to sleep.

She dreamt of Ben and Mike and their excitement as they left with the sleigh Daddy had built in secret in the shed last fall. The brothers roared at each other for an extra turn while Liz dodged a hard snowball on the bumpy harbour ice. She was taller, older, somehow. She slipped, clambering over the fresh frost newly formed on the black rocks at the harbour's edge. It was across the road from Mr. Jack Foley's. "Wait, b'ys! I'll go galleyin' wit' ye now! Wait! Wait!" Her shouts turned to frantic shrieks. The ice beneath her boots trembled for a second before giving way, and she slipped. Backward and downward she went. Her double-knit red and white mitts allowed no grip on the glittery rocks. She twisted her body, and screamed to her friends on the harbour for help. They didn't so much as look her way. The boys' shouting and the laughter and the squawks from her frolicking friends became muffled as she slid beneath the broken ice. The freezing, salty hands of the sea had her. Then she woke.

Afraid and shivering in a cold sweat, Liz was relieved to be in her damp, chilly bed and not in the icy water of the harbour. It was still dark, and she wanted to get up and go down to the kitchen, where it was warm. She could hear Mammy rocking next to the stove, the clinking of her rosary beads, and the crying whispers of her prayers. The storm door opened and closed when Daddy finished his tea. The door never opened once he was in for the night, unless it was really cold and someone took pity on the cat. The poor old cat. How did anyone ever know she was out by the door when she was too cold to bawl? Mammy would look out the window, after troubling herself getting up from her rocking chair, and barely see the cat for frost. The cat would have the look on her face like she knew she had no business in the house but that she'd likely freeze to death if someone didn't let her in soon. Mammy would move the folded quilt lying across the bottom of the porch door with her feet, which were always cold, and lift the latch on the storm door. "Come in, ya poor devil," Mammy would say. The cat would head straight for the side of the stove and lay on the floor, panting and purring before closing her eyes for a little snooze. Mammy wouldn't be comfortable in her chair when the cat would be up bawling, too hot and heading back to the door, yowling to be let out again. "And that's the last blessed time you're getting in the house this night, s'posin' ya freezes to death," Mammy would say. But she always got up to let her in, and out, and in. Every time.

Mammy probably wouldn't say much if Liz went downstairs. She might enjoy the company but would warn of the long day tomorrow, which was already here. And what if Daddy came home and Liz was up when she was supposed to be in bed? But what if the boys were with him? Mammy would make them tea to warm them, and they'd share their dark Christmas cake because they were so hungry. And they wouldn't fight, too tired from the ordeal.

Instead, Liz stayed in bed, wishing her window was on the side of the house facing the road. With each crash as an icicle fell from the eaves, she bolted across the little room, stood on a chair, and tried raising the window. But it was frozen shut. Perhaps the noise she heard wasn't icicles at all. Maybe it was the boys, sneaking around the house making sure everyone was in bed, asleep, before they came in because they heard Daddy talking about the arse-trimming they'd get for wasting lamp oil. She slept no more until later that night.

The days and nights repeated themselves, as visitors, conversation, and flour and molasses became scarce. For the first time ever, there was silence in Sampson's kitchen at Christmastime. Night after night, people, sometimes crowds, sat around surmising, humming, praying, whispering, smoking, and drinking. The rattling of prayer beads and the drone of the rosary could be heard around the harbour through the downstairs windows kept opened when the heat from the stove was too much. Bright dresses and colourful woollen sweaters were replaced by garments of black dyed in preparation of the worst, which most already considered at hand but wouldn't mention.

The rest of December and most of January in Fox Harbour were filled with worry, anger, desolation, and utter hopelessness, as each day bared nothing of the boys' whereabouts. Each trip in over the hills in spring to haul out wood on the last bit of snow carried with it expectations of at least a hint at what might have happened. Talk grew. Optimism faded. New schooners, like the *Annie Healy,* were carved from deep in the woods to bring in what could only be a better century than the last.

When the days got longer, the ice eventually left the harbour. Men in schooners, skiffs, and dories plowed the waters in search of Ben and Mike. The windswept shorelines around the harbour and in The Sound were scanned in the rain and on sunny days, which were scarce.

Desperation grew with each new blade of goose grass visible at low tide in springtime. The arrival of each new dandelion behind Sampson's house was accompanied by a wild depression poorly disguised in the compulsory nods and smiles. Everything seemed as black as the clothes on their backs. And the dreary, bony fingers of light creeping past the closed, dusty window blinds of every room did little to lift anyone's spirit.

Where the strength came from to carry on, no one knew. Mammy said that until the day she died. People's gestures of sympathy became old and meaningless. Nothing mattered. The boys weren't coming home. God's will. Sooner or later, it seemed all words had been said, and, for the first time in Fox Harbour, finding something else to talk about was a problem.

CHAPTER SEVEN

The Kellys

Roaring flames from the wind's vacuum send crackling flankers against the glass door of the Parlor Stove in John and Ellen Kelly's front room. The stovepipe rattles. Creosote dust hovers where the shaking pipe meets the chimney. Some flankers fly under the chrome-plated footrest and begin to burn into the sail canvas covering most of the floorboards. The edges of the dory-green canvas curl in places, exposing the unpainted spruce planks beneath. Eager hands and a little birch broom sweep up the sparks and smidgens of ash left behind.

Another heavy gust of wind draws air quickly up the chimney, rolling the damper key of the stovepipe shut. A large puff of smoke is sent through the vent and other seams of the stove where the asbestos rope lining is rotted and worn.

Gran Kelly coughs from the smoke between lines of the rosary. Her voice is soft. Relaxing in her son's comfy chair is all she sometimes needs to get a good rest.

Uncle Mick Duke, Gran's brother, stands in the doorway of the front room chewing on frankum and talking about the weather. Murmurs of prayers find their way to his own lips.

"'Tis goin' t' be fine for a spell, 'cardin' t' the paper," Uncle Mick says of the weather forecast.

Uncle Mick is one of the best readers in Fox Harbour, and he has no trouble filling a kitchen with listeners when he's lucky enough to get hold of a newspaper.

Like most families in Fox Harbour, John and Ellen Kelly have a house full of young ones, and the barrel from relatives in the States often provides enough used clothes to keep the children out of their bare skin and warm most of the year.

When the wind gusts pass, the clothes on Ellen's line hang toward the ground again.

A Coaker engine resumes its distinctive knocking, echoing through the sparsely wooded hills of the harbour. Two men in an open boat let go their ropes and slowly head out around The Point and down the harbour.

Another boat's motor replaces the racket of the one just left, sputtering plumes of black smoke before shutting down. A tall man stands, reaching his long arms upward, to tie the boat on as she brings up sideways to a small wharf. A stout woman sitting firmly in the front of the boat holds a patched quilt over her shoulders to ward off wind that's never warm to old bones on the water. Even in August month. Her back to the shore withholds her identity from curious wives, daughters, and sons in gardens and house windows above the dirt road.

John coughs and barks incessantly as he opens the front door of the stove. Although the common cold seems to have the best of him, he's determined to go out on the *Annie Healy* today and, in a day or so, be fit to fish.

Ellen reiterates her serious concerns over his not going anywhere in his state. She doesn't think too much of Captain Mullins and the crowd, either, barging over here today like a bunch of savages, tormenting John to go.

"The next thing ya know, you'll be in The San wit' the TB," she says, gathering things he'll need for the trip.

Gran Kelly complains of her legs.

"I'm nairly killed from standin' an' beatin' out mats all marnin.'"

She continues rocking and knitting in the low chair. She hums a lovely tune between complaints of the heat, but says she'd rather be too hot than cold any day. She nods off now and then from the warmth. Both her feet jump when one of her needles slips from her hand and falls to the floor.

Two of the Kelly children, Marg and Liz, are sitting up on their knees in front of the stove. They're entranced by the wonderful orange glow coming from the nest of driftwood they collected from the beach near King's Meadow earlier this morning. They stuff alder branches into the fire for devilment and wait to hear what Gran will say.

"Get outta dat, the two o' ye, 'fraid ye burn the house down," Gran says with a scowl.

The stove's front door is left open, and the smell of driftwood burning is heavenly.

The girls, having spent most of the morning since daylight in the garden with their mother and father digging potatoes, also enjoy the fire's warmth.

The base of the fire falls in and more flankers fly onto the floor. The moment John bends down to close the door of the stove, the girls take off like a shot out into the kitchen.

John sits on the chair painted dory yellow next to the stove. He says a prayer for his little brother, James, whose picture hangs on the wall near where Gran sits. Uncle Mick, godfather to James, makes the sign of the Cross over his breast.

"'Tis too bad," the old man says.

Gran Kelly lets out a cry and John pulls his chair closer to his mother, holding her hand.

"He t'ought he was doin' the right t'ing," Uncle Mick says.

"He shoulda listened to his poor auld mother," Gran cries.

"Ah, who could blame 'im," John says. "He had sense enough to get away from the fish, an' had a few dollars in his pocket. Got to see a bit of the world, unlike any of us. Who could blame 'im?"

When John's brother, James, was sixteen, he took the ferry from Jerseyside to Halifax, lied about his age, and enlisted in the army. He'd made the mistake of telling a couple of people in Fox Harbour about his exciting plans. When Gran found out, she had the telegraph operator at Argentia wire the authorities in Halifax, who immediately dismissed James and sent him home. The day he turned seventeen, he took off for Halifax again and signed up to go to war. Sometime later, Gran received a telegram saying her son had been killed in action, his body unaccounted for, somewhere in France.

The fire in the kitchen's Waterloo is down to a dull roar. The remaining heat from the cast iron has made away with the damp morning air.

John goes in and out through the porch door, gathering

necessities for his sea box: molasses and buttered bread, his tin quart kettle with the copper bottom, his share of splits for the *Annie's* small stove, pork fat, potatoes, a small piece of pickled beef, a second pair of knitted drawers, and an extra suit of clothes besides his Sunday best for Mass in St. Bride's.

Now that the wind has passed, Ellen slides the heavy frying pan full of cabbage hash back over a damper.

"Be good, the two of ye," she says in a loud whisper. "'Fraid ye wake Mr. Watt."

Ignoring their mother, the girls give old Watt a few pokes in the ribs and run around down the hallway, into the front room to hide. Their worn, wooden clogs that came in the barrel do nothing to hush their getaway.

"Take them off yeer feet, and save 'em for the fall," Ellen said.

Sneaking back into the kitchen, they take Marg's red silk scarf and dangle it in front of Watt's flaring nostrils.

Ellen goes on sweeping the floor, doing her best to get in and around Watt's big boots hove over the side of the daybed. Lying on his back, he snores at the top of his lungs.

The size of him, Ellen thinks, noticing how he seems to go halfway up the wall on account of the low ceiling.

"'Tis a wonder he don't go through the bed, floor an' all," she says under her breath.

The girls burst out laughing at their mother's droll observation, as the scarf sticks to Watt's nose. He jumps up snorting, coughing, and cursing. The springs of the daybed squeak, and the iron frame rings out as the heel of his rubber boot slams against it.

The girls take off running through the porch door, laughing

their heads off, pretending to do the Lancers as soon as they get outside the house.

"By de Jaysus! I'll have yeer heads yit! De little fookers!" Watt says, no longer half-asleep.

"Get out, the two of ye, an' give up yeer divilment. Go find someone to play with," Ellen bawls out, even though she knows they are long gone down the lane.

Standing outside the back door, John takes off his knitted salt and pepper cap and shakes it at his girls.

"Mind yeer titterin'," he says, knowing they're up to no good.

The girls run off without a care in the world, singing a local rhyme in brazen voices at the top of their lungs.

> *Mickey Bom from up Along*
> *Catches fish in Drummer's Pond*
> *Sadie fries 'em in a pan*
> *And Mickey ates 'em like a man*

After scraping cabbage hash onto a plate for John and Watt, Ellen fills the big black pot on the stove with water to wash the babies' clothes.

"Them that rears none, rears the best, Mary Briney said," Ellen says with a little grin.

"If they don't make ya laugh, they won't make ya bawl, the wife used t' say," adds Watt.

Both are laughing away when Pad Bruce walks into the kitchen. He takes his woollen cap from his head and bids Ellen a grand day. His dark hair flattens against the ceiling.

"Mind yer head on the beams, Pad," Ellen says with a chuckle.

"Might do 'im a bit o' good," says Watt, rising from the daybed. "Might beat a bit o' sense into 'im."

They all laugh.

"Comin' over to see us off, Uncle Watt?" Pad asks, laughing.

"I s'pose I am. I'm sayin' the Benediction," shouts Watt. "If ye had any sense, I'd be goin' wit' ye. Show ye how t' fish."

"Now, Uncle Watt, you knows the women and youngsters needs you more in here, at home."

"Das true, I s'pose, Pad. Das true. Have Liz got dinner ready?"

"Soon, b'y, Uncle Watt. I'm in Jim Spurvey's skiff now, and I can't be long."

"Here ya go, Mr. Watt, luh, a plate of lovely cabbage hash for ya. That'll hold ya over till ya gets back to the house," Liz says, handing Watt the steaming plate of potato, cabbage, and turnip, fried with a piece of fat pork.

"Ya might even find a piece of salt beef in there, Mr. Watt," Ellen says, winking at the hungry old man. "Who was with ya in the boat, Pad?" she asks over the racket of Uncle Watt wolfing the leftovers into him.

"Mrs. Mart Mullins. She's gone in o'er the hill t' see Bridge King. I told her t' send for Jim, so he should be 'long the once."

"She's liable to bust any time a'tall, the poor soul," Ellen says of Bridge, tut-tutting.

"Yes. I s'pect Jim an' Bridge will have another young one be the time we gets back next week," Pad says. "We'll have lots t' celebrate with a boatload of fish, Mary Jane Sampson's birthday, an' another new youngwan for the community."

"'Deed we will, Pad. 'Deed we will," Ellen says. "Poor Mon's some sick, though. Who's goin' in his place, Pad?" she asks.

"Young Michael Mullins."

"Sure, 'tis his birthday today. He don't think much of that, now, I know," says Ellen. "Poor Mon, he's not the same since poor Johanna died," she goes on.

"Sure, 'tis only four months ago she passed, Ellen. 'Tis most likely what's wrong wit' 'im," Pad says.

"Yes, an' poor baby Michael McCue, an' he not even two yet, livin' all the way up in Long Harbour wit' his aunt," adds Watt. "Not aisey on Mon, eider, I tell ya."

The three shake their heads at once, tut-tutting and sighing for their friend.

Jimmy Kelly, named for his dead uncle, scuffs past Pad and plops on the chair next to the stove.

"The barrel's handy filled up," he pants to his mother.

"Good b'y, Jimmy. We'll have lots of water for a couple of days now," Ellen says with a big smile for her boy, kissing him on the head.

John comes down over the stairs with his extra shirt in his hand and kisses Ellen on the cheek. Little Nellie, eight, has been a little sick herself and is just up from a big nap in the front room. She lifts her arms for John to pick her up.

"You're sick, Daddy. Ya shouldn't go out in the boat t'day," she says softly.

John smiles and kisses her on the forehead before gently laying her down on the daybed. He turns away, wheezing.

A quaint voice drifts into the kitchen from the front room.

"Oh, Nellie, honey, one of these days you'll know them men don't listen t' women. And we knows best," says Gran Kelly. "Have ya got the toutons I made for ya, John?"

"In the trunk, Mother," John answers.

"Go out to the barrel an' get yourselves a nice cup of water to wash down yeer bread an' budder an' molasses," Ellen says to her children.

Jimmy springs quickly to his feet and runs past Pad and Watt to the porch.

"I'll be 'round t' see how yer makin' out when the lads are gone, Ellen."

"Thank you, Mr. Watt. You're very kind."

Watt grabs the bib of his cap and casts Ellen a wink and a nod.

"We'll be lookin' out the harbour to watch ya leave, John," Ellen says with a sigh.

John tries his best to avoid the extra displeasure in his wife's eyes. He nods his goodbyes to everyone. Then his eyes search the ground to pass the awkward seconds.

"Don't take that salt pork off yer neck, now, till yer throat feels better, mind," Ellen warns him.

The three men cross the dusty road and make toward the wharf.

Pad and Watt grab the leather handles of John's homemade sea box and pass it down to John in the boat.

Jim King walks quickly down over the path past Kelly's house. At the wharf, he flings his brin bag of food and clothes down to Watt. The old man grabs the full sack with one of his big hands and tucks it safely in the cuddy of the skiff.

The six–spark plug engine soon ignites while a thick cloud of black smoke temporarily hides them from Ellen and her children watching from the front of the house. Baby Jack is in her arms. Tom and Dennis stand clinging to her apron, more concerned with their bread and molasses than their father's leaving. Little Nellie, resting her elbows on the kitchen windowsill, waves to her daddy with her fingers. He's too far away to see her as the boat putts away.

The buzz of blue-arsed flies gathering over the opened molasses barrel in the porch breaks Ellen's trance.

"We better get back inside an' close the door before the flies goes off with the puncheon tub," Ellen says. "Put the cover back on it now and make sure the spout is twisted in all the way!"

The youngsters do what they are told while Ellen closes the door and goes about her chores.

CHAPTER EIGHT

The Midwife and Bridge King

The bittersweet scent of newly scythed grass and dandelion blends with the fresh smell of evergreen needles after last night's showers of rain. A nervous hare retreats from the path of scuffed tree roots and rocks, back to the shelter of thick brush, as Mart Mullins makes her way in over the hill on The Green toward King's house, near The Neck.

Waiting for the woman to pass, the hare crouches, still as a rock; its eyes shoot lightning-fast glances around the periphery. The forest floor beneath its furry paws is blanketed with red needles, buds, twigs, and cleverly placed slips set by young boys in their spare time. A dewy spider's web catches beads of sunlight sifting through the dark branches of the evergreen trees.

A couple of robins land on the path, pecking at crumbs of hardtack scattered from the hole in the corner of Jim King's brin sack.

The last stretch of the path winds around an outcropping of disfigured trees shaped by the ever-changing winds of the rugged coast. Perforated mounds of dirt show Mart where the ants are, and she lifts her long skirt with both hands, doing her best to step around the nests. While she uses a cane, her steps are quick, but three or four black ants manage to climb quickly over her worn leather boots and onto her legs. She stomps, one leg at a time, to shake clear the ants, then stops to bend over to smack the others. A couple of ants, still moving, are stuck to her legs by their own blood. She quickly flicks them away, wiping the tips of her fingers in grass on the side of the path.

King's bungalow is small and nestled in the hollow of a meadow kept neat by a couple of sheep. One side of the house rests partially in the shade of old trees hanging precariously off a bank of rocks wearing nothing but a thin layer of dirt and roots. The almost-even natural walls of sod-clad earth surrounding the property may have held a pond long ago. And although it can't be seen, the ocean cupped between The Neck and The Green on the other side of King's property is heard clearly. Mart pauses to catch her breath and to watch the masts and sails of the *Pauline* as she makes her way out into the open water before turning to head into the harbour, where she'll be loaded with men and supplies.

In her swampy garden, Bridge King is busy untangling the clothes on her line. Her lips pressed tightly on a mouthful of pins, she huffs and puffs, waddling her way along the clothesline strung between an old knotty pine on the hill and an uncut fence post on the other side of the little patch of land.

Bridge's stomach hangs low. The child in her womb kicks like the devil to get a glimpse of the world. Her tightly tied apron seems to be the only thing keeping her bulging body together. Hens cluck about her feet while a shitty-arsed sheep wearing a yoke strains in vain to get through the rickety fence made of skinny longers.

"Ye'll be on the choppin' block before long," Bridge snaps at the hens, trying her best to kick them out of her way.

"How are ya, me child?" Mart asks with a little laugh to break the tension she knows the pregnant woman is feeling.

"Oh! Mrs. Mart," Bridge says, startled. "I've had better days. Have ya laid eyes on Peter and Francis this morning?"

"They weren't over our way. Not that I see. A few young ones were playin' rounders, but n'er sign o' yer b'ys."

"They knew their father was leavin' today, an' they have to keep 'head of the wood for the week, the little divils," Bridge says, tut-tutting loudly. "I'm after fetchin' 'em once already, but they took off again."

"Ah, they'll be fine, Bridge, girl. The tide is droppin' and they're liable to be gone 'cross The Neck, out to The Isaacs lookin' for buried treasure," Mart says with a hint of childhood excitement. "Or perhaps they're gone to the pools in Billy's Brook catching prickles. Meself and Roselle will be in there tending to me garden by 'n by. If I sees 'em, I'll be sure an' send 'em home. Don't fret, child."

"I s'pose, girl," Bridge says, unconvinced, tossing her head.

Mart walks along the fence, crossing over a trench Jim dug years ago.

"Mind the ditch, Mrs. Mart! 'Tis all right for gettin' rid of the rainwater, but 'tis the sea water comin' in behind the house that keeps it filled with auld kelp an' the like. I'll see if I can get them little shaggers to clean it out by 'n by," Bridge says of Peter and Francis while beckoning Mart for a mug-up with swift flicks of her hand. "C'mon!" she says.

Bridge straightens the centre pole, lifting the clothesline as high as possible, out of the reach of the sheep that think nothing of standing on their hind legs and eating a shirt or pair of pants.

As Mrs. Mart nears the garden gate, two grey jays, perched on the posts, hop along the fence toward her before leaping to the ground to snatch a few crumbs from the nervous hens. Leaning on her cane, she lifts the piece of rubber keeping the gate closed and tries her best to slip neatly through the opening and into the garden without the sheep getting out. But it's too late. One of the dirty animals comes quickly and quietly and, brushing alongside the midwife's long apron, bolts to freedom.

"Oh, Scared Heart!" Mart bawls out.

"No odds, me dear. It won't go far. The b'ys will round it up later, if they ever comes home," Bridge says.

Mart carefully watches Bridge raise one heavy leg after the other to get up over the four damp steps leading to the open door of the porch. The smell of wild roses permeates the warming air as the women stomp on a colourful mat made from thin strips of old clothes, to rid their boots of wet grass and mud. Dust from the mat dances wildly on the shaft of sunlight coming through the small porch window. The heat from the kitchen stove hits them in the face, and Bridge remembers why she was glad to get out in the first place.

In the kitchen, four-year-old Josie rocks her little brother, Billy Henry, while singing quietly.

Little Tom Tit, his wife could knit
And she could card and spin . . .

The baby is barely two and enjoying his late-morning nap.

"Have ye names for the new baby yet?" Mart asks.

"Jim, after his father, if 'tis a b'y," Bridge says, out of breath and leaning over the rectangular wooden table.

"You sit down, child. I'll mind the kettle," Mart says, shooing Bridge toward the daybed.

"Put your brother in the front room, Josie, an' let yer poor mother sit in her chair before she falls in a pile," Bridge says, grimacing over the pain in her back. "An' put the big quilt 'round him, 'fraid he roll onto the floor."

Little Josie gently slips from the barrel rocking chair and does what she's told without a sound. The cool canvas is refreshing to her feet, having been next to the hot stove for so long. Mart scolds Bridget while kneeling on the floor alongside the daybed.

"You had no business out on them flakes this marnin'. 'Tis half yer trouble, me dear, ya won't pay heed."

Mart has been a midwife for more than forty years. She and her sister, Ellen, attended births with their mother since a young age. When Ellen died as a teenager, Mart continued delivering babies with her mother and then on her own. This morning was spent delivering baby Dorothy Whiffen into the world.

When she wasn't delivering babies or looking after new mothers and their families, Mart got the dead ready for burial. If someone didn't have a habit to be buried in, Mart gave them hers to be replaced later by a relative of the deceased. With plenty of plenary indulgences to her credit, Mart is sure she's guaranteed a safe path straight to heaven.

"Now, Bridge," warns Mrs. Mart, "yer liable t' go any day a'tall, so ya have t' mind yerself."

"Jim was some nervous 'bout leavin' me here," Bridge chuckles, laying back on the daybed, showing no signs of uneasiness.

"Oh, he'll be all right, dear. The men will take good care of him," Mart says, laughing. "Now, let's get ya up an' into yer chair for a lovely mug o' tay. I brought buns I baked a spell ago this mornin.'"

CHAPTER NINE

The Sampsons

A brace of rabbits stirs in the wind. They're hanging on a wire from the half-rotten eaves of a shed. When Maude Sampson's eyes meet those of the dead animals, she gets the fright of her life. The curved corners of their mouths, with the exception of a few trickles of fresh blood, offer expressions as solemnly unaware as the moment they entered the slips. Although their eyes show no signs of death, Maude has seen enough of this in her ten years to know they won't be going anywhere but in a stew with carrots, potatoes, and an onion.

She picks up a stick and gives the rabbits a few pokes. Just to make sure. Their fuzzy little paws will soon be eight lucky charms for her and whoever else wants one. Their insides will help make the garden soil fertile, giving her family better vegetables.

Maude throws the stick down and adds more Gillett's Lye to the slow-bubbling animal fat mixed with scalding hot water she lugged from the kitchen stove. The sloshing liquid flicks over the side of the sawed-off wooden tub and onto her apron. She doesn't bother about the mess. Her work is far from done. She stirs and stirs until the mixture is just about even. In a couple of hours, the contents of the tub will be cool enough to be cut into square cakes of soap.

Maude leaves the yard to help her brother and sister lug kelp from the landwash to the family's vegetable garden. Scuffing a path with her bare feet through drifts of sawdust and woodchips, the young girl makes her way onto the garden path, toward the daunting shadows of Healy's flakes.

Charlie Sampson, Maude's father, is busy making ready what he needs for what could be a long spell at sea. Like Jack Foley, Charlie has fished for the Healys forever, since the *Queen of Providence* was in her prime. Charlie, like everyone else who borrows food and supplies from Healy's, hates having his name in that black book alongside sticks of tobacco, packs of matches, sugar, tea, and flour, and other things he'll need during his time away. He stands in the middle of the kitchen, scratches his full head of thick black hair, and looks around, making sure he has all he needs for his time at sea.

"I've got a barrel of salt heads 'board the boat, Mary Jane, girl, but I haven't got time to bring 'em in now," he says, cupping his strong, square jaw in his hand, combing his moustache with his index finger. "Next time we're in, I'll bring 'em home. They'll do us the winter."

"That's all right, b'y," Mary Jane says hurriedly, with more important things on her mind. "Oh my, Charlie, b'y, I s'pose you'll have the crowd in for a time on me birthday next week. I'd better make an extra batch of bread, I s'pect."

Charlie says nothing, only smiles, and Mary Jane lights up at knowing he's already told everyone in the harbour to drop by. He has done that for every birthday of hers since they were married.

All hands from the community will be by at all hours on the big day. Some will bring a drink while a good many more will come empty-handed and leave loaded. But they're all welcome, for it's not every day you turn forty-five.

Charlie smiles at his wife, putting a sack full of food in a sea box he made about thirty years ago. Besides an extra top-heavy shirt and a pair of knitted stockings, he puts in a breadbox Mary Jane has packed with tea, sugar, milk, tinned sardines, pork fat, and onions. Standing to the drop-leaf table under the front window of the kitchen, she wraps two letters of Beaver tobacco in cloth and puts it in the box. She makes sure it's near the top.

Charlie remains quiet, even when the string tied around the crumpled brown paper lets go. Seeded raisins are sent into every nook and cranny of the old box. He tosses his head and lifts his mug, taking a good whiff of his favourite smell: molasses and tea. He shows no sign of being in a hurry with the last couple of drops. He picks up the sea box before much eye contact or words might take place between him and his wife.

"See ya next week, Mary Jane, girl," he says, heading out the door.

"I might be down 'round the wharf, but I doubt it," Mary Jane says, knowing how little room there'll be to move there. "Ya never know, though. Good luck."

Charlie goes to the shed for his splitting knife and file.

Mary Jane has always watched her man leave each morning, whether he's going to sea or just going to the shore to work or chat with the other men. She hates to see him go away, but he'll always be back home, she prays. The strength of the worn, brown scapular hanging from his neck, if nothing else, will keep him safe.

The young ones are wound up like watchsprings. Finished most of their morning chores, their raging appetites lure them to the smell of bread baking in the kitchen.

"One, two, three, four . . . ten loaves," they count together.

The tops of the bread are immaculate, shining with butter. Some loaves sit on the table to cool, while others are in the porch where there's never any heat. The young ones are off their heads over the toutons. The leftover small pieces of dough fried in fat are smothered by a coat of molasses on a plate fresh out of the oven.

"If only ye were as quiet as yeer fadder," Mary Jane bawls out.

By the time she goes back to the window, the lock is back on the shed door and Charlie is out of sight.

Liz Kelly bursts through the porch door, giving Mary Jane a start.

"Can Billy come out?" Liz pants.

"Yes, my child. 'Deed he can. Take 'em all, if ya like," Mary Jane jokes. "How's yer fadder, Liz, girl? Any better?"

"He's still coughin' an' barkin', but he's gone down to the wharf with the men, anyway," Liz says. "Mother's not too pleased."

"Is that right?" Mary Jane asks. "Sure, 'tis no good talkin' t' them men, Liz."

"That's what Gran Kelly always says," Liz laughs.

"Like two starvin' gulls, ye are," Mary Jane says, as Billy and Liz scoff down their toutons and take off out the door and down the lane.

Mary Jane is barely back to the window when she sees them bolting out from underneath the flakes and running up the road.

Crossing the road, dragging a cartload of kelp from the beach, an old man sings in a lovely tenor voice, making his way up the steep, rocky path to his home and garden. He turns his head to have a good look at the majestic schooners freshly scrubbed and anchored in the harbour, ready to set sail. "Mind where yeer goin', ye!" he says to the young ones as they just about knock over his cart.

Billy and Liz pay no mind to the man and carry on up the road.

Mary Jane calls out to her son, Arthur, still down on the wharf kicking what's left of the fish-turned-ball. He obediently gives the tattered fish one last kick, sending it into the murky water around the busy wharf. Crewmen are going to their boats with trunks of personal belongings, sacks of salt and coal, and armloads of firewood.

Charlie walks down the plank of the *Annie Healy*, picks up a large coil of manila, and tousles his little boy's hair. Arthur looks up at his father and smiles, then takes off to catch up with his mother, who is already halfway to Roselle Foley's.

"Be good to yer mudder!" Charlie says, but not loud enough for anyone to hear with all the noise.

Michael Mullins flicks the last of his cigarette into the water, grabs another coil of rope for the *Annie Healy*, and goes up the plank. Still feeling a bit gloomy over being away from Katie, he's pretty sure the crew will share their booze with him on account of it being his birthday. He doesn't crave the drink, but hopes a drop will numb his loneliness; it will dull the image of her fallen face last night when he broke the news that he wouldn't be around for the next week or so.

He won't stew in her absence. Not in the presence of his father, Captain Mullins, or of those older men. He enjoys their company too much for that. This bond, unattainable on shore, has handed him many of life's lessons—the things that matter, and, more importantly, all the things that don't. Michael loves to sing. He'll sing for the men and some of them will sing for him, knowing his great love of song. There's something about being at sea, with nowhere to go, when the little bit of free time while sailing to the fishing grounds is your own, and it's there Michael finds his best audience, an audience that cares to listen. Not like those Saturday night parties where everyone vies for the lead role, until the fight breaks out. There's none of that nonsense at sea, not with this bunch, anyway, and although he'd never give Katie the impression he'll be okay without her, it's hard for him to cast aside his silent longing for the moments he'll get to sing with the sun on his face and the salty wind all around. For Michael, the sea is where he learned his favourite stories and songs, where he learned to do what his grandfather and great-grandfather did to survive here: catch fish. And until he can afford to get to Dublin, he'll long to be no place else, except by Katie's side when the work is done for the day and the night is theirs.

Roselle Foley has been blind since she tripped over a bucket when she was five. She struck her head so hard the sight went from one eye, and two years later she went completely blind. But this hardly slowed her down. Not a bit. Her mother taught her to sew and knit, and, by the time she was a teenager, she was the best hand in Fox Harbour to make and mend clothes. Unable to work on the high fish flakes, Roselle makes a living sewing and knitting, ensuring women and children and men as much comfort as possible while working the land and slaving for fish in a variety of foul weather.

Down over the road they come. Mary Jane is linked arm in arm with Roselle while Arthur struggles with Roselle's cloth bag with the wooden handles. Making their way along the busy shore road, men and boys scurry in every direction. They're making last-minute preparations for the schooners about to sail. Wives and daughters run past with fresh buns and other treats for their husbands and fathers. One woman looks at Mary Jane, smiles, and rolls her eyes.

"T'anks be to Jaysus he'll be outta me hair for anudder spell," she says.

"I'll be some glad t' see the arse of that boat with him on it," says another.

"They won't be gettin' on like that when they're home be themselves after a couple of nights," Roselle is quick to say.

"I misses Charlie already, sure," says Mary Jane.

"Where are we now, Roselle?" Arthur asks, trying to fool her.

"We're just past Jim Nowlan's now," she answers gently.

Arthur's head rolls up toward his mother's, his face held in familiar amazement.

Having walked it for half a century, Roselle's feet know every bump, dip, and turn in the road. Arthur is astounded and wonders aloud how he'd ever be able to find his way around Fox Harbour, let alone play with his friends, if *he* couldn't see.

"Oh, you'd manage, me child. Same as I do," Roselle assures him.

With her free hand, Roselle makes sure to keep her long black skirt from dragging along the dirty road.

They're not long in Mary Jane's house when the kettle is boiling mad. Seventeen-year-old Marianne Sampson pours tea for herself, her mother, and Roselle while Mary Jane takes a plate from the warmer oven atop the stove. If she hadn't hid the toutons from the young ones, they'd have eaten the works.

"A bit of fish hash left over from last night, Roselle?" Mary Jane asks.

"That'd be lovely, me dear."

"A piece of rum an' molasses cake for yer tay?"

"Yes. All right," Roselle answers, standing and leaning on the sideboard to eat. "Is there anyt'ing on me apron?"

"There's a little spot of tay on yer apron, Roselle," Marianne answers.

Without a word, Roselle feels her way along the kitchen wall and out to the water barrel in the porch before Marianne says the tea spot isn't big enough to worry about.

Roselle cleans the small stain with a rag she carries in the pocket of her white apron. Arthur isn't far behind, making sure she's okay.

When she comes back into the kitchen, Roselle walks to the far wall where the clock sits on a wooden shelf Charlie made "a hundred years ago," according to Mary Jane. Opening up the small glass doors of the clock, she feels the hands tell her she has plenty of time for more tea and gossip this afternoon.

To the relief of Mary Jane's crowd, Roselle finally sits in the rocker by the stove and digs the heels of her high-buttoned black boots into the seams of the wide plank floor for a good rock. Leaning over to one side, she opens her knitting bag and takes out a big black sweater.

"This should keep Charlie nice an' warm," she says. "P'raps Marianne will run it down t' the boat an' give it to her father?"

"'Tis a dandy, Roselle," Mary Jane says cheerfully, as she turns one of the youngone's coats for the fall.

"Charlie has his auld one with him, and that'll do him for the sake of another week. Put it up in the room, Marianne, an' he'll be delighted t' see it when he gets back."

"Very good, me dear. Time for a snuff, I 'low," hints Roselle.

Mary Jane reaches up and takes a package from a nook in the low, open-beamed ceiling. From a piece of cloth, she takes out a stick of tobacco. With her good knife she cuts off a letter, wraps it in a piece of cloth, and bangs it nine or ten times with the hammer. Roselle gets up from the rocker and sits on a chair next to the table. Mary Jane takes the snuff out of the cloth and, with the back of her hand, pushes it in front of Roselle.

"Was herself out yet the summer?" asks Roselle, motioning with her head toward Healy's big house.

"I don't believe so," Mary Jane answers. "I would've seen her go in the back door wit' Annie when she come yesterday."

"The poor dear. Sure, the last time she was out, sure, they made fun of 'er that much they said never again would they be takin' the poor soul to Fox Harbour."

"'Magine, now," Mary Jane says.

"Who ye talkin' 'bout?" one of the young ones asks.

"Mrs. So-and-So," Mary Jane answers quickly. "Now, don't be askin' questions and go outside and play!"

"Sure, did ye hear the postman fell off his harse ag'in?" Roselle continues. "That fella's goin' to be killed yet if he don't mind himself."

The exchanging of news continues until Marianne comes back in the house.

"The boats are gettin' ready to go," she says, "and Mrs. Biddy Mullins is out sittin' on a chair in front of her house."

"Is dat true? Sure, she's been in the house, the poor t'ing, since poor Peter died. 'Twill do her good. Good for her," Roselle says with a few quick nods of her head.

"The men are singin' from their boats. So are the crowd down on the wharf," says Marianne. "I'm goin' back down."

"You have them mats beat out yet?" Mary Jane asks.

"They're hangin' o'er the fence," Marianne says.

Half the community's people stand and sit around the shore to see the crews off. Many, especially the old men, bid "good look" and "good fortune" to the crews of the schooners *Pauline*, *Lady Jane*, and *Annie Healy*. Although it will be a while before they'll be leaving.

Mary Jane's view of the wharf from her kitchen window is blocked by Healy's store. She runs out of the house for a look and a wave, hoping to catch a glimpse of Charlie. Roselle continues knitting the sweater she started after dinner.

"When Mrs. Mart gets back from Bridge King's this evenin', we're goin' into Billy's Brook to weed the potatoes," says Roselle.

Roselle and Mrs. Mart Mullins are the best of friends.

"Come on, Roselle, we goes down to the water to join in the send-off."

The swarm of people keeps Mary Jane's attention while the tune of voices on the wind sings to Roselle. Even the gulls seem excited, circling the mastheads of the schooners. Neither of the two women speaks as they make their way through the crowd. Mary Jane knows she hasn't a chance of seeing Charlie, as he's busy aboard the *Big Annie*.

Work continues along the way. The young people, who had lined the shoreline all summer looking for a bit of work to earn a few coppers, are now flat out doing what they're told. Young girls in homemade cotton dresses, and underwear made from flour sacks spread fish and curse at snickering boys peeking up through the flakes.

"Pillsbury's Best, me arse," the boys shout, reading the print on the girls' homemade drawers.

The strong smell of oil paint fills the air. Freshly painted dories, skiffs, and schooners set the harbour agleam. Crisp white sheets on taut lines dance to the rhythms of summer's wind while tough, glowing women, mostly pregnant, banish hungry cats and kittens from the fish and the flakes with boughs and brooms.

Lead sinkers break the water's surface while young lads catch tough conners, banging their slimy heads off rocks, allowing little delay to their endings. A barrel-chested gull rips the head off a struggling tomcod and balks at a couple of crows hopping around in a circle. It's like some lost tribal dance, natives offering respect to the gods for the unexpected feast they're sure they'll get. But the gull swallows the fish in one gulp when the brazen crows get too close for its liking.

"Hello, Bern'dette," says Mary Jane.

Bernadette Foley is on her way to Healy's to see if that new bobbin is in for her mother's sewing machine.

Liz Kelly and Billy Sampson fall up the road, ahead of Bernadette, laughing their heads off about the "tarmentin'" Liz and Marg gave Mr. Watt earlier.

"That's a sin fer ye," Bernadette says.

"Go on, girl! He loves it," Liz proclaims. "Wanna come into The Falls by 'n by? We're goin' spyin' on Michael Mullins an' his missus."

Liz and Billy can't stop laughing.

Even if she were allowed, Bernadette wouldn't go. She's

expecting a letter from her sister, Laura, who left in the spring to join their sister, Nell, to work in service in Grand Falls. Bernadette can't understand why Laura didn't just stay here and work at Healy's store, or as one of their servant girls like everyone else.

"Sure, that's where me mother worked, at H'aly's, when she met Daddy, and *she* come all the way from Conception Harbour," Liz says proudly.

Bernadette dreads every moment of life without Laura around. At least her daddy's not going fishing anymore. She's glad of that. Now that she's able to go up the hill and cut the grass on Gus's grave by herself, it will give her daddy more time to do other things. Although his thoughts hardly ever make it to his lips, a slight nod of his head and a little wink from his intense eyes sometimes tell a tale of gratefulness. On Sundays they visit Gus's grave, mindlessly pulling weeds eager to take over the small plot. It gives her parents a chance to reflect, to say things like "I s'pose God had a plan for our b'y," and "He's probably better off, the poor soul."

God is second to no one in Fox Harbour, no matter how many losses He sends their way. Bernadette said she'll never forget Sunday past making their way down from the graveyard, what her mother said, and then what her father said.

"Jack, b'y, I thinks 'tis time ya had yer habit made."

"Lize, girl, t' tell ya the truth, I'd just as soon be buried in me rubber clothes."

"Jack, b'y! Ya knows ya can't be buried in yer rubber clothes. P'raps Mart Mullins will lend ya her habit."

When Jack said nothing, Lize just sighed and said something to Bernadette about how queer her father is.

Bernadette and Laura are the best of friends—inseparable until Laura went away. Sharing the same birthday, Bernadette will soon be eleven and Laura eighteen. And this is the first year in Bernadette's life the two will be apart on their special day. Laura's absence adds awful hours to Bernadette's never-ending daily chores, with just herself and her mother left at home. The only excitement is when the barrel comes once or twice a year from her sisters, Margaret, Helen, and Jane, in the States. It never fails to include nice hand-me-down dresses and, every few years, shoes which Daddy puts on the last and makes good as new.

The day Laura left Villa Marie for Grand Falls Station, a bit of good left Lize. It's been all right having Jack around for the past little while, between trips, good and bad, to Golden Bay, although his coming and going in and out of the house gets on her nerves.

"Go on down, b'y, an' see what the men are at," she says, up to her elbows in the bread pan, as he traipses back and forth over her clean floor in his dirty boots.

Bernadette can still hear Liz and Billy shouting and carrying on, although they're nearly out of sight. She scuffs over the gravelly lane leading to their back door, takes the dry mats from the wood-horse, and goes in the house.

CHAPTER TEN

Uncle Watt

Liz Bruce snaps out of her daydream. Young Johnny is sound asleep at the table, chin on his chest. His berries are cleaned to near-perfection. Liz figures fifteen or twenty minutes must have passed since she got lost in that awful past of hers. She breathes a sigh of relief when hearty laughter from the yard rings through the kitchen walls.

Pad and Jack Foley are in the stitches, laughing at Uncle Watt telling stories. When they enter the kitchen, the room immediately seems smaller because of their large frames.

"The H'alys won't be drivin' ye back t' sea for more fish if I goes wit' ye," old Watt says, plopping down on the daybed. "Never ye mind Golden Bay," he continues. "I knows a spot up be The Rams where the fish are so plentiful they'll jump right into yer boat if ye talks nice 'nough to 'em."

"Now, Uncle Watt! Ye knows I wouldn't make do here without ya while the b'ys are away," Liz says cheerfully.

"I s'pose yer right, girl. I s'pose yer right," old Watt says, tossing his cap on the back of the chair next to the stove and wiping the sweat from his head with the back of his hand.

Watt's real name is Walter Sinnott. He comes from The Rams, a small island north of Fox Harbour, about a four-hour row by dory for Watt. After his wife, Mary, died, he moved to Fox Harbour with Pad, his nephew. Watt is tall and lean, not unlike Pad, but with silver-grey windswept hair and a small forehead mapped with strong lines of hard work and adversity. Below two shadowy slits for eyes is a long, wide-bridged nose *he* says is capable of detecting fish a hundred fathoms below a boat and of smelling the direction of the wind. His thin lips seem to hold a permanent smile and his mouth appears to be always open, showing a sharp tongue once hidden by good teeth.

"Jaysus! Yer not eatin' again," Pad says to his uncle.

"I don't know why the good Lard ever give me teet' when I can chew anyt'ing wit' me gums," Watt says behind a big piece of salt beef, ignoring Pad altogether.

"Luh! He can't even hear me o'er the racket he's makin'," Pad says, trying to get Watt going again.

"I hears ya, ya foolish fooker!" Watt says, not bothering to uncross his eyes fixed on the fatty meat dripping grease over his chin.

He gives the sleeves of his black Sunday coat a flick with his long fingers, but there's little room for the garment to move on his big arms and the sleeves continue to soak up the grease. His once-white dress shirt is a bit small on him, buttoned tightly around his wrinkly neck. Worn rubber boots hide the shortness of his pant legs.

"Not much outta you, Fowlou!" Watts spits out to Jack from behind the vanishing fat and stringy beef.

"No, b'y," Jack says with a close-mouthed grin and a toss of his head.

"Sure, 'tis not like you'd hear 'im, anyway, ya contrary ole fooker," Pad says.

"That's 'nough now, Pad," Liz interrupts. "Let Uncle Watt eat in peace."

"Pay no mind t' him, Liz, me dear, he don't know any better. His mudder dropped him on his head when he was small, ya know. I was there," Watt says matter-of-factly. "He never had the sense of a suckin' duck."

The other three laugh at Watt's drollness while enjoying their tea and raisin buns. Watt waves his big hands, shining with grease, to draw attention to another of his stories. And for the next twenty minutes he seems unaware he's sitting in comfort in Fox Harbour, as his actions and many facial expressions uncover a few details of life on The Rams.

"Yes, b'y, the pack ice kept the trader away for the whole winter, that year," Watt sighs, "an' we soon had ne'er bit o' shot left for our guns. No, sir, an' never a bite t' eat, eider. The last sacks o' flour we had between us, about twelve big fam'lies, there were, was 'bout half flour an' half ker'sene, where they has the two stowed togedder in the holds o' the schooner, see. We'd take out a bit o' offal from the liver barr'ls an' spread it on the rocks, an' when the gulls were hoverin' above, we hooked 'em wit' our jiggers. They waren't bad wit' a bit o' bread, even though the bread tasted the same as lamp oil. Eat anyt'ing when yer starved."

Watt gives thanks for the gulls and the bad flour that kept most of his people from perishing.

"My God, I say there were three or four young ones starved to deat', p'raps more. Shockin', 'twas." Watt's volume drops way down. "Hear 'em bawlin' from the hunger in the middle o' the night, an' when *their* bawlin' stopped, the mothers'd be howlin' like the Divil. No wan else howled the way the women howled when a youngster died. They never had the strengt' t' bawl too loud, I s'pose. The other wans, 'specially the youngsters, barely 'live demselves.

"You knows what 'twas like some winters out there," Watt says, looking at Pad. "You were reared there, same as meself."

"That's true, Uncle Watt."

"Another couple or three women perished givin' birth, an' no wan had the strength to bury 'em right, so we'd put 'em down just 'nough so the dogs couldn't dig 'em up an' when the trader would get in ag'in with 'nough food t' get our strengt' back, we'd take 'em up, the poor souls, an' dig 'em a proper grave."

"Thank the Lord we never had too much of that to deal with," Jack says, "with a doctor in Little Placentia, an' Ville Marie Station, the train."

"And the dogs that eat each udder, sweet Jaysus, I never see the like," Watt adds.

"Now, Uncle Watt, they were awful times, 'deed they were," Liz says, "but for the love of God, p'raps you've a happier tale to tell the b'ys before they heads back to sea?"

From his eighty years, Watt quickly hauls out a story which they're sure they've all heard before, but their faces show no disappointment when it begins with a new twist.

"Meself an' me fadder were on Burke Island, bright an' airly one marnin' in December, cuttin' next year's wood, see," he begins.

"Jaysus, we must've been choppin' away at one side o' this one tree for half the day when Fadder said, 'Walter, I 'lows 'tis time we takes a spell.' So Fadder lay down be the tree an' closed his eyes, an' I walks around our tree to make me water, an' what do I find, but two other fellas choppin' away at the other side. O' the same tree, mind ye. They were there all mornin', too, they said, an' we never heard a peep from them or their axes."

"'Tis a job to find a tree like that anymore, Mr. Watt," Jack says.

"I guarantee ya!" Watt says dryly, almost believing his own foolishness.

"I s'pose ya lugged that tree out on yer shoulders, did ya, Uncle Watt?" Pad mocks.

"Pad!" Liz warns again.

"Yes, b'y, we made the strangers limb it an' then paid 'em off with a plug o' 'baccy an' lugged the tree to the water, carved a big hole to sit in, then paddled our way back t' De Rams, towed our own boat behind," Watt carries on, never missing a beat. "An' after we made a skiff out o' it, we had 'nough leftovers t' make two stores an' a wharf."

"A wharf?" Jack plays along.

"Only a small wharf, now, mind ye," Watt says.

"Is that so," Pad says, waving his arms and hands like Watt.

"Not hard t' know he was dropped on his head, is it, Fowlou?" Watt says, lifting the front damper and spitting tobacco juice in the stove.

Jack replies with a toss of his head and his usual slight grin.

"Ah, Uncle Watt, ya knows we'll miss ya," Pad says, reaching over and squeezing Watt's shoulder.

Pad proudly boasts how the Healys, the crew, and the shore

boys loved Watt's company all last winter when they stripped the *Annie Healy* of shrunken caulking and filled her seams with new oakum.

"Yes, b'y, Mr. Watt, yer after helpin' mend an' make many a net an' boat in Fox Harbour with your fine stories an' chunes, too," Jack says softly.

Watt responds with a series of deep snores.

"Uncle Watt! Uncle Watt!" Pad shouts.

"Jaysus, b'y, wha's the matter wit' ya?" Watt snaps, not bothering to open his eyes.

"I thought ya were dead, b'y," Pad says. "Go on back to sleep."

"With dat yap o' yours goin' steady, I'd have a job t' die 'round here," Watt mumbles. "In a bitta peace, anyhow."

"Jaysus, Pad, will ye leave 'im 'lone," Liz says. "He had Mick Mullins's roof tarred by eight o'clock this marnin', ya know."

"I know, girl, I know. I'm only coddin' 'im. Ya can't open yer gob 'round here." Pad lets on he's mad, crossing his legs and turning toward the window with his cigarette.

With Pad silenced and Watt asleep, all three work on their second helpings of tea and watch people coming and going from Healy's wharf.

Pad knows Watt will be heaving the tunes out of him down by the wharf soon enough, and this bit of rest for the old man will go a long way. A favourite amongst the youngsters of the harbour, Watt is under constant torment and, although he never lets on, he loves the attention. He's fond of all young ones like the ones he and Mary never had. Having lived through Newfoundland's toughest times, he can't get over how easy everyone has it these days. Much of his time is spent walking around the town, talking with people, holding ladders, and tying mops, brushes, and pails onto pulling ropes for men and boys tarring rooftops on nice mornings between trips to Golden Bay. Under the flickering light of oil lamps at night in stores and stageheads, he sharpens axes, knives, and saw teeth. On mornings with men away and company scarce, he cleans longers of their bark for flakes and fencing for chicken coops, pigpens, and gardens.

Watt is strong and well able to eat twenty meals a day if he has the mind to. Wherever he has dinner is where he takes his long nap each afternoon. Two slices of fresh bread dipped in stewed cods heads chased with a couple of mugs of scalding hot tea and he's as good as dead when sleep strikes. Tables shake, rattle, and squeak as women knead dough for bread and buns. Lifters lift dampers, scraping stovetops while long iron pokers stuff junks of wood into dwindling fires. Lids clank and puff out steam as boilers of dancing hot water tremble in waiting for pudding bags, soiled diapers, or potatoes dug fresh from capelin and kelp-laced gardens. Heavy oven doors screech when opened and bang when slammed shut, rattling flues and dishes as Watt heaves off on daybeds, or "stretchers" as they're known in some Fox Harbour homes. Not even the brazen crows cawing noisily on the ground outside kitchen windows can wake him. "Some day on De Rams," he says when the sun is shining, no matter where he is.

Johnny wakes up, finishes his dinner, and is playing with one of the Mullinses' young ones next door by the time Uncle Watt is upright again and finishing his next mug of tea.

"'Tis some nice to have me men back in the house," Liz says, glad her mind is reeled back from old thoughts of which she's sick and tired.

The day turned to rain again, just as quick as it changed from rain to shine this morning. Liz worries about Ellen catching her death, with the mid-August wind not that warm.

"She's not long left with Maurice Whiffen," Liz answers Pad.

Ellen and Maurice are the best of friends, even sharing the one birthday, and, according to Pad, are joined at the hip.

Liz sees them going up the other side of the harbour with pails in their hands while they are supposed to be heading in the opposite direction, to Billy's Brook, for water. Maurice always carries a strong stick his father cut for him to carry two pails of water at a time. He always carries Ellen's water home for her. They get awfully mad when Pad jokes, "Ye'll be married yet."

"God knows, now, with the two of them, where they're to," Liz says.

"There's plenty in the barrel in the porch to do till tonight, anyway," Liz assures Pad, as he and Jack head out to the shed.

Liz sends Johnny up to Healy's shop for two sticks of Jumbo tobacco for his father.

"Have a look an' make sure that shawl is still hangin' on the wall by the window," Liz says to Johnny as he's running out the door.

With Pad and the young ones out of the house, Liz gets a taste of that bitter loneliness she so dreads. The thought of Pad leaving again is hard, but at least they'll be able to get a handle on most of their debt to Healy's when he returns. The thought of the new shawl keeps her happy, although Pad said no way can they afford it and her old one will have to do. Watt will help out lots and keep her entertained. It could always be worse.

Jack walks up the road with Pad and gives him a hand putting Jim Spurvey's belongings back in his skiff.

Jack and Lize have lost two of their eight children: first Lizzie, then Gus.

"I was some proud of him, our only b'y," Jack says, avoiding Pad's eyes, pretending to scan the harbour. "He was a real joy to have 'round, on the water with meself soon as he was able t' stand in a boat. He was good, ya know."

All through the years, when one daughter after another was born to Jack and Lize, Gus graciously accepted the role of big brother, the one who knew everything. They all adored his gentleness and, like his father, he was quiet as an old dog. When Lizzie was the baby, she held Gus's full attention.

"He treated her like she was the Pope," Jack says. "She always had to kneel up on a chair an' watch for him comin' home."

When she was four, Lizzie got tuberculosis, keeping her out of the window and away from just about everyone, except for Gus, who refused to leave her side. One night late in the fall, returning home from the woods, through the storm windows of the kitchen, Jack and Gus heard the bawling. They threw down their bucksaw and axe and stormed into the house. On the kitchen floor lay all the girls, slumped over their mother's legs, as Lize tried desperately to rock and rub life back into little Lizzie's body. She was blue and cold in the cradle of her mother's arms. Through torrents of angry tears and shrieks of horror, each person mumbled the rosary in their turn. Words were hard to find in times like these and everyone turned inward. It wasn't proper to speak of such things, let alone how you felt about it. November soon turned into Christmas, and with Lizzie in the hard ground, Lize longed for another child, someone to fill the void left by her little girl's death. The next August, Bernadette was born.

Although Gus dutifully resumed his role as big brother with the new baby, Bernadette, the sadness he held over poor sweet Lizzie never left him. He wore it openly in his sullen expressions: the downcast eyes that grew smaller with disgust over time, the mouth with one corner risen in perpetual doubt, and the strong jawline that showed his teeth were always clenched behind lips that rarely smiled. And in the few words he spoke. Jack said he couldn't blame his son for being withdrawn. Lize told Gus don't be so black, but she was no better herself.

"Gus had a poor appetite an' could hardly gain a pound; n'er bit of energy, Pad, b'y, an' no wan knew what was the matter with 'im for a few years. We just figured it was to do with Lizzie dyin'. God knows none of us were good for much for a long time after that."

Pad tut-tuts and shakes his head, summing up his thoughts on the awfulness of Gus's condition and little Lizzie dying so young.

"An' ya never heared the like of the bark he had," Jack says, making a coughing sound much milder than the one he's trying to describe. "Biverin' with the cauld one minute, he was, an' his clothes drenched with sweat the next, 'specially in the nighttime. Goddamn TB! "

"Why couldn't He take me instead of Lizzie?" Gus said for a year or more after Lizzie died. "'Tis not like she did anyt'ing to Him!"

When Mrs. Lize said how the Lord could take any of them any time He pleases and there was nothing anyone could do about it, it only made Gus worse.

Lize was no stranger to tuberculosis before her little girl died. She lost her own sister, Sarah, to the disease when Sarah was only twenty. But Lize never had the strength to tell this to any of her children, even then, even if it held a chance of showing Gus and the girls she really knew the hurt of losing a sibling.

Life went on, with special Masses offered up to Lizzie and the other poor souls in purgatory.

"There's fish to be got, an' food to grow, I always told 'em," Jack says.

"I'm lucky, I s'pose," says Pad, "never to have lost someone young the way you're after losin 'em. An' two, at that."

Pad imagines he might comprehend Jack's sorrow the way he tries to envision Liz's grief over the loss of her two brothers, but nothing consoling comes.

"I don't know, Jack, b'y," is all he manages to get out. But that means more to Jack than Pad will ever know, the fact he listened.

By the time he was twenty-five, the tuberculosis was robbing Gus's every breath. By the middle of November, his strength hid in places far from his mind's reach, and his time amounted to screaming, though not very loudly, fighting for life on the daybed, coughing up great globs of blood into his sheets when the galvanized bucket on the floor seemed too far away, and trying to stay warm.

Jack was back in the woods by himself again, the first time in nearly twenty years, to fend for his crowd. Even though Gus hadn't been a big help alongside his father with a saw and axe for a few years, Jack was lost without him long before he was even gone: another man, his own flesh and blood, to say a few words to without fear of ridicule or judgment.

When Gus drew his last breath on Easter Sunday, 1924, Laura, fourteen at the time, held young Bernadette's hand while Lize said, yet again, she'd think twice about lugging firewood to the church. What was the point, she yelled, of spending half her time on her knees praying to a god who does nothing but steal her young ones before they get a chance to try to live a decent life? Why should everyone stop what they're doing when the Angelus rings at noon every day and then again at six o'clock when there's so much to be done, and it's not like there are angels sweeping down from above to help make the fish?

"We're reared t' larn the catechism an' have the answers to every blessed question the Church asks, an' who has answers for me when me youngsters are tortured with the TB, better off dead than alive, tormented just to get the next breath . . . an' then they dies? Who has answers for me, Jack? 'Tis certainly not you!" she would bawl at him. "An' 'tis certainly not the church, nor the Lord. We here livin' on tea an' raisin buns, with a job to keep ourselves warm an' alive, an' me, foolish as a hen, frettin' over the likes of Fadder Dee, an' all the other priests they sent our way, 'fraid they be cauld in a church they have nuttin' to do with, hardly, twice a year. We'll see now, the next time ya sees me luggin' wood all the way to The Bottom. 'Tis not good enough! Can't even have a few prayers answered."

Jack says how he never said nothing back to Lize, and he tells Pad how she often wonders if she was wrong to raise her hand to Gus when he was suffering and cursing the Lord because of it. She should have thought more about Gus's suffering than the Lord's, Jack says. It was hardly the Lord who kept fresh water in the porch barrel, and splits and shavings by the stove on cold, damp mornings throughout the year, he says. And it certainly wasn't the Lord who went in the woods with Jack for all those years and carried out sticks, big and small, miles to the lane by their house. And it was no one but Gus who played games with his little sisters and chased them around the house and harbour for years and years.

The worst part, Jack says, is the torture she endures from the guilt placed upon her for stooping so low as to question God's ways, God's will, God's everything.

With some of his strongest feelings unearthed, Jack feels a thousand pounds lighter, and something in the summer air stirs him. He stands gazing out the harbour and then down toward the *Annie Healy*. A little smile comes to his lips.

"What brings all that auld stuff back, I wonders, Pad," he says, not expecting an answer, and shooing blackflies away from the grey hair under the sides of his cap.

"Uncle Watt talkin' 'bout people dyin' on The Rams, I s'pose, Jack, b'y." Pad tries to bring light back to the day.

"See ya in an hour or so, Pad, b'y."

"I thought ya said ya weren't goin.'"

Jack doesn't turn around, and keeps on walking toward home.

Pad smiles and heads across the road to give Jim Spurvey a nip from his flask of 'shine.

Not long after Bernadette gets back home, Jack is back to say he's going out with the crew.

"Mon's perishin' with the cauld, an' Pad Mullins was hurt fallin' off the house. John Kelly's goin', but he's liable to be in the bunk the whole time. He's awful sick."

Jack can't let down those who've helped him earn a living his lifetime. Lize knows that. Bernadette doesn't understand. She watches him lift his other shirt from the nail in the wall behind the stove. All of a sudden the mess he brought over her clean floor doesn't matter much. His week's rations are prepared in no time.

Stroking his thick black moustache, Jack looks around, making sure he's not forgetting anything, and heads out the door.

"Run down to H'aly's an' put down two sticks of Jumbo for yer father, luh," Lize says to Bernadette. "Ya knows he can't live without his baccy."

Lize throws a handful of raisins into a batch of dough and baking powder, knowing she has plenty of time to make buns for Jack before he leaves.

Left: Jim and Bridget (Bridge) King (Photo courtesy of Bride Ruffalo, granddaughter of *Annie Healy* crew member Jim King)

Right: Bridge King in old age (Photo courtesy of Bride Ruffalo)

Johanna and Mon McCue. Mon was a crew member too sick to take that last trip and who, as a result, lived. (Photo courtesy of Mary McCue Culletin, granddaughter of Mon McCue)

Children of lost *Annie Healy* crew members. L-R: Maude Sampson Kelly, Ellen Bruce Whiffen, Jimmy King—born four days after his father was lost—Bernadette Foley Murray, and Beth Maher (Liz Kelly). (Photo courtesy of Shirley Houlihan Duke, granddaughter of *Annie Healy* crew member Jack Foley)

Left: Annie Healy, age nineteen, 1898 (Photo courtesy of Bob Hyslop, grandson of Anne Healy and Edward Furlong)

Right: Bernadette Foley Murray (Author Photo)

Schooner *Pauline King* aground (she was one of the schooners to leave Fox Harbour with the *Annie Healy*) (Photo courtesy of the late Mary Duke McCue, daughter-in-law of *Annie Healy* crew member Mon McCue)

Left: *Annie Healy* crew member Charlie Sampson (Photo courtesy of Maude Sampson Kelly, daughter of Charlie and Mary Jane Sampson)

Right: Edward and Anne (Healy) Furlong (Photo courtesy of Wallace Furlong, son of Anne Healy and Edward Furlong)

Children of Edward and Anne Healy Furlong, their spouses, and a grandson visiting Fox Harbour where their grandfather's (Rickard K. Healy) home once stood (Photo courtesy of Joann Fantina, granddaughter of Anne Healy and Edward Furlong)

The Bottom, Fox Harbour, with Murray's Island at low tide, from the Crow Hill (Photo courtesy of Shirley Houlihan Duke)

Left: Eliza Whiffen Foley, widow of crew member Jack Foley (Photo courtesy of Maggie Burns Widell, great-granddaughter of Jack and Eliza Foley)

Right: Gus Foley, son of crew member Jack Foley (Photo courtesy of Bernie Houlihan O'Reilly, granddaughter of Jack and Eliza Foley)

Left: *Annie Healy* crew member Jack Foley (Photo courtesy of Shirley Houlihan Duke)

Right: Midwife Martha "Mart" Mullins and her husband, Mick (Photo courtesy of Mary Murray Hawco and Susan Murray Mandville, granddaughters of Mart Mullins)

Jim and Mike Healy, proprietors of M J Healy Ltd. and owners of the *Annie Healy* at the time of her loss (Photo courtesy of Wallace Furlong)

The Isaacs, and the body of water between Fox Harbour and Little Placentia (Argentia) known as The Reach, where the *Annie Healy* left and entered her home port (Author photo)

Fox Harbour, with The Isaacs in the background and the shoal entrance to the community (Photo courtesy of Shirley Houlihan Duke)

Fox Harbour, Placentia Bay, circa 1905, with schooner *Annie Healy* to the wharf in front of Healy's large home (Photo courtesy of Maritime History Archive, Job Brothers's Collection, Memorial University of Newfoundland)

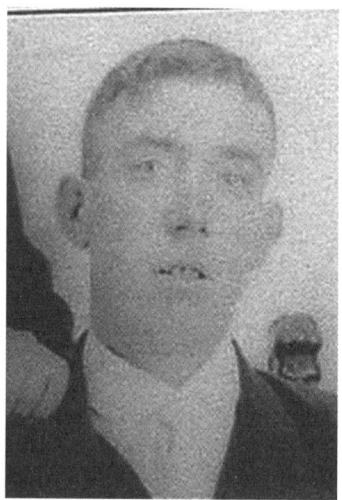

Left: Midwife Martha "Mart" Mullins and Johnny Whiffen, grandson of crew member Pad Bruce (Photo courtesy of Mary Murray Hawco and Susan Murray Mandville)

Right: *Annie Healy* crew member Pad Bruce (Photo courtesy of Ellen Whiffen Bruce, daughter of Pad Bruce)

Beth Maher (Liz Kelly), daughter of crew member John Kelly, and the author following his play, *Thursday's Storm: The Annie Healy Story,* at the Marquise Harvest Theatre, Argentia, 2000 (Photo courtesy of Amy Smith)

Men and boys aboard Healy's boat, *Revels* (centre), with Richard K. Healy in the smaller boat, right, and the *Annie Healy,* left, circa 1909. *Annie Healy* crew member Jack Foley is looking toward the camera with his son, Gus, standing in front of him. (Photo courtesy of Wallace Furlong)

Fox Harbour, Placentia Bay, Newfoundland. Murray's Island and The Isaacs in silhouette at sunset. (Author Photo)

Left: *Annie Healy* crew member Jim King (Photo courtesy of the late Anne King, daughter-in-law of Jim King)

Right: *Annie Healy* crew member John Kelly (Photo courtesy of Beth Maher, daughter of John Kelly)

Jim and Laura (Foley) Houlihan and their first child, Mary, Fox Harbour, 1930 (Photo courtesy of Betty Houlihan Howard, granddaughter of crew member Jack Foley)

Left: Mary Ann Mullins, daughter of Captain John Mullins and sister of crew member Michael Mullins, age nine, 1929, Corner Brook, Newfoundland (Photo courtesy of Eneida and Bill Valenti, grandson of Captain Mullins, and Annmarie Naimo, granddaughter of Captain Mullins)

Right: *Annie Healy*'s Captain John Mullins (Photo courtesy of Eneida and Bill Valenti, and Annmarie Naimo)

Grave of James Mullins, son of Captain John Mullins and Bridget Murphy, Crawley's Island (Long Harbour), Placentia Bay, Newfoundland (Photo courtesy of Eneida and Bill Valenti, and Annmarie Naimo)

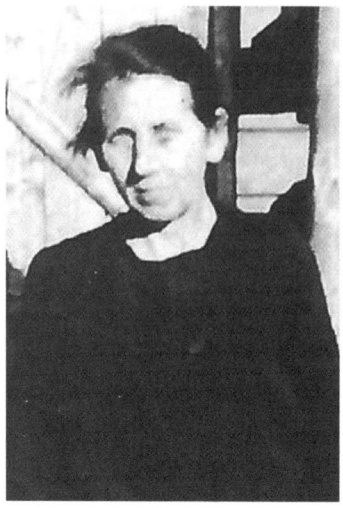

Left: Bridget Murphy Mullins, widow of Captain John Mullins (Photo courtesy of Eneida and Bill Valenti, and Annmarie Naimo)

Right: *Annie Healy* crew member Michael Mullins, circa 1925 (Photo courtesy of Eneida and Bill Valenti, and Annmarie Naimo)

Michael Murphy, the last person aboard the schooner *Annie Healy* the morning she was lost. He was twenty-two at the time, and lived to be ninety-four and a half. (Photo courtesy of Harry Murphy, son of Michael Murphy)

LOST WITH CREW OF 7 IN SIGHT OF HOME

Another Addition to Storm's Toll is Loss of "Annie Healey", Crew of Seven, All With Large Families

Argentia, Aug. 29—(Special to Daily News)—The schooner "Annie Healey," owned by M. and J. Healey of Fox Harbour and commanded by John Mullins was lost with all hands in Thursday's storm. Seven married men with large families, all of Fox Harbour, comprise the crew of the schooner which was lost with in three miles of her home port.— Correspondent.

Daily News article, August 29, 1927: four days after the storm (Photo courtesy of Centre for Newfoundland Studies)

This anonymous poem appeared in the *Daily News* following the storm (Photo courtesy of Centre for Newfoundland Studies)

TOLL FOR THE BRAVE

Dear Mother Newfoundland, we children pray
Accept our loving sympathy to-day
Whilst thou art mourning thy beloved sons -
our brothers called so soon from thee away

These few have seen the wonders of the deep
And in its cradle sleep their long last sleep
Yet, as we ponder o'er their courage and their strength
Our pride in them restrains the tears we fain would weep

Yet, Mother, still among the sons thou gave
Others there are, as willing and as brave
That thou mayst keep thy children in thine arms
Are ready yet to battle wind and wave

August 27, 1927, Page 6.

TERRIBLE LOSS OF LIFE IN THURSDAY'S STORM

Feared not less than 33 perished - many vessels wrecked

..........A schooner reported off Merasheen Bank with men clinging to the wreckage has disappeared. She probably had a crew of seven.

Daily News article (Photo courtesy of Centre for Newfoundland Studies)

PART II

CHAPTER ELEVEN

Leaving Home

The *Annie Healy* is just about ready to set sail. Skipper Bill Murray moves his schooner, the *Clare Murray*, from the middle of the harbour to allow room for the others to pass freely. The *Nellie* is the first to leave, passing The Isaacs, heading into open water. The *Pauline King* and the *Lady Jane* lay anchored farther out the harbour. Both boats are alive with activity, as men in smaller boats deliver their crews' provisions.

From rickety, horse-drawn carts men and boys step into the crowd near Healy's Wharf. They carry sacks and crates of goods and casks of fishing supplies to go aboard the boats. Standing with their hands in their pockets, old men chat away in small groups beneath scores of young legs hanging and swinging from the edges of the high flakes above. Women, in their blue bandanas, scan the surroundings for things and people to talk about. Others murmur prayers for the men about to leave and for their safe return with fish stacked to the hatches of the schooner holds.

Bernadette Foley squeezes her way through adults and youngsters alike with a tin full of buns for her father. He sees her from the deck of the *Annie Healy*. Although they're meant to be spared along to provide energy between breakfast and supper at sea, Lize's tea buns are the best Jack's ever had and he jokes he's liable to have them gone before Red Island is at their backs. Bernadette smiles shyly, silently wondering if her father noticed the sadness in her mother's eyes. She searches for a way to ask him. The look she's thinking about is the same one her mother always wears every time her father's about to sail away, even though most of the time he's around she tells him to get out of her sight and go down to the wharf and see what the men are at. The look on her mother's face seems more intense this time, since her father spent a week saying he wasn't going back to sea. Now, all of a sudden, he can't wait to leave again.

Lize's forced smile is never wide enough to cover her inner conflict when Jack heads out the door. Even when Lize tells him he doesn't know his arse from his elbow, always changing his mind, Bernadette knows her mother never wants to see her father leave, knowing his back is probably even worse than he lets on and he has no business out baiting hooks and setting and hauling trawls in a damp, cold dory on the open sea.

Bernadette's thoughts keep returning to her mother's sad eyes and the child struggles for a way to talk about it. Even if she could find the words, she knows she'd never have the courage to speak them. The most her father ever says to her is, "Do what yer mother tells ya." That and a pat on the head, the one that comes with the little twinkle in his eyes.

When Jack lays his hand on his daughter's thin shoulder, his eyes speak of words he's never known how to utter. He only hugs her when he has a few drinks in. She likes that and wishes he'd drink more often. But those expressions of love are rare, as Mammy says she's too young to be allowed downstairs when company's in on Saturday nights, when they have a few nips of St. Pierre rum or homemade moonshine, and there's no talking or complaints of poor weather for making fish or good weather with no fish at all—just songs, stories, and jigs and reels the young girl hears from her room upstairs.

Jack and Bernadette nod their goodbyes and turn away from each other quickly. She runs back through the crowd toward home.

"Bern'dette!" Jack shouts.

Bernadette stops and leans around several big women in aprons to see her father beckoning her back to the side of the schooner with a toss of his head.

"The weather's goin' to be fine. Don't forget to cut the grass on Gus's grave. I sharpened the sickle not long ago. Mind yourself. It can cut ya."

Bernadette presses her lips into a smile, nods her head, and turns for home again.

The Isaacs look on complacently, like old friends of the place, as Liz Kelly and Billy Sampson run up and down both sides of the harbour road, skipping over potholes, and singing to the top of their lungs.

> *Mickey Bom from up along*
> *Catches fish in Drummer's Pond*
> *Sadie fries 'em in a pan*
> *And Mickey ates 'em like a man*

"If only 'twas rainin', the fun we'd have," Liz says, as the lack of water and dirt momentarily dampens their spirits. Neither can help looking back and forth to the water, no matter how much fun they're trying to have on the road. Nothing could be more majestic to the youngsters than the sight of schooners, their gigantic sails hoisted all the way to the sky. Especially when their daddies are on board. The smaller one, the *Annie Healy,* looks as big as the rest lying alongside Healy's Wharf. All schooners have their mainmasts raised to let the sun soak up any lingering moisture. The huge sails will be lowered upon leaving while the motors, jibs, and jumbos will take the boats out the harbour.

Biddy Mullins, Captain John's stepmother, is in her glee. With each thunderous *whomp* from the gusts of wind hitting the schooner sails, her old heart jumps. She's thrilled to be outdoors, and takes a big breath, laughing when her old bones rise off the wooden chair.

"I couldn't be more contented," she bawls out across her front garden to a few people she knows heading over around the wharf.

Watt and Michael Mullins lead the crowd on the wharf in an old sea shanty for leaving. Biddy says the Our Father aloud with the swarm of onlookers and well-wishers and, with the sun shining warmly, she knows the Lord, Himself, likely has His neck stuck out over the Crow Hill to keep an eye on all hands.

Biddy's thoughts of her late husband, Peter, are plentiful and, if she looks hard enough, she imagines it won't be too hard to see him in the crowd. For scattered moments she's a little girl again on Sound Island, farther up Placentia Bay where she was born, watching her father leaving on big schooners for the same fishing grounds the *Annie Healy* is headed for this day. "My, the stories he'd tell when he come home," she often said of her father. How the world always seemed better when he smiled! And the rare times he found no reason to smile, she, too, felt his hurt. And then, when she got married, the best time of her life! All the times Peter took to the sea and those heavenly feelings when she'd finally see the schooner's tall masts coming past The Isaacs and into the harbour again. How they, together, took suffering and good times all in stride. Guilt skirts her happiness as she breathes the crisp salt air full of all things summer in Fox Harbour. She whispers a prayer for Peter, and asks for a little forgiveness to help brush away the guilt for enjoying herself for the first time in years.

Smiling sweetly, she acknowledges her thoughts, accepting it all, one day at a time. And there, now, is John, her stepson, but no less her own boy, all grown up and to the wheel of the *Big Annie*.

In the eyes of the locals, the old schooner still glows from her fine reputation of long ago.

Biddy imagines old Richard Healy standing on the wharf, his tall frame bent over from hard work and heavy winds, making sure every detail is seen to.

Jim and Mike, old Richard's sons, are in their fifties now, with Henry not far behind. And half a century on that same wharf that has been repaired hundreds of times only hardens their image. They are tough when it comes to their business, too. They have to be. Good men, they are, like most in Fox Harbour, always counting on one another in the hope tomorrow will be one blessed with less TB and more fish. "If you've yer health, what else can ya ask for, besides plenty of fish?" Biddy always says.

Peter's permanent absence makes her miss those important men more than ever now. She never fails to thank God for her sons, the way they continue to fill the unrestricted emptiness of widowhood, and for that she's as well off as anyone. Although it's not her true home, Fox Harbour is like no place else.

There will be no fretting over whether or not she'll feel Peter's loving presence again and again. She can see him now, hunched over the stove, one of his big hands resting on the top oven, making sure it's banked safely for the night. The flue is adjusted so the chimney draws just enough air that it's not freezing down in the kitchen in the morning. John has never failed to take care of her since his father died, and what would she ever do without him, especially now that Pad has a bad back? Biddy often sees Peter in the kitchen, standing, one arm behind his back, leaning over the daybed and looking out the window to see what's going on in the harbour or who is coming and going up and down the road. How could she not feel him? If Peter was here now, she knows, he'd proudly watch John and talk about life when he, himself, was a shore boy, just like young Billy Penny on the wharf now, about to let go the *Big Annie's* lines.

Once the men from the *Pauline* and the *Lady Jane* have rowed out to their berths, the *Annie Healy* slips gently from the wharf and turns gracefully on her way with the help of her twenty-horsepower Acadia engine.

Biddy watches with pride and joy at the sight of the three schooners sailing away. A few small boats coast alongside.

From the deck of the *Annie Healy*, Michael Mullins sings, in his beautiful tenor voice, a lovely old Irish ballad to his little sister, Mary Ann. She's smiling from the shore but is sad to see him leave. Earlier today she overheard Michael telling someone of his bad dream, about falling in the water and of a boat sinking. He was making a joke out of it, but she felt he wasn't happy about it. She longs for his return. He'll help celebrate her eighth birthday next month.

Once faired up, the *Annie* slips through the tricky shoals and glides out behind the other schooners. When the boats disappear from sight, Biddy Mullins stands up and walks her chair back into the house.

CHAPTER TWELVE

At Sea

The crewmen of the *Annie Healy* are big and strong, most of them
well over six feet, except Charlie Sampson, who's five-ten. Their
hands are massive, deeply torn, scarred from years of jigging and
baiting hooks and hauling trawl lines and traps. Thick white lines
in their palms and on their fingers and thumbs remind them where
hooks of all sizes have caught hold, and where they'll likely catch
again. Not to mention the slivers and slices of flesh taken by splitting
knives, and those other scars on arms and legs, from axes, bucksaw
blades, and spoke shaves used for wood in fall and winter. Some old
wounds to the hands have a job to heal, reopening and washed clean
with the salt water. Again and again. Year after year. Getting cut is
as natural as breathing, and each trip and the dangerous excitement
it brings is worth a bit of lost blood. They take great pride in their
strength while hard-sung shanties help them through the many
tasks required for fishing. Really, it has to do with where the fish are,
and whether or not they can find them. Nothing else.

The *Big Annie* is on her way to Tide's Cove Point for bait. The trip across Placentia Bay to the Burin Peninsula is a time for the crew to catch up. When enough squid is aboard, it will be steady belt. No time for chatting once they take to sailing again. They'll cut up bait until they reach Point Lance Rock, at the other side of Golden Bay. From then on it will be a vicious cycle of lowering dories, loading them with gear and bait, rowing, setting and hauling trawls, rowing back to the schooner, pewing fish aboard, carrying and packing it into the hold, and salting and stacking. Then back into the dories to do it all over again. They'll be lucky to get a couple of hours' rest before each dawn. So, now is the time to have a laugh, sing a song, to size up the lands they pass, tell a story or two.

Once clear of Fox Harbour's shoals, it is clear sailing for the *Annie*. The daylight dances merrily on the water outside Pond Head, Argentia, where children and dogs run wild on dark, sandy shores. Little girls sit on big rocks worn smooth by time. They hold dying dandelions to their lips and blow the feathery seeds to the breeze. The white backs of young boys swimming just off Sandy Cove glisten in the water. The whitewashed clapboard of Point Latine Lighthouse glows, too, in the peaceful afternoon.

The white oil paint and dory-green trim of the schooner shines. It catches the attention of the Argentia children, who cease all play and run to a big rock to wave frantically. The crew hoists the sails to catch the Placentia Bay wind always stirring in one direction or another.

The small schooner makes a north-northwest tack to get around the outcropping of jagged rocks fortifying Argentia's deep black bog from the great combers of the open sea.

To the right of the schooner, Fox Island lifts from the green sea like a round pan of bread in rise, buttered by the late August sun. The sea laps at the tiny island's wild edges of limestone and granite while dozens of gulls circle above in a frenzy of perpetual hunger. Lighthouse Keeper Power sounds the foghorn to salute the Fox Harbour crew.

Tacking westward, the *Big Annie* joins the fleet of schooners, big and small, en route to Golden Bay. In the distance, to starboard, the sheer face of Red Island ignites in rugged splendour. The forest of schooner masts is carried along by wind and tide.

To port, scattered along Argentia's rugged coastline, tiny figures lug seaweed. They're tending to vegetable gardens planted along the edges of old graveyards walled in layers of rocks long since picked from the land. Leaning towers of marble still stand after a hundred years or more of punishing winds and salt spray from the sea. Farther along, Merasheen Bank basks graciously in the overflow of sunshine from Red Island.

As they sail past Argentia and First Beach, the crew has a gander in at the broken heart in the big hill of rock just outside Freshwater. The French named it *Creveceour*. With bigger sips of rum and moonshine, some of them take a stab at uncovering the poetry restless in their Irish blood. Each gives his spiel as to why the French christened it so, aside from its shape.

At times the crew sings together, while other moments are handed solely, respectfully, to one man. With tunes passed around on the wind, time often seems to stand still. Each mind lost in its infinite passion for the Old Sod from the patriotism handed down so strongly through generations of legend and song. At such times, thoughts lie neither in yesterday nor tomorrow. The words and tunes they love to sing came with their great-grandfathers and great-grandmothers and their few possessions on the filthy boats carrying them from Cobh. Other verses they've made up along the paths of their own lives in this little corner of big Placentia Bay.

Michael Mullins finishes his cigarette, coughs to clear his throat, and spits, the way he always does before singing. No one dares open his mouth, except to take a drag on a pipe or smoke.

The young man sings softly and passionately about Dublin in days of old and a lovely girl named Molly Malone. A few moments of silence follow the song's end, and one by one the crew says how they envision themselves walking the alleyways and streets of Dublin. All but Michael say they're sure they'll never live long enough to have the means to go there. The older men wish they had Michael's nerve for singing without the drink.

"You'd swear he was alongside her when she died," Charlie says under his breath of Michael's singing. Tears are in his eyes as he remembers the tune from his own younger years.

". . . cockles and mussels," he sings, looking into the horizon.

"Alive, alive-o," the rest help finish the line.

"I doubts we'll ever see cobblestones to walk on in Fox Harbour," Pad says, laughing.

"Ah, but b'ys, don't we have the good-looking girls like they says are in Dublin an' Galway an' Cork?" Charlie says proudly.

"Such brazen beauty could only be born of Irish blood," Michael says, thinking of his Katie. He's inspired to sing another.

I went to a dance one night in Fox Harbour,
There were plenty of girls as nice as you'd wish.

There was one pretty maiden a-chawing on frankum,
Just like a young kitten a-gnawing fresh fish.

Jim King reaches down and grabs John Kelly by the arm, helping him up from his bed of twine. Arm in arm they swing around the deck, singing the chorus to Michael's song.

We'll rant an' we'll roar like true Newfoundlanders,
We'll rant an' we'll roar on deck an' below . . .

"All right, b'ys! Get to work out of it!" Captain Mullins roars, keeping his smile back-on to the dancing men. "Hard to port," he yells, as the *Annie* makes her third tack, this time on a southwest course for Tide's Cove Point, near the entrance to Mortier Bay on the western side of Placentia Bay.

Several miles off Marticot Island is a black curtain of fog. Inside the fog bank a peculiar but familiar feeling of night prevails. The three-second blasts every thirty seconds from the horn at Marticot Light doesn't stop Jack Foley talking about Gus. He's talking to Pad again, finishing what lack of time wouldn't allow earlier. He imagines if his boy was here with him. Leaving him at home the way he had to, sick on the daybed, to go to the same godforsaken place to fish never made a bit of sense. Then, to come home excited, as much as Jack got excited, from a boatload of cod to find poor Gus dead in the bed upstairs, then to bury him and get back in the boat to do it all again for the past three years. There's little wonder why he spent the past week or more bitching and complaining to Lize.

"Gus was a great hand to salt fish," Jack says. The rest of the crew nod in agreement.

"One of the best," he says. "Curse the TB, anyhow."

"Goddamn TB," two or three of them say.

Tossing his head, Jack spits a mouthful of black tobacco juice into the white, frothy mass of water being pushed aside by the boat. Looking into the evening of the day, he tastes his pipe and whispers prayers for Lizzie and Gus, Lize, his daughters, Nell and Laura in Grand Falls, Margaret, Helen, and Jane in the States, Angela and her crowd in Fox Harbour. And Bernadette, Lize's saving grace in his absence. Bernadette can bake a Christmas fruitcake as good as her mother, and her molasses and raisin bread is as good as any Jack's ever tasted. A little smile comes to his lips. Someday he'll tell her.

Knowing the jigging of squid will soon put a dent in his strength, Jack turns his attention back to his fellow sharemen, whose good humour never fails to calm his nerves.

John Kelly comes up from his bunk and joins in on the chat. He's still white in the face but says he'd rather be no place else. The fog, he says, is better than the sun draining the life out of them.

"A boat cuttin' us down in this blackness might drain the life outta ya, too, John," Pad says.

They all nod to his good point, then laugh because it's rare for Pad to say something without a smirk. The skin of salt pork tied around John's neck hasn't helped his sore throat one bit, and he flings the failed remedy overboard.

"Here!" Pad says, holding a small glass bottle to John.

"Wha?"

"Take a few swallies of that an' yer throat will be better in no time."

"What is it, b'y?" John wants to know.

"Kerosene an' molasses. Uncle Watt said you'd be needin' it. 'Tis good for what ails ya."

"Here's to Mr. Watt," John says, raising the bottle to his lips. Pad waits for a reaction but doesn't get it.

"Wha?" John asks. "Ya didn't think 'tis the only time I ever drink this stuff, did ya?"

Michael stands next to his father at the wheel, watching how the captain allows the schooner to glide effortlessly over the water. And although he's been on a schooner a fair amount in his life, Michael is still amazed how the staysail and jib are able to catch the slightest breeze and carry a big boat along. He watches the sails breathe in the light breeze and takes a drag on his cigarette, letting the smoke out slowly. The *Annie* clips along at six knots.

Jim King paces the sixteen feet from port to starboard, tapping the bait barrels and trawl kegs lashed around the mainmast along the way.

"I wonder if Bridge'll have the baby while I'm away," he says, his fidgeting large frame doing little to hide his nervousness.

At Jim's request, all hands kneel where they are and say a few prayers for Bridge and the baby she's carrying.

Up ahead, another boat comes into view. Captain John Stevenson from Fox Harbour gives a quick wave from the helm of the *Lady Jane* and points ahead to the sunshine peeping through a hole in the bank of fog.

The crew remains united in a bit of gossip and in wishing Michael a happy birthday.

"Young Katie will wait for ya, Mick, b'y," mocks Jim King.

"If Bridge heard ya talkin' 'bout young Katie, King, she'd have yer head," coughs John Kelly from a bundle of net near the stacked dories.

"I thought Mullins told ya stay in the bunk till yer better, Kelly," Jim says.

The rest of the crew, including Michael, joins in on the fun.

"Ah, sure, b'ys, I was handy to takin' Mr. Watt on this run," the captain bawls out from behind the wheel. "That woulda been somethin'."

"Uncle Watt could show you a thing or two, Mullins," shouts Pad, rolling a barrel of salt up the deck.

"'Deed he could, me son. 'Deed he could," returns Mullins.

All hands agree.

The *Annie Healy* breaks through the fog and into the view of dozens of other schooner crews taking bait on near Tide's Cove Point.

With the *Annie's* head to the wind, Captain Mullins turns her wheel all the way to starboard until she slows in the lop. With orders to lower the sails, the crew gets to work. Pad takes the halyards of the jib and jumbo down and zigzags them around the cleat gunwales, letting the ropes slide slowly through his hands. The weight of the boom brings the sails down to the deck. Jack does the same with the foresail while Jim grabs the downhaul from the trip boom for the mainsail, allowing the biggest sail to fall more quickly.

"Let go," roars the captain.

With that, Charlie trips the trigger and the bow anchor hits the water with great force.

Clouds of squawking gulls circle the *Annie's* mastheads in hopes of a meal. Bullbirds and turr lounge patiently on every perch, without the cheek of the boisterous, dirty gulls soiling every exposed inch of the boat.

One by one, silhouetted schooners loaded with bait cross the shimmering horizon on their way to Cape St. Mary's and Golden Bay.

Preparing to haul anchor nearby is Captain John Power of Marystown and his crew on the schooner *Chase*.

"Off to Golden Bay, Cap'n Power?" Captain Mullins bellows from the *Annie's* stern.

"Yes, sir. Soon's the last dory's aboard. We left ya plenty of squid, John. Ya needn't worry."

It is suppertime and over four hours since the Fox Harbour crew left home. With the *Big Annie* safely moored, the three dories are uncovered and removed one by one from the stack and lowered onto the sea by a boom. The men drop their three-inch pieces of lead and hooks over the side of the dories. Captain Power was right; the squid are plentiful, going mad for the red jiggers, ignorant of their many hooks. As fast as they can be hauled up, the squid are removed, covering the men in their greasy ink. They're tossed into wooden tubs in the dory. Aside from the sound of lead hitting the water, all is quiet for about an hour.

"Mind the freeboard, b'ys," Jack yells to Jim and Michael, who have a tendency to load the boat to the gunwales.

"The last thing we needs is a dory gone," Jack grumbles.

Within three hours the dories are hauled up, stacked, and fastened back to the schooner's deck and covered with oilcloth. With the last barrel of squid covered, the crew hauls anchor and heads across Placentia Bay.

Darkness creeps in from every corner of the earth as the *Annie Healy* cuts through the black water, soaking up the late summer night. Michael makes sure the oil lamps are full before placing them inside the red and green glass casings of the port and starboard lights. The clear light casing of the mainmast lamp gets snagged while Michael is running it up the line. He climbs up and down the masthead and fixes the tangle in no time.

The *Annie's* freshly barked sails of reddish brown smoulder in the last ashes of evening light as the schooner breaks on a southeast tack into the open sea for Golden Bay. Within the hour a splendid gibbous moon sends slivers of light on the water in the schooner's wake while the North Star twinkles like a guardian angel. To the starboard bow, smiling dolphins play quietly at great speeds. Humpback whales grace the surface now and again, sending sprays of their misty sighs into the cooling air. The tranquility helps prepare the crew for the hard work that lies ahead. Not another word is spoken.

As the *Annie Healy* nears her destination, the treacherous Cape Shore coast spits back the ocean with each impotent attempt by the surf to climb the craggy cliffs. These are the same cliffs that reminded the Irish of the Cliffs of Moher so long ago, enticing them to embrace the endless miles of beautiful coastline as their own.

Under the spotlight of the moon, white, frothy masses against chiselled rock faces allow plenty of warning to ships' captains and crews to keep a safe distance. The houses dotting the cliffs shine like patches of spring snow in the woods but are no match for the beauty of the dancing dippers in the night sky.

Rolling combers gently lift and pass beneath the boat, travelling great distances to break heavily on beaches far from the reach of land lovers sleeping in their homes hundreds of feet above. When the waves hit the cliffs, thunderous crashing sounds reach far back across the sea, giving the night a different feel altogether.

It is impossible for the crew to look at the majestic walls of rock and tremendous surf along the Cape Shore without mentioning the Virgin Rocks farther up the coast, near Barasway.

"Uncle Watt often talks 'bout the 1887 August Gale an' the ship *Ocean Friend*. Cracked right off on the Virgins, she did, takin' all of the crew down with her," Pad says.

The men aboard the *Annie* know all about the Virgins and are glad they're nowhere handy to them.

"'Twasn't uncommon to see boats big and small, Uncle Watt says, impaled on the Virgins where they stay till beat to bejaysus by the water," Pad adds.

Pad looks down at the off-coloured stitch in his sweater where the burn hole had been. He misses his family, closes his eyes and gives thanks for Liz. And her patience. How he'd love to have Uncle Watt here poking fun at everyone and everything on board, and doing his fair share of the work in the meantime. Pad admires his uncle for being such a grand sport after all he's been through: the hard life on The Rams, loving one woman, marrying her, losing her to childbirth along with the child, and never again looking at another woman, let alone remarrying and having children like so many do. Watt's willingness to stay with Pad's family while he's away is immeasurable in Pad's mind and, although the real work of this trip hasn't really begun, he wishes himself home in the kitchen already, carrying on with Watt, and watching Ellen and Johnny grow up so fast, the way they all seem to these days. And Liz keeping it all together, the way only a good woman can. He can't imagine life without Liz, the way Uncle Watt manages to carry on without Mary. The calm night conjures images of Uncle Watt rowing gracefully out the harbour in his dory—the one he made himself when he was a young man—with no compass, just the light of the moon and his big nose for smelling the wind to guide him back to The Rams for a visit. While there he'd see his old friends, share a bottle of moonshine, a walk to the graveyard, and a lifetime of memories before parting ways again. Pad wonders if he ever lost Liz would *he* move back to The Rams to forget her? Not that he could ever forget her, the way Uncle Watt moved to Fox Harbour after losing Mary. When someone asked Watt where he lived, he'd never say one place or the other. He lived where he was, one moment to the next. Pad wonders if he could ever be half the man his old uncle is.

It's an hour before midnight. Jack thinks of Lize and Bernadette, home by themselves, long since gone to bed, after blowing out the lantern to save oil, with the drop of cold tea from the pot used to dout the fire in the stove.

With the *Annie Healy* hove to, all hands turn in on their bunks for a nap. The sound of the sea rolling beneath the boat is just enough to help them drift to sleep.

CHAPTER THIRTEEN

August 25, 1927
Thursday's Storm

The fog has been bad for the past week. Most mornings the men do nothing, only stay aboard the schooner, drink tea, and nibble on the bits of grub left in their sea boxes. And wait for the fog to lift, move on, or burn away enough to create visibility to find their floats and trawls. When the fog burns off or blows away, it's time to set the dories back in the water, bait the trawls, wait, and haul them in again. When they do get to their trawls, fish are plentiful.

The wing walls of the schooner's hull are packed solid with heavily salted cod of all sizes. Once this day ends the Healys will have no need to gripe about a bad trip the way they did the last time.

"We'll take everything up 'round ha' past two t'day, an' we'll be well under sail for home no later than four o'clock," Captain Mullins says of the fishing gear in the water. "No need of overloadin' the boat. There's always next week."

The captain is still vexed after Michael and Jim took off in their dory earlier and got lost in the fog, leaving no choice but to use the

Annie's engine to creep around looking for them. The risk of hitting another boat was one thing, and the possibility of killing innocent men in their dories was another. But using precious engine fuel always put the captain in a bad way. The few dollars worth of gas and oil will be taken from the entire crew's share.

"No need!" the captain mutters. "No need, an' we with plenty of fish. Ye knows better than that, b'ys. Ye should have more sense."

Mike Murphy, a young man fishing from a Dunville schooner, is not long gone from the *Annie Healy* in his dory. He was welcomed aboard earlier for a chit-chat and drop of tea, waiting for the fog to lift before returning to his boat not far away.

The smell of fried rashers drifting up from the *Big Annie's* galley is enough to torment the men. The fog left earlier than usual and there's precious time to use up eating bread soaked in fat and the remaining handfuls of tea. Jack picks a few raisins and dough from his tea bun, shoves them in his mouth, and stuffs his last bun crumbling into the pocket of his oilcoat. He dreads the thought of wet rope and twine tearing through the cuts and cracks of his hands, not to mention the cold salt water necessary to wash the blood and fish slime away. He'd sooner perish, he says to Charlie, than have to haul another big, ugly sea sculpin with thorns for a head off a hook caught deep in its belly. He prays to the heavens for no sign of a dogfish to have to club to death with the moll or, worse again, a wolfish like the one that bit through his boot and almost through his foot yesterday.

"'Tis bad enough," he grumbles, "t' have t' spend another day wit' one foot soakin' wet an', thanks be to God, 'tis the last day for this trip."

He jokes he's liable to be a week with his foot up on the oven door to thaw out, with Lize bawling at him, wishing he would get out of her way.

Despite their tired, aching bones, and water-soaked, wrinkled flesh, the early morning air and the absence of fog like pea soup bring smiles to the men's dried and cracked lips. Golden Bay is a wondrous sight, they agree, even Jack with his wet, sore foot. Dozens of schooners and a hundred or more dories are revealed when the blanket of fog is pulled back.

"Not like 'twas one time," Jack says, remembering years ago, before people started going away to the States to live. "No trouble to walk along the schooners here then, b'y, they all tied up together."

"Yes, Jack, but there were more fish long ago, too," Charlie reminds his friend.

"Yes, b'y, I s'pose, Charlie. I shouldn't complain, I know."

The rising sun reveals speckled fingers of sand laced with bits of kelp and sea urchins clawing at crevasses in the steep incline of black and grey rock. Crouching tuckamore crawling along the meadows above cling to overhanging rocks. They make fine resting places for busy birds. The face of the land watching over the lengthy crescent of beach stands like a fortress protecting the endless miles of wilderness at its back.

Around eight o'clock all hands aboard the *Annie Healy* finish their tea, having stowed away the fish from their first haul of the morning. It's time to head back to work.

With enough bait cut up and put in their dory, John and Pad are the first to row away from the schooner. Charlie and Jack untie their dory at each end, slinging the lines in over the rail, and shove off from the schooner with their ten-foot gaffs.

The voices of other men singing in their dories fade quickly, and the air is swiftly replaced by the screeching of gulls and gannets swarming in clouds overhead.

"Lard Jaysus, Kelly, will ya stop makin' such a racket," Pad sings out, making fun of John, who hardly ever opens his mouth.

"'Tis a queer thing," Jack says, "the birds gettin' on like that and no one splittin' fish on our deck."

Beneath the bright sun the shadows of the birds are cast upon the *Big Annie* and then on the men in their dories. The birds race toward the walls of rock above the beach, directly in from the schooner. Jim King curses and swears on the bird shit raining down, covering the boat, dripping from the ropes and booms, making the deck slippery in places.

More seabirds in the hundreds make like mad for the shore. Some fly to the *Annie's* mastheads, but only long enough to land, let out a few squawks, and they're gone again. They join the rest bolting in over the water to the harsh layers of cliff wearing a soft cap of sunshine.

Closer to the land the gulls keep pace with the kittiwakes, murr, and terns while smaller birds fumble through the air. Some are struck and maimed by bigger, faster birds, and they fall into the water, easy prey for schools of dogfish never far from fishing boats on the water.

"I never see the like," Charlie says, standing up, holding his hands above his eyes to get a better look.

"Sit down out of it, b'y!" Jack says, looking over his shoulder to the *Annie Healy*.

"I never see the like," Charlie says again, settling into his oars.

"What a Jaysus racket that was, Jack! P'raps their mothers are callin' 'em home for a bite t' eat," Charlie says dryly.

Jack sees Captain Mullins running to the rails on the opposite side of the schooner. Jim and Michael follow him. They seem to have no intentions of getting into their dory.

A strange drone is heard, and it's getting louder by the second. The sky is clear and blue, but raindrops of all sizes start pelting the men sideways. Quick gusts of wind take the knitted caps from their heads and send them skidding across the water.

"'Tis salt water, Jack!" Charlie says, wiping his mouth with the cotton cuff of his oilcoat. "'Tisn't rain at all."

The words are no sooner out of Charlie's mouth when a living gale comes barrelling from the southwest. Jack and Charlie topple over backwards into the twine, hooks, and bait in the bottom of their dory.

The sea is in a fit of rage. It throws large crests of water over the *Annie*, knocking Michael and Jim to the deck. Michael is carried along the rails of the schooner by a surge of salt water until he brings up solid on the handle of the windlass. He lets out a roar from the pain in his chest, and quickly scrambles back to his feet, clinging to the rope of the foresail masthead. He barely has his breath back when another surge picks him up, rips him from the masthead, and sends him head first over the bow. Blood spurts from his forehead. He wraps both arms around the bowsprit to keep from falling into the sea. The schooner tips forward and dips into the water. Michael disappears. He manages to keep hold of the bowsprit until the *Annie* rises upright again. When the water retreats from beneath his lower body, he crawls backwards to the bow, finds his legs, and turns. He lunges at the foresail. But one of his rubber boots is half-off and he buckles on one leg. He's taken a third time by the next rush of water, but he grabs hold of the foresail mast and is secured long enough to get the boot back on. Then, he's picked up and thrashed off the windlass again.

The captain's body lifts on the same wave that just threw his son face first into the windlass. John Mullins is picked up and dropped over the wheel. One of his legs falls between two of the wheel's spokes, his body left twisting. His head and arms bash off the deck until the wheel turns enough to allow him room to manipulate his leg from the iron spokes. The boot from the caught leg is lodged between the spokes. He tries to stand but can't, and drags his body backwards with his arms. The boat is out of control as another surge rolls him to the stern. He manages to stand on his good leg and hops back to the wheel to retrieve his boot. He screams as he forces the hurt leg to bend while trying to keep an impossible sense of balance.

Jim is on his hands and knees, spinning around the deck in a couple of feet of water until it runs out through the scuppers. When he hits the rail, he grabs hold, looking straight into the sea. He's sure the schooner will roll over. The *Annie* rises up and evens out again. Jim tears a piece of kelp from across his face and sees Jack and Charlie rowing toward him. He ties a coil of three-inch rope to the rail and casts it toward the dory half-full of water. Charlie's hands are bloody from the hooks. He grabs the rope and twists it around his big arms and begins hauling while Jack keeps hard on the oars. There's no time to bail, and the dory is just about full when they smack into the *Annie*. Jim braces his legs under the schooner's rails and hangs out over the boiling sea to reach both men. He hauls them aboard and watches their dory, still tied to the schooner's rail, vanish beneath the surface. Charlie and Jack are exhausted and collapse. Jim yells there's no time for that. The *Annie* is doing circles around her anchor while the three men look for a sign of Pad and John.

"Over there!" Jim roars.

About sixty feet from the schooner, Pad and John are leaning back on their oars. The next thing the men on the schooner see is the dory's keel. She hovers momentarily above the water, then tips back altogether, sitting on her stern before turning bottom-up.

"We got to get to 'em!" Jim screams, still holding on to the coil of rope.

"Where's me father?" Michael yells.

Michael staggers, hauling himself along the rail. Blood is oozing from his head.

"Take this!" Jim says to Charlie, handing him the rope.

Jim and Michael struggle along the railing toward the stern of the schooner. They find Captain Mullins lying against the base of the wheel with a knife between his teeth, tying a piece of sailcloth around one of his legs.

Another wall of water nails the three men to the deck, scattering them in different directions. Charlie and Jack's dory is thrown over the rail and across the deck. Michael is on his back and puts both legs up, preparing to be crushed by the dory. Another wave comes over Michael's head and washes the dory a few feet away. The schooner levels off again. Michael heads back to the ship's stern.

"Father!" Michael screams, taking the knife from the captain's mouth and shoving it into the leather case on his side.

"The leg is broke off at the knee, b'ys," Captain Mullins yells, wincing from the pain. "Get me up and tie me to the wheel right fast."

As Jim and Michael go to pick up Captain Mullins, the ship is lifted out of the water for a second and dropped. All three men are swept about the deck again. When the water on the deck subsides, the captain screams and curses louder. He panics, as Jim and Michael are nowhere to be seen. Then they both come crawling up the deck, lifting themselves up by holding the jumbo spar. They hang on until the next wave passes. Captain Mullins is hanging onto the wheel. Michael makes it to the wheel and does as he's been ordered—ties his father to the wheel.

When the captain is lashed to the wheel, the *Annie* rolls on her side and almost doesn't upright. Michael and Jim are sent flying face first into the rail, and it is five or ten seconds before they regain their senses. Both men have bloody faces now. The captain regains footing on his good leg and does his best to steady the ship.

Jack raises the jib and staysail to give the captain enough canvas to safely turn the vessel, and staggers back to the helm. They look in every direction for John and Pad, but there's no sign of them or their dory.

The *Annie* bucks like a wild horse, rising over one big wave and crashing headlong into another. Her nose is buried in a mass of white froth and water, sending more waves crashing and rolling around the deck.

The cold water washes over the shoulders of the men. They cling to whatever's closest. Jack's spine is numb, right to the top of his head, and he's sure he's paralyzed and soon to be drowned. Captain Mullins shakes his head like a dog to rid his face of water and seaweed while he tries to navigate the schooner toward where the men agree John and Pad might be.

Other schooners, with masts cracked off and lying across their decks, limp close to the *Annie Healy*, and Captain Mullins is just able to keep clear of them. Jack and Jim are portside, yelling John and Pad's names. Michael and Charlie are at the starboard doing the same.

"They're liable to be run down by a boat," Jack sings out, his voice trembling. The remaining crew is helpless and they know it. Jack's talk with Pad last week flashes through his mind; they'd been walking up along the road to Jim Spurvey's skiff. Pad listened, and how good Jack felt afterwards. He's guilt-ridden, knowing if Pad were here, he'd have the good dory over the side and out looking for someone missing, but Captain Mullins has already forbade Jim and Michael from doing that. All of Jack's wishing his son was alongside him returns and, for the first time, he's glad Gus is where he is.

Pad and John's dory appears alongside the schooner. It's upright and full of water. There's no sign of the men. Jim unties a grapnel from the deck, near the masthead, and flings it with both arms into the centre of the submerged dory. He hooks it on the first try and Michael helps haul it to the *Annie*'s rail. The sea lifts it up as both men are pulling hard, and they're barely able to get out of the way when it comes crashing onto the deck. Jack, holding onto the swinging mainmast spar, stares at the dory full of water.

"Jack!" the captain roars.

Jack doesn't respond.

"Go down below an' check on the stove; make sure the place is not on fire," Captain Mullins orders. "And stay down there in yer bunk and hold on. Won't do your back any good being up here."

"Mind, now!" Jack says, but he knows the captain is right and does what he's told.

"Ya all right, Charlie?" the captain asks.

"Yeah!"

"All right, b'ys, check over the hatches, make sure they're battened good! Swing 'er off," he shouts, and the men give the schooner the double-reef foresail.

"The b'ys! Jaysus Christ, John! We can't leave 'em!" Jim screeches.

"They're gone," the captain roars, and continues screaming orders.

The weight of the wind on the foresail alone swings the schooner to port, dragging the anchor chain screeching across the bow. Michael holds a rag to his head, stopping the blood. He and Jim fight their way to the bow and grab hold of the windlass. They pump up and down until the anchor chain snaps under the strain. The gale continues to pound the schooner, shoving salt water up the noses and down the throats of the men.

The foresail topmast cracks off.

"Look out!" Charlie shouts, as wood and sail fall to the deck, just missing the men at the windlass.

The jib topsail tears away from the bowsprit and disappears on the wind. Jim and Michael dive to the deck to avoid flying debris.

Captain Mullins knows he has to take a northwest course to get the schooner past the False Cape and Cape St. Mary's and into the deep waters of Placentia Bay. She'll be safe there.

Mountainous seas throw the schooner on her beam ends. After

a long thirty seconds or so, she uprights again, sending dory oars, trawls, and kegs into the seething sea.

Atop the massive waves, the crew sees several boats attempting to navigate the dangerous reefs outside Norther' Head, likely on their way to St. Bride's, where just Sunday past they sat in a lovely meadow, enjoying a spell, chatting with other men after Mass.

"Up with the mains'l. All the way," Captain Mullins orders.

"Jaysus Christ, Mullins, 'tis too much wind. She'll never handle it," Jim shouts.

"Get it up! 'Tis out of here we're gettin'!" Mullins screams back.

"Christ have mercy," Charlie cries, as he, Michael, and Jim put all their weight into hoisting the mainsail. The heavy boom beats them in the guts after each pull as the *Annie* is knocked about like the toy boats their fathers once made for them.

The rope around Charlie's right forearm keeps him from falling completely overboard when the wind carries him backwards and over the rail. His broad back smacks off the water as the *Annie* rolls. Jim grabs Charlie's boot, twisting it so it doesn't come off, and pulls him back to the deck. They continue with the harrowing strain of raising the mainsail until it's all the way up and secured. With that, the schooner rises out of the water and turns running. The mainmast light casing shatters, sending shards of clear glass to the deck. Michael gets another cut to his face. The lantern from inside the casing flies through the air fifty or sixty feet before crashing into the wall of sea surrounding the schooner.

"We can make St. Bride's, Father," Michael shouts, staggering to catch his balance, holding his chest still searing with pain.

"Too many boats headin' to one place, Michael," his father roars back. "No room, an' we'll end up on the rocks. We'll fare all right once we're in the middle of the bay."

"Father! Your leg!" Michael yells.

"Can't even feel it," the captain yells back.

A few hundred feet from the *Annie*'s stern, across maddening waves, Captain John Power struggles to keep the *Chase* intact.

From another schooner nearby in the race for St. Bride's, Mullins's old Long Harbour friend, Peter Murphy, doesn't like what he sees: the *Annie Healy* under full sail and heading away from land.

CHAPTER FOURTEEN

The Storm At Home

The storm batters Fox Harbour. The wild, howling wind scratches and tugs at homes, stables, stores, stages, and flakes. Felt is ripped from rooftops and fish from flakes, shattering glass in windows, sending it crashing to the rock foundations below. The tallest wild rose bush branches in gardens snap and large trees on all sides of the town are torn from the ground. Roots and all.

Mothers and wives are headlong into the rosary, praying for the safety of their sons and husbands at sea. With Mary Jane Sampson's birthday time on the minds of many, prayers are said so the gathering will go ahead. The whistling and whirring of the wind in stoves, pipes, and chimneys is deafening. Breakfast is quickly forgotten by youngsters peeking outdoors to catch a glimpse of the wind's wonderful command.

Drying codfish and their coverings of branches and birch rinds are whisked through the air like paper, much of it ending up in the harbour. The rest flies over the road and into gardens, smacking off fences, houses, and stables where sheep are baaing and cows mooing and moving about with fright.

Shore boys chase fish, slipping and sliding, gathering what they can. They can't get over the wind with the sun still shining, and how last night's red sky had promised nothing in the way of this. No one hears their curses and complaints.

Around Healy's premises, shore boys Billy Penny and Cyril Leary have an awful job collecting fish and everything else blowing around. The wind lifts their slim bodies as they scramble down and fumble over the steps of the wet and slippery flakes. Sheets of water lifted and thrown from the sea slow them down even more. Their hands and the sides of their legs are scraped and torn by nail heads and large splinters impossible to avoid. Running in every direction, the young fellows do what they're told without hesitation. They dump fish under the shaking and squeaking linny of the big store, yelling at one another to watch out for this and that flying through the air. Through a broken window of the store, Jim Healy's pet crow bawls a few words at the lads. The linny is jumping up and down, its four-by-four wooden support posts pounding the ground. The nails attaching it to the house twist and screech until the whole thing collapses on top of the fish and rain barrels beneath. They knew this would happen and there's no sense in trying to fix it now; at least that much fish is safe, trapped under the linny.

Overturned punts by the water's edges somersault across the road, demolishing fences, outhouses, and well covers. The few clothesline poles still attached to their lines spin and leap in every direction.

The wind howling across the mouth of the harbour picks The Green clean. Everything not nailed down is sent through the air, making it increasingly difficult for men fighting to save their small boats. Gear once stowed in wooden boxes, barrels, and tubs on wharves and stageheads floats in a huge mess along the shore, all the way to where the sea meets the brook.

Clothes that managed to stay on lines are taken in and hung above stoves to finish drying when it's fit to light a fire. Brave boys marvel over the speed of their iron barrel hoops rolling madly under the sway of the wind until their mothers or older brothers grab them by the ears and point them back home.

The noise of scattering debris is unbearable, with the whir of the wind leading the band of destruction. A mangled chorus of disturbed horses and cattle and chickens mixes in with the great blows of the gale. The harbour's water level rises to meet the road and, in places, washes over. Muddy trenches are carved and men have to lay wooden planks down to move scared horses across.

Children who managed to sneak out are soon rushed indoors and led beneath stairs and under tables where they're told they'll be safe. Bottles of holy water are emptied while windows smash and crash all around them. Babies bawl, cats gale, and dogs whimper and howl while mothers and older children try in vain to quiet and comfort all.

Brittle kerosene-stained pages of old prayer books rustle beneath the crippled fingers of elderly women praying in loud whispers, rubbing the faces off the saints of their rosary beads. Plastic and ceramic statues of Jesus, Mary, and Good Saint Joseph stand guard. On windowsills they face windows and doors, except where wind and debris have broken panes of glass. It's the end of the world, some say, with all the booming and breaking, and the Lord Himself in pieces on the floor.

Oblivious to the storm, some old men are lured toward the water. They trudge through flattened grass and broken flowers, fretting over their sons and friends, boats and gear. They're helpless and can't stand the shame accompanying the feeling.

"Will Daddy be home soon, Mam?" Ellen Bruce asks her mother.

Liz holds her daughter close to her side, unable to get a word out. The very thought of never seeing Pad again is heavy in their breasts, stealing most of the air in their lungs.

Uncle Watt scratches his grey head.

"I don't know, me dear. I don't know. I never see a gale like this in forty year," he shouts over the racket. "I never see the like. 'Tis a good t'ing for us The Isaacs are there, keepin' the waves down. "'Tis a good t'ing. The poor crowd on The Rams, too."

Watt stands, unusually quiet, peering out the front kitchen window. The usual strength in his voice is absent, and what traces of vigour are left fall into mumbled prayers for Pad and the rest of the *Annie*'s crew.

Around dinnertime, fifteen loaves of bread lie cooling in Mary Jane Sampson's kitchen. She peeks through the window past Healy's big house to the water for a sign of the *Annie Healy*. People are going in and out of Healy's store, and by the way they mope out, she knows they have nothing to tell. She's better off waiting for someone to come to her door with the good news that the men are back safely. Her boiled molasses cake has fallen in the middle, but that's no odds. She pities the poor shore boys still chasing fish in such a state, while Billy begs to go outdoors, certain his best friend, Liz Kelly, is out enjoying the bit of excitement.

"When this storm is over, ya can go out beatin' the paths, Billy. Not a bit sooner," she warns him.

Mary Jane knows that when the *Annie* is anchored in the harbour this day the fish won't be brought in until later, on account of all the mess to clean up. But perhaps they might wait till tomorrow and her birthday time might start a bit earlier. Her baking will be the talk of Fox Harbour once all hands have a few drinks in, and being an old woman of forty-five won't be so bad after all.

Making his way in over the hill to check on Bridge King and her young ones, Bridge's father, William Dreaddy, can hardly catch his breath. With one hand he holds onto the needled branches of the spruce trees lining the path while the other keeps his cap tightly to his chest. Stopping at the top of the garden, he wipes his eyes left watery from the wind. He can see the waves pushing in over the land behind the house, and the dirty foam of the angry sea blows through the air. The small house seems to make a face at him, tilting back slightly to get out of the way of the wind. Trees around the soaked meadow dance like savages, trying hard to free themselves from the ground. William hops over the overflowing trench in his hip rubbers and carefully unlatches the length of rubber stretched over the post, keeping the gate closed. He quickly changes his mind, undoing the latch and driving the few scared sheep from the garden up into the woods where they might find a bit of shelter.

Inside the house, Bridge is cursing the storm and fretting over Jim. The baby in her belly kicks like mad for a way out. She's worried the stress of it all will send her into labour this day and she wonders if Mrs. Mart will be able to make it in time to deliver the child. She's scared by the possibility of complications from the stress, and of dying in childbirth the way many poor women in Fox Harbour have, leaving Jim alone to fend for himself and their growing family.

"They'll be in soon, I s'pose, Daddy?" Bridge says, trying to cover her nervousness, and as if he will have an answer.

"I s'pect the b'ys are gone in to S'n Bride's, or perhaps Trepassey, 'pendin' on where they were when the wind struck," Mr. Dreaddy says.

Through a continuous stream of salt spray hitting the rattling windows, the sunlight casts strange, ever-changing shadows on the faces of the young ones. They're huddled together on the daybed, where they're scared, seen, and not heard.

CHAPTER FIFTEEN

Southeast of Merasheen Bank
11:00 a.m., August 25, 1927

The sun is shining brilliantly. The wind rages from the southwest at ninety miles an hour.

Hurled atop giant waves and thrown headlong into even bigger mountains of water, Jim Harris's schooner lists starboard, almost capsizing.

Walls of salt spray and dirty foam darken the water and air. A schooner, half-submerged with both masts gone, is in a sinking position, her nose underwater. The last thing the captain from St. Joseph's needs.

Barrelling by the derelict hulk, Harris's schooner smashes through lifeless bodies, puncheon tubs, and heavy scraps of sail canvas. The crewmen aboard Harris's boat are reluctant. They have their own lives to worry about. Their own families are at home. But orders are given to try and rescue a man in the water.

Two of Harris's men grasping their schooner's rails wait for the right moment to reach out and snatch the drowning man. Freezing salt water slaps their faces, rushing over their tired bodies already numb from the cold. They wait forever.

When the moment comes, one of Harris's men extends an arm to the fisherman struggling to keep afloat amidst a mess of trawl lines, kegs, and spars. The drowning man has one arm savagely wrapped around the cracked, splintered mainsail spar of the battered schooner. Reaching for the man trying to save him, he bawls out. Their hands miss by a couple of feet, and the undertow caused by the passing schooner robs the drowning man of his last words. He is sucked violently, head first, into the black water, along with a pile of wood and canvas from the battered boat. The yellowish froth of the sea turns brown with his blood.

Harris's crew is helpless. They can hardly see each other for the water washing over them and their boat, let alone spot the man in the water. They try to remember the place where he went under, but it's impossible with the sea rising and falling, twirling and crashing upon their deck. One second they're watching the sinking schooner lifted high by the sea; the next a wall of water comes between them and the wreck. The wall drops without warning and the wreck rises up in front of their boat. They're sure it will land on them. The heavy current of the waves rushing across the deck and out through the scuppers and over the rails keeps the men clinging to whatever they can find. They shout to one another that they think they see the drowned man. But it's always a piece of wood or something. They're sure the poor soul is long dragged far away by the undercurrent, or tangled on the ocean floor in seaweed and in the nets of their forefathers.

The sea exhales, throwing Harris's schooner on her beam ends.

When the boat is uprighted, they decide to keep going. It's too dangerous. Until they look back. Like a wounded beast on the swell, the sinking schooner rises again. Another man is seen, lashed to two dories stacked on deck.

The boat's wood splitting, cracking, and snapping can be heard through the roar of the wind and lashing sea. Forged nails and iron spikes shriek as they're warped and plucked from the schooner's hull.

At first the men on board Harris's boat presume the second man is dead. Then he screams. In the mayhem his words are indecipherable.

Captain Harris orders his crew to turn his schooner around again.

The man has moved from the dories. He's clinging to a rope, and being thrashed like a bell clapper against the schooner's deck, a warping spruce wall at his back.

With another agonizing roll, a thunderous roar comes from within the ship. When she comes back up, the man is nowhere to be seen.

Then, about ten feet from the wreck, he's spotted again.

Harris's weary men manage to manoeuvre their vessel around the sinking ship. Passing by the man, they extend ten-foot gaffs. He doesn't have the strength to raise his arms.

Harris's schooner is thrown headlong, again, into a mountain of water. It tips back and climbs the wave, crashing through the crest. This time it keeps going.

The schooner wreck, picked up by another massive wave, falls on her side like a dying horse. After a violent jerk and a few spins, she turns bottom-up and is carried across the bay, toward Argentia.

CHAPTER SIXTEEN

Argentia, 2:00 p.m.

People stare into the ocean. From meadows above the beaches, they gasp, and sigh, and wonder, both silently and aloud. Who owns the boat? Who's on it? If anyone. Their eyes comb the stretch of rounded boulders where the salt water continues to pound the land. The edges of the eroded cliffs of black bog are littered with trawl kegs, nets, spars, and other wooden objects too mangled and mashed together to make out. In the marsh covering the bog lie long lengths of wood—old schooner masts clawed up from the ocean floor by the storm. They were thrown there this morning when the winds were at their peak. They're useless. Too heavy to lift and too waterlogged to burn.

The crowd is growing despite the remaining strong winds. The clouds are scarce and it's raining hard. The sun is still bright. With the wind they figure the rain could be blowing from anywhere, far away.

The freshly sharpened, worn-down blades of their father's scythes reflect the sun in the uneven meadows of flattened grass.

The first of the crowd here today came to check on their crops. Most expected the worst and got much more. Seaweed blown off potato beds fills the drills running through and around the fenceless gardens. Tiny skeletons of capelin—dug into the topsoil to feed the turnips and carrots—are exposed, their dirt blankets gone on the wind. A summer's hard work ruined. They're furious over their great losses.

Clumsy lupine stalks on the periphery of the fields wobble and dance fiercely before cracking off. Their grey, fuzzy seed pods scatter. Pitcher plants in the surrounding bog act as if nothing's going on, continuing to make meals of oblivious spiders and flies busily lapping rainwater from the cups of the flowers.

The sea has gone mad. They've never seen the like. The eldest of the men in the crowd says it's liable to wash in over the entire Argentia peninsula and they should be home preparing for the worst. The debris spread along the shoreline is the least of their concerns. The schooner, bottom-up and spinning viciously with the savage tide, comes into better view. The women in the crowd start to roar and bawl. A few husbands belonged to Argentia are out fishing with crews on boats from Dunville and Red Island. They're unaccounted for and speculation is taken to a new level.

Another old man mumbles how the Lord is about to pull the plug in the bottom of the bay, taking the works to Hell. Some tell him he's off his head and don't be so foolish, while others know he's just scared and move closer to offer a bit of comfort.

Nervously, pant legs and soiled apron pockets are emptied of worn rosary beads, whose tiny crucifixes spin and twirl recklessly in the wind.

Some folks fight the wind and, at best, are bent over in all directions. The rest are now on their knees. Frantic calls to saints Barbara, Christopher, and Thomas Aquinas to quell the storm go unanswered as the sea continues its fit of rage.

Although they figure the worst is probably past, the prayers continue. Hail Marys are seized by storm and trampled. The surge moves the beach of massive boulders with ease. The pounding of their hearts is topped only by the noise of the wind and the shifting of rocks big and small.

A man is halfway through a verse of Amazing Grace when his missus says get a bit of sense, there's probably no one on the boat, anyway.

"My God! I s'pose they were able t' get off, all right," another says.

Miraculous medals hand-sewn by mothers onto tattered and earth-stained clothes glisten in the sun. But, as far as anyone can see, no miracle occurs.

Disappearing and reappearing again and again behind mountainous walls of murky water, the drenched bulk of wood moans her final moan and hastily takes one last swig of the tempestuous sea. With breath held deep in their lungs, those on shore watch and wait, until on the swell the schooner appears no more.

After an hour or so, the storm subsides. Like gnarled lines of trawls, strange strings of passing clouds cling to the sky. With them comes a heavier rain. The sun never misses a trick.

People stand, squint, and blink. Necks stretch forward for reassurance that what they just witnessed is real. Rosary beads hang from limp arms and hands while half-open mouths utter little sound.

They dare to clean up the mess, with the rest of their lives to talk about it at night around kitchen table card games, and in twine lofts making and mending nets to fish the same sea.

A young lad, cap clenched tightly in hand, bolts away from the murmuring crowd. He runs across ripening bakeapple marshes, over fenced meadows, and past nervous horses and cows fresh out of stables. His lean body, trimmed by the long, hard childhood of a man's work, is twisted slightly now and then by the lingering gusts. Down dirt roads, dustless from the fresh sheets of rain, curious, weather-beaten faces emerge cautiously from their two-storey homes. No usual nods of the head, winks, or "How're ye gettin' ons," occur, as weary eyes gaze in every direction at the storm's handiwork. There's little to say. Only it's too bad they've missed half a day working. They pause the odd moment to watch the strange, moving sky.

Thomas S. Keats, the merchant, stands in the doorway of his store. His arms are folded. His eyebrows lift and he takes on a curious stare when he sees the gritty lad racing toward him.

Fixing his woollen cap back on his soaking wet head, the boy leans over, his hands resting on his thighs.

"A boat . . . just sank, out there," he pants, pointing to the open sea, his eyes wild. "A schooner."

CHAPTER SEVENTEEN

The Bad News

It's still pouring rain. Puddles form quickly in potholes farther in The Bottom where the sea didn't reach earlier. Rainwater running off the hills and down over lanes create small rivers in places where the road is eaten away.

It seems harmless enough now for most people to leave their homes, and they make their way out. House to house, store to store, stagehead to stagehead, they ask if the Fox Harbour crews are back yet, or if they're someplace else, safe and sound. But no one has anything to tell.

The *Pauline King* and the *Lady Jane* were fishing farther up Placentia Bay and likely took shelter in the nearest port, some say. The *Annie Healy*, no doubt, with Captain John Mullins to the helm, is safe in St. Bride's harbour, or perhaps forced to beach at Point Lance, as the *Annie Healy*'s crew is known for fishing near Point Lance Rock.

More fish is picked up, washed with water from the brooks and ponds, and restacked in piles under tree rinds until the weather clears. Henhouses and fences lie in piles with the odd dead bird sticking out from beneath the rubble.

Dories and flats are rowed to pick up what the storm has laid to waste. Oars blown from boats, longers plucked from stages and flakes, and coverless barrels half-emptied of rotting fish livers lay around the harbour.

Billy Penny and Cyril Leary use long gaffs to pick up debris from the water around Healy's Wharf. Mike and Henry Healy bail their boat, *Tojori*, to make ready for leaving.

Word of a schooner sinking off Argentia has come in a string of versions to Cis Davis's telephone, so the Healys agree it's best to have a look. A handful of men who were fishing outside some of the Cape Shore communities walk by the wharf, saying they barely beat the storm and made it to The Sound. Some even say they saw the *Annie Healy* bashing her way through the storm and wished they were on a big boat like that instead of in their little jaunters. They say their bodies will be bruised for a month. They imagine the *Annie*'s not far behind now.

Tojori's Mianus engine spits the usual dirty black smoke. Its loud knocking echoes through the dripping trees and soggy hills.

Jim Healy manoeuvres the wide vessel past smaller boats partially submerged and barely visible behind the pelting rain bouncing on the water. Mike does his best to clean the glass in the end of the rectangular wooden box their father bought in St. John's years ago for looking under water. Jim says it hasn't been touched for fifteen years, when the *Queen of Providence* sunk right over there, and it's not like they needed it to find her then with her masts sticking thirty or forty feet out of the water. But the old man said the box was a good one, and any chance to use it was worth what he paid for it.

"The way the water's stirred up, 'tis a waste of time, Mike," Jim says to his brother. "Be the time ya gets the cobwebs outta the box, we'll be home again."

In the harbour, gulls hop and run and jump and squawk in one place on rolling and bobbing barrels, while punts and dories, if not too damaged, are right-sided and set back in the water to join in the cleanup.

More men in small groups scuff wearily from the path leading to The Sound and onto the lane leading to the main road. The weight of their wet clothes drains them of their last reserves of energy as they step onto the road and turn either way toward their homes.

"Go out now an' ask 'em if they heard tell of yer father an' the crew," Lize Foley tells young Bernadette.

Leaning over her kitchen table, looking out the window, Lize watches the Healys head out the harbour again. She sits back on the chair and barely has strength enough to crank the wooden handle of the Singer sewing machine. She frets over the flannelette she's after writing down at Healy's shop since Jack left. He told her to get a new dishpan, nothing else, and he'll square up with Jim and Mike when he gets back with his share of the fish. In late fall and winter, when it's too windy to leave the fire in at night, the bedroom floor is too cold to kneel upon for prayers. The nightdress Lize is making will help comfort her bad knees. *Jack will understand*, she tries to convince herself. Although she'll never admit it, she wishes they were like their daughters in the States, with real money to buy things, instead of fish to barter for the meagre necessities of their ordinary existence.

With her mother's woolsquare covering her head, Bernadette reluctantly walks back and forth alongside O'Brien's house, just up the lane, waiting for one of the passing men to say something. As Bernadette trudges uncomfortably in her bare feet, there are more potholes than places to step. Muddy water flicks on the lower back part of her flowery skirt.

No schooners have entered The Sound, according to one nice man, a friend of her parents, who's sure there's great concern about, because Lize would never allow her child out in such poor weather, miserable, cold, and alone.

Bernadette runs back down the lane, glad to have something to report to her mother, even if it isn't what they both want to hear.

Neither the *Annie Healy*, the *Pauline King*, nor the *Lady Jane* have returned yet, but Lize guarantees they wouldn't attempt navigating the shoals of Fox Harbour in such wind.

"They're liable to be gone in someplace else," she says to herself, continuing to sew.

At four thirty Mary Jane Sampson finally lets her son, Billy, out of the house. He finds Liz Kelly at her grandmother's. With their coats over their heads, the friends head out Dreaddy's Road in the rain, laughing and shouting. They jump over some puddles and land in others with shouts of joy. They couldn't be happier.

When it's time for Billy to go home again, young Liz goes into Mrs. Anne Murphy's for a visit and, hopefully, a bite to eat while she dries off. The rain eventually lets up, and with the bit of wind left over from the storm, Mrs. Murphy says what a lovely evening it would be for drying clothes if she hadn't already dried them over her stove.

On her way home Liz sees two old men standing by the road, in front of Mon McCue's woodpile. One is nodding slowly, the other shaking his head. They're not carrying on, the way most men in Fox Harbour do, and the great smiles they're known for are absent from their lips.

Liz jumps over a big puddle of muddy water and runs up a lane, a couple of houses away from where the men are standing. She bolts around the back of the houses, hurries over a section of fence blown down by the wind, and creeps alongside Mon's house. She sneaks down the lane and hides behind the pile of wood to hear what the men have to say. Three other men come walking up the road. They stop to ask the two old fellows if they've heard the latest news.

"Yes, b'y, that's what they're sayin'," one of the men says. "The *Annie Healy*'s really gone. They found her hatch an' something else belonged to her in Long Harbour."

Numb with shock, Liz stumbles forward from where she's crouched. She puts her hand out to catch herself but fumbles farther when it slides over the loose, wet bark of the wood. She stays on her knees and elbows, afraid the men have heard her, waiting for one of them to grab her.

"Did anyone tell their women yet?" a man asks.

"Tell 'em wha?" the oldest man says.

"That the b'ys are gone, lost."

"Jaysus! Ye can't go tellin' the like of dat when ye don't know if 'tis true," the old man says angrily, shaking his head.

"Well, b'y, that's what all the crowd is sayin'."

"What about Mon? Do he know?" asks another.

Liz bolts out from behind the wood. She feels like attacking the men, but takes off racing for home, instead. She tries to block it out, deciding she won't utter a word of what she's just heard. She won't stand for such nonsense.

"Likely story," she says to herself. "No way is the *Annie Healy* gone." But the horrible thought gets bigger with each step.

Her legs grow heavier and the muddy road has lost all appeal. She can tell the rumours are spreading like mad by the expressions on the faces of those she passes on the road and the closed mouths of those with their necks stuck out windows and over garden fences. No matter how she tries to erase the dreadful notion, her skip is reduced to a walk. Her mind is all a spin as she thinks back to last week when she and her mother and daddy were in the garden at the potatoes and Captain Mullins and the men came over the road like an army—that's what her mother said—insisting her daddy go with them; she thinks of how her poor daddy wasn't well enough to be at the potatoes, let alone go fishing, and how he should have listened to her mother when she said, "You needn't think yer goin', sick like that."

No! What those old men said isn't true. It can't be. People in Fox Harbour love to make up stuff, something to talk about, especially old men, bitter because they're no longer able to fish. The *Annie* is safe somewhere else and will soon be seen coming in the harbour right full of fish so Liz and her family can have lots of flour and molasses and salt beef for the winter. Mommy will give Daddy her chair and he'll rock the little ones, telling of all the big boats in Golden Bay, and the small ones, and the thousands and thousands of birds at Cape St. Mary's, where Liz would love to go someday and have a picnic and go to the edges of the high cliffs and throw crusts of bread to the birds, not that anyone could afford to throw away crusts of bread. *We're looky to have a bite to eat areselves, let alone give it away to the birds*, her daddy would say. *Say nothin', saw wood*, he also says. And that's what Liz intends to do. She starts running again.

After a brief yarn with the shore boys at Healy's Wharf, Billy Sampson runs up under the big flakes toward his house to tell his mother the news of the boat sinking off Argentia. Mary Jane's stomach falls again, as someone has already been by with their own version of the story's growing details. But she shrugs off the idea of it being the *Annie Healy* and says nothing to Billy, only go wash your hands and face and get ready for supper.

Soon word comes from several sources of the horrors taking place only miles outside The Isaacs. Dismal stories trickle in from Patrick's Cove, Ship Cove, and Point Verde, where three schooners foundered earlier in the day, with swollen, lifeless, bloodied bodies bashing against the ragged rocks of the rugged Cape Shore coastline. The Virgin Rocks are blamed immediately as the culprits.

Word from Magistrate Sullivan's office at Placentia tells of Ship Cove men attempting to tow a submerged schooner in to Placentia. Bodies of drowned sailors have been recovered, they're told, but all are believed to belong to Burin Peninsula crews. This brings some relief to the people of Fox Harbour.

Crowds of people near Placentia Gut watch in fright and hopelessness as a submerged schooner is carried closer and closer to the land by the strong current below Castle Hill. The ruined ship all but disappears, except for the masts, and then heaves above the surface again like a wounded whale. The body of a dead man is lashed to the boat's riggings. Each time it appears the shouts and screams of those on the beach echo off the surrounding hills. The ship's tons of screeching and moaning wood seem to plead for the drowned man, as his head rolls from shoulder to shoulder, whiplashed from chest to back. The shrieks from the women and children grow louder as the schooner barrels in through The Gut. The dead man's eyes look their way. The sight of his ghostly, torn, and bleeding flesh sends young girls and boys alike bawling behind their mothers' aprons. The women pray while the men stuff their pipes and rolled cigarettes into their mouths, fumbling for a light.

If we can get the boat ashore, the magistrate wires the newspapers, *we'll be able to see a name and if there are more bodies on board her.*

Ellen Kelly is pacing her kitchen floor when her daughter bolts through the door. Liz stands with her clothes dripping wet against the wall, putting on her best face for the almost-silent crowd. Her younger sisters are sitting on the floor, rocking back and forth, holding a stick between them and quietly reciting a nursery rhyme.

Gran Kelly rocks furiously in the chair next to the stove, quickly passing her prayer beads through her fingers and thumbs. Although her eyes are open, she doesn't bother to look in Liz's direction, and never misses a word of the rosary whispering past her lips.

The opening of the porch door and the stomping of boots on the floor gives the crowd a few seconds of hope. Until Uncle Mick Duke pushes the kitchen door open. He stands there awkwardly, cap in hand.

He looks at his sister, Gran Kelly, around the room full of youngsters, and then to Ellen sitting on the edge of the daybed.

"Ya needn't tell me they're gone, 'cause I already knows," Ellen says. "I heard someone throwin' lumber down behind the house earlier."

"'Tis a sign," Gran Kelly says in a low voice. "An omen."

"I've bad news for ya, Ellen," Uncle Mick barely manages to get out.

The moments between these words and the next seem an eternity.

"The *Annie*'s gone," Uncle Mick mumbles. "There was never . . . there was never a body got on 'er."

Ellen stares out the window, to the water, and watches the *Annie Healy* float in the harbour, the way she's done for years. John comes into the house, the boys struggling with his black wooden sea box with the leather handles, and the girls in their Sunday dresses and freshly washed hair clinging to his dirty clothes. He tells them all to sit, right excited to paint on their little minds images seen only from the deck of a schooner on still nights: sunsets over Red Island, dolphins so lovely they make the salt water look the thickness of fresh cows' cream, strange and beautiful birds from God knows where silhouetted on Point Lance Rock, and the commanding Isaacs, oh what a sight to see, like two burly soldiers in the distance standing guard over Fox Harbour. His smile upon every word speaks of the joy in his heart.

"Mother! Mother!" the youngsters cry.

Ellen's mouth is half-open, almost smiling, but there's no sound.

John. Her John. Gone? No more shaking his cap at the young ones when they're bad—the maddest he ever got. No more admiring him quietly while he turns the little ones upside down looking for gold, tickles them first thing in the morning, and tells them stories by the Parlor Stove during long winter evenings. Tales of storms and ships pounded to matchwood and dead men seen walking the beaches of Argentia and in The Sound, for years.

The emptiness in Ellen's guts since yesterday gets heavier and heavier. The weight of it takes her slowly to the floor. She screeches and roars, frightening the young ones who stay where they are, looking at one another. One after the other, their crying shakes their mother back to the present.

Gran Kelly drops her beads and stumbles from the rocking chair, holding her chest, past Uncle Mick, and into the porch.

"Noooo!" she cries aloud. "Not John. Not my son. Oh, John! No!" She opens the outside door and collapses.

Uncle Mick catches her and holds her against the wall, easing her heavy body to the floor. When she comes to, her shrieks of agony grow even louder. Her voice belts past the driving rain, echoing off every house and hill in the town. She doesn't notice when Uncle Mick puts her beads back into her hands.

Young Maurice Whiffen drops the stick from his shoulders holding two pails of water he's drawn for his father, and takes off for home with the fright at the sight of the old woman falling around in the doorway.

The Kelly children shuffle and stumble beside their screaming mother on the kitchen floor. They fall all over her, clutching at her head and waist and legs.

Grief-filled bawls soon occupy the air around the little town as the bad news is delivered to every home. Some of the widows stumble mindlessly outdoors, falling to their knees at the water's edge, grabbing wet rocks and sand. They shout the names of the lost souls, begging them to please come home. Their children, laden with grief, anchor themselves to the wet earth and bawl for daddies they'll see no more.

CHAPTER EIGHTEEN

Friday, August 26, 1927
From the Crow Hill

People are up early, continuing the cleanup and putting the town back together. Wracking bars and hammers draw bent nails from the wood of collapsed stores and animal pens. Mauls pound the tops of new fence posts cut to replace old ones ruined by yesterday's storm. Axe blades grinding on sharpening stones will be used to chop the hundreds of trees needed to repair or replace wharves and flakes knocked down and hauled away by the sea. The level of activity is not a whole lot more than some summer days, but this morning no one is whistling or singing or laughing.

Tired old men, driven from their homes by loneliness or busy wives, sit quietly on rocks by the roadside whittling sticks, carving toy boats for their grandsons and ragged birch brooms for their granddaughters.

The morning sun works hard to dry up the rain's mess. Clumps of unruly grasses along the side of the road and next to paths start to rise again. Rose bushes bloom shiny leaves of lively green while the few September mists not cracked off sprout triumphantly.

Gloom clouds the minds of many as they kick pebbles on the paths and skip rocks across the harbour. The late afternoon sky, white with light at the earth's rim, blends heaven-like with the soft glow of baby blue above. The Isaacs and their craggy silhouettes face the fearless sea swells of deep green while armies of whitecaps patiently advance upon the beached meadow connecting the two great rocks. Harmless ripples are sent around the coast and in to Fox Harbour, rinsing kelp and sand from the feet of young boys and girls playing by the water.

In the evening, after the rosary, people gather in homes. They talk about the same things they've talked about every day, year after year, generation after generation: the heat of the sun staying in the house if the windows were shut early enough to keep out the coolness of the creeping dusk; the smell of fall already in the air, with the cold of last winter hardly left their bones; the water of the sea, just as cold now as it was in April month; how no wood stove stays cool for long these days; and how their backs won't last another year in the woods. The clothes they took in off the line were just as damp as when they went out—a nuisance, weighing down the line strung above the kitchen stove, then smelling of salt pork, cabbage, onions, and smoke until washed again.

Stumbling like a wounded animal, Michael Mullins's girlfriend, Katie, drags herself to the top of the Crow Hill. Her surroundings are blurred by her tears. She lugs her feet over rocks, lands in puddles of water too big to cross, and scuffs each next long step to the place she feels she needs to be.

From a sloped rock face at the top of the high hill, The Isaacs look helpless out there, all alone, sitting in the middle of it all—the place where her parents took her every fine Sunday of her life, in their dory, where they'd all sit amongst the rocks of the beach, the grass of the meadow, and at times in the shade of the trees of the woods. Hordes of families did the same. It was where youngsters, like Michael and her, ran freely over the uneven land and through the refreshing edge of the sea. And always a meal of smoked capelin, and fresh bread, and molasses. She and Michael always talked about that, but Michael could describe it best: *the smell of capelin, molasses, and freshly fried toutons; those mouth-watering scents teasing scavengers of the sky spying boisterously on youngsters exploring the thick evergreen woods; where parents, too tired before their time, rested on rocks painted with dried bird droppings, rotting coral, and fungi of orange and white. Water in blackened kettles was always on the boil over fires made with alders and driftwood; started with a few handfuls of Old Man's Beard, for a drop of tea boiled from loose leaves.*

Katie ponders life. More like how their lives are hardly their own. What kind of a place is this, anyway? When young women her age are on their way to the States to make real money, where they will never have to look sideways at a fish again, if they don't want to; where women don't have to live their lives looking out the window for their men to come home from sea. She pounds her fist against the rock beneath her. She *could* go to the States. If she could convince Michael, that is. She'd hardly leave without him, though.

Katie's thoughts leave the States and wander back to Michael and his way with words, and childhood Sundays at The Isaacs: women on their sides near steaming pots of tea, on the sharp blades of grass kept neat and tidy by someone's goats. The women relaxed, with no fish to turn over, except the ones in the blackened frying pan lying on the rocks, over the fire. The usual signs of stress on their faces erased by the soft breezes and the little change of pace they deserved and sometimes granted themselves once a week. Squinting babies in white bonnets babbling happily to themselves when they weren't being whisked around by everyone else's youngster. The men couldn't stay away from the water if they tried; standing, dressed in their best suits of clothes, they smoke from their pipes, talking about the weather and fishing and ships.

The lifelike quality once possessed by The Isaacs is gone. They're nothing but two useless lumps of rock, unable to reach out to Michael, and his father, and God knows how many more men.

Katie's anger attempts to ward off her grief as she scans the sea for a trace of the *Annie Healy*. The people milling around Healy's Wharf below look like crawling ants. She grinds her teeth, and the tears come again when she sees the Healy brothers tying *Tojori* to the wharf for another night.

Her eyes dart back and forth to paths in the woods below, and to all the places from where you might be able to make your way up here. What she wouldn't give to see Michael walking to get her, to hear him say he's okay. She's haunted by the empty space next to her on the big rock face of the hill. She cups her hands, the left caressing the right throbbing with pain from pounding the rock. Her head falls to the right, and as she leans into the air, she imagines she's in Michael's embrace: his big arm around her neck to draw her into the warm curve of his body; the breath from his nose moving behind her ear, and along the top and side of her head. The fresh smell of Sunlight soap, from the bar her mother keeps on the kitchen shelf, fills her lungs. There, Katie sits on a chair, washing her long locks in the big oval galvanized pail filled with water from the brook, warmed by the fire in the stove, the whole while dreaming of being alone with Michael where their breathing is the only sound they hear. She waits for his hand to cross her leg, for his fingers to slide between hers. The chill sends a freezing pain all the way to her elbows. She reaches back and slides her fingers along the rocks, hoping to feel the quilt he always carried when they came up here. She wishes he were here to drape it over her bare legs, below her dress. When he knew she was cozy and warm, he also knew she was all his and he could share his dreams, the ones he'd never let past his lips in the small town 300 feet below.

Michael would sit here, staring out into the big world, dreaming of Ireland, of living there, where fellows like him, he said, could earn an honest living singing. And although it's close to England, the Protestants wouldn't even mind, he imagined, and there'd be no end to the songs. Because everyone loves music. And he'd send for her and they'd be married. In their spare time they'd look through old church records to find out where they're really from and who their relatives were all over the Isle. He could even go to a good school if he wanted. And he wanted that, too. He said she and Mary Ann were the only ones who knew his secret. And she believed him.

The damp breeze chills the nape of Katie's neck as her head rests in her hands. Her ringlets send chills down her back. Her blue cotton dress is stuck to her.

She wishes this was just one of those times when she'd be here waiting for Michael, knowing he'd show up as soon as he could. She'd like to scream his name but is afraid someone will hear.

She looks out over The Isaacs again, scanning the bay, with her hand over her eyebrows to block the orange glare of the setting sun. Sometimes the clouds give her arm a break, and her brown eyes are drawn down to the flat mass of Argentia and the white lines of smoke rising from houses, where it is always twice as cold as it is here in Fox Harbour.

Another rush of tears lands on her bare forearm. She looks down. She's full of goosebumps, but needs the cold to keep her awake. She'll never sleep again. Not until she's back in Michael's arms; not until she feels that gentleness that erased the boredom of Fox Harbour; not until Michael's arms cradle her in unspoken love. Her safest haven. Her fingers fumble over the goosebumps as she glares past the rocks and trees, the wind and cold, her despairing existence, into Michael's eyes where she's always sure to feel protected.

It's the day before he left—that day last week in to The Falls, the steep rocks and the refreshing smell of alders alongside the river running all the way to The Sound. The sticky sap of the spruce trees clings to their hands as they haul themselves back up the path through the woods, to the top of the waterfall. The rush from jumping back in and the great relief when everyone else leaves, except for a couple of youngsters spying from the woods. What odds about them, Michael says. On their last jump, she holds his hand. Underwater, his smile blows her away. He hardly has time to take a breath when she throws her arms up over his shoulders and wraps herself around him. He treads water for them both as the cold of his shoulder stings her lips. She wishes for the nerve to say *I love you*, but it never comes. The closeness is good enough. Each time he smiles at her, a chill runs up and down her body. They sit on a flat rock, about two feet below the falls, and he kisses her softly. He's so sweet. Then, he talks of Ireland. What else? And sings his favourite song. Katie almost feels jealous at his passion for this girl peddling cockles and mussels, and a bit relieved when she died of a fever so long ago. And with all the talk of the pretty girls in Dublin, sure, how can she wait for him to send for her when the day arrives?

All the while he sings, Michael caresses Katie's arms until she's warm again. The sunlight dries her hair. She drinks up his rugged beauty. His big smile and green eyes not unlike the colour of the sea this miserable evening.

A blanket of black quickly covers the land and sea. She closes her eyes again and prays like mad for another glimpse into that dream, a dream that was real only nine or ten days ago. Will she ever have it back? How she wishes the tears hitting her arm are drops of water from her hair that day and Michael is here to rub the cold from her body. How she longs for more of those new feelings that arose each day they were together, and on days when time was not their own.

With clarity she recalls that night last fall under Healy's flakes when she first heard him sing. The boys were after getting into their first batch of moonshine and Katie did her best to ignore the wisecracks and grabs and sauce of the boys ready to drag her off into the shade of night. Michael said nothing, only cleared his throat. No one expected to hear what came out of him, and all the foolishness stopped. The wild fire in his eyes told her he was nowhere near Fox Harbour. Katie was the only one really listening, and he knew it. After much talking and dancing at three or four kitchen parties throughout the winter, they were considered an item. Someone told Katie how Michael calmly offered to beat the heads off the boys, all the one time, if necessary, if they so much as looked her way again.

That meant he really liked her, because he always walked away from fights.

A crow's caw steals Katie from her happy thoughts. Every time she closes her eyes to get back to Michael, all she sees is him smiling, underwater. The scary dream he kept having before even knowing he was leaving. How could that have been?

If people didn't talk so much, she'd gladly jump off this hill. She can't bear to think of Michael without a smile, let alone drifting alone in Placentia Bay. Michael always talked about how the bay was legendary for stealing the lives of men and the contentment of wives and children. He didn't want to be one of those men. Lost. Girls don't pay much mind to that stuff. But how can *he* be one of those who may never come home again? As big as the bay is, Katie knows, it's also very small with the way people talk and know one another. If Michael made it to shore somewhere, word would have reached here by now. Has the fire in his eyes died with him? If it is true angels go to heaven, and if heaven is what you think of as the best place to be, then surely Michael is strolling the streets and lanes of Dublin city, singing the beautiful Irish ballads, with people handing him shillings galore for another one just like the other one. If she could ever get there, would she run into him, somehow?

When they sat here on the Crow Hill, there were the games of which island is which in the bay, and who owns that schooner coming 'round The Isaacs. But all she ever really noticed was Michael. Her quick glances to the sea, just like her swift answers, were only to please him. She really loved him. Loves him. Oh, if only she'd told him. Her mother always said only some married people said the like of that to each other. For the first couple of years, anyway. But the young crowd isn't that old-fashioned. She could have told him. It's not like she would do anything other than give him a nice, long good-night kiss. Anything beyond that, they knew, had to wait till marriage.

God knows what time it is, and Katie gives jumping over the hill another full measure of consideration. She'd rather die than have to walk back down. What if she just lies on the ground where she stands? Surely Michael will soon wake her and carry her in his arms. He'll be wet, but she won't mind that. She'll marry him, if he asks. Indeed she will.

Tomorrow she'll be back, rain or shine, and play the game of "name that schooner" until the *Annie Healy* sails in the harbour, battered and bruised. Then she will vanish from the hill faster than she ever did in her life, until she has hold of Michael, says how much she loves him, and walks him to his mother's house. He'll warm up by the stove, and she'll make him tea and butter his bread, like she's always done.

But in her heart Katie knows there'll be no *Annie Healy*. No Ireland. And no more Michael. Afraid of what news she might have missed, still hoping she's wrong, she takes off back to the path. She screams her way through the woods, away from that mountain of memories. Helping herself over the first pile of rocks to the path, she grabs hold of a tree. She shoots a quick glance back when her fingers latch into sticky grooves. *Michael and Katie*, she reads through great sobs, nearly dying from the weight in her chest. The fresh whiteness of the tree inside each carefully carved letter gives off a glow in the growing twilight. A little bit of hope, maybe? It's just like him to do something like this and not tell her, until she noticed it herself. But they'd been here since and why hadn't she noticed it? It's no surprise. She could look at trees anytime.

From the heart Michael has carved around their names, Katie blows away a stream of black ants. She lets her head fall into the tree and her tears to the soft, uneven ground where the tree's roots make it difficult to stand and rest. Gripping the tree a foot or so below the inscription, she scratches her fingers through more stickiness. She swings around the front of the tree slowly to see what else he might have carved. When her eyes clear from a wipe of the back of her hand, she sees *Mary Ann* in block letters. *Of course,* Katie laughs to herself, *his littlest sweetheart had been with him.*

CHAPTER NINETEEN

Friday, August 26, 1927
More News—Better Off Buried—Letters

Uncle Mick Duke fumbles through the pages of the *Evening Telegram* with his big fingers. Scores of family and friends squeeze into the kitchen of John and Ellen Kelly to hear him dish out the news. Those who can't fit inside stand outdoors on a wood-horse and crates with their heads stuck in through in the windows.

One article tells of a ten-foot wall of water that swept up the Humber River, on Newfoundland's west coast. Boats are damaged and much of the railway around Seal Head is destroyed.

"At Humbermout," Uncle Mick reads, "a man was swept from the boom an' killed."

"But what about the *Annie Healy*?" someone asks.

There's nothing to tell them, only that wreckage litters Placentia Bay, as told in the endless reports from fishermen out in search of survivors.

. . . picking up rails, bulwarks and hatches, woodwork
. . . pieces of dories . . . trawl kegs . . .

Another article tells how the storm began a week ago off the south coast of Africa and then made its way across the Atlantic Ocean to the Bahamas. After scraping the edges of the US eastern seaboard, the storm struck Nova Scotia on August 24. It wasted little time raging across the Gulf of St. Lawrence to Newfoundland. With all communication lines down, no forecast could be made to warn men to stay off the water. No local boats had wireless radios on board. Out of a cloudless sky, ninety-mile-an-hour winds swooped across the water and the land. By the time it struck Placentia Bay Thursday morning, the storm was at its worst.

The schooners *Pauline King* and the *Lady Jane* made it to Port Royal. When the crews of both schooners returned home to Fox Harbour, they told of the terrific gale, and the seas, mountains high, breaking from the bottom miles from shore. Schooner hulls were rendered useless, they said, and sails out of the control of any man. No matter how great his might.

While many say the *Annie Healy* is lost, some friends and relatives of the crew still have hope the men are alive. Perhaps they were forced to shipwreck and are gathered around someone's stove, drying off, warming up, drinking tea or moonshine and talking about how close they came to losing their lives. They'll manage to get the *Annie Healy* off the rocks. And once things settle down, they'll have her mended enough to tow back to Fox Harbour for repairs in no time.

Telegraphs inquiring as to the whereabouts of the fathers, sons, and brothers aboard the missing schooner are sent around Placentia Bay. And from some of the things people are hearing back, the storm was gracious here compared to other places on the Island.

The newspapers out of St. John's dish out reports from all over Newfoundland concerning the storm's havoc.

A story of the *Pride of Detroit*'s landing at Harbour Grace, and its pilots flying to beat the around-the-world record, stirs no excitement here. They prefer to read or hear about what happened to this boat and that one, this fellow and that.

Cis Davis has the only telephone in Fox Harbour and it hasn't stopped ringing since yesterday. Charlie Sampson, Jr., finally gets through from Arvida, Quebec, where he works. He has to settle his nerves about a nightmare he had last night. A man, he says, appeared next to his bed, soaking wet in oilclothes.

"I believe 'twas Father," he told his mother. "I heard 'bout the storm. Were they out? Are they all right?"

From other communities, relatives of the missing men and their families trickle in to Fox Harbour to offer support, however possible. They're from Placentia, Argentia, Long Harbour, Ship Harbour, Red Island, Merasheen, and beyond. They, or their fathers, have fished for the Healys at some point in their lives. Some come in larger boats, anchored outside the harbour, while others arrive in skiffs, jackboats, dories, and punts. Heavy rope, gaffs, hooks of all sizes, and dip nets are carried on their big arms. They want to know the rights of the rumours and news, and they offer to join the locals in searching for men. One skiff is full of leftover sail canvas for bodies they're certain to recover. At least they'll be able to do the poor souls a bit of dignity, covered from the flies, what the fish haven't already taken. Bock Barry from Red Island, known around the bay for his brute strength, says how his father fished from the *Annie* in 1902. He tells Mon McCue he'll haul the schooner in himself if he has to.

Most of the Fox Harbour men are long gone this morning, searching the coves and beaches up and down the bay for signs of the *Annie Healy* and her crew. The few men left around put down their hammers, mauls, and axes and walk to the water and what's left of the wharves to help tie up the visitors' boats. Together they walk to Healy's premises and gather by the water. Billy Penny and Cyril Leary make a fire in a hurry and the kettle is boiling in no time.

The men take sacks from their shoulders, lay them on the beach, and hand the shore boys rations of beans, peas, sugar, molasses, and mason jars of rhubarb, blueberry, and raspberry jams wrapped in linen seed cloth. These men, like most in Newfoundland, are poor fishermen themselves, but they haven't lost anyone in the storm and there's always a mouthful of food to be spared.

"Take this stuff to the fam'lies of the men aboard the *Big Annie*," one of the visitors says to Billy Penny, "an' bring back the cloth, too."

The men drink tea from dirty, old mugs brought down from the store by the shore boys. Henry Healy pretends to count the mugs, and he gives a few dirty looks. No one pays him any mind, only to give him a drop of moonshine. He doesn't speak, only grunts to let them know he knows they're using his father's mugs. And how many. He climbs the high flakes, sits where he can see the mugs, and keeps busy by calling out to Billy and Cyril to hurry up and get back to work. The men waste no time discussing all aspects of the storm and the best possible methods of search. They try to match stories and reports of debris with where the schooners were last known or thought to be.

A cousin of Lize Foley's has rowed all the way from The Rams.

He says there's wreckage in the bay, but mostly small stuff and nothing that looks like it might've come from the *Annie Healy*. The new schoolteacher, Jimmy Houlihan from Argentia, she tells him, will be here in a couple of days, and someone said they heard he has a radio. What a relief that will be. The Foleys' daughter, Laura, is on her way home from Grand Falls. Lize will send her over to meet the new teacher and see if he'd mind sharing a bit of news from the radio.

The next day little is different from the day before. Uncle Mick continues reading news from the papers to a houseful of people.

Saturday, August 27, 1927

The *Daily News*, St. John's

The Storm's Aftermath

. . . At the time of writing, ten deaths of Newfoundland seamen are recorded; whilst other messages point to the almost certainty of the number being considerably larger. The storm seems to have been general and other lands than ours have similarly suffered. Again the unsparing hand of death has brought tears and sorrow and suffering to the South West coast . . . Yearly the tale is told, and sometimes blows fall when least expected. A fair sky, gentle breezes and sparkling wavelets invite; and within a few brief hours the sky frowns, breezes become storms, and the placid sea is transformed into a seething, swirling cauldron of angry waters, and the toll of the sea is paid in the lives

of men and the agonies of their wives and children:
"For men must work and women must weep."

Devastation caused by the storm has set Newfoundland's government into immediate action. It solicits donations to feed the Permanent Marine Disaster Fund, an account set up following the immense loss of life from the SS *Newfoundland* while sealing thirteen years earlier. Personal and business monetary contributions pour in.

> *. . . Thanks to the generosity, the sympathy and the*
> *active aid of our mariners, travelers . . . and the*
> *public of Newfoundland, the Permanent Marine*
> *Disaster Fund has, so far, been enabled to bring a*
> *measure of relief to those in dire need. The work*
> *continues, and must continue, and it is inspiring to*
> *note the practical sympathy extended by those "that*
> *go down to the sea in ships, that do great business*
> *in great waters." To the victims of the terrible storm*
> *the sympathies of the public go forth, and that this*
> *sympathy will find practical expression, if the need*
> *arises, the unfailing response of the last twelve years*
> *inspires confidence.*

Earlier in the summer, the Nova Scotia schooner *Bluenose*, famous for its speed, ran aground off Argentia, causing speculation the big race scheduled for September against the American schooner *Columbia* might not take place. But the *Bluenose* was repaired in time and ready to go. The storm, however, settled the score on this match. The *Columbia* was snatched by the sea, with all hands on board, off Sable Island, Nova Scotia, on Wednesday night.

The Newfoundland Railway coastal steamer SS *Argyle* was on her way to Lamaline on the Burin Peninsula when her captain beached her at Morgan's Island. Her full load of passengers and freight were safe. While riding out the storm, the *Argyle*'s anchor snapped. Forty-five fathoms of chain went with it. The mail boat lashed to the port side was smashed. With no guarantee of the steel ship floating at high tide, the steamer requested assistance. The coastal boat SS *Glencoe* came to the rescue, but after thirty-five minutes of strain in the heavy seas the tow lines broke. After the failed attempt to free the *Argyle*, the *Glencoe* was ordered to Merasheen Bank to assist a schooner in that area. The message came from another schooner en route from Cape St. Mary's in the storm. The messenger described a schooner, a total wreck, about five miles southwest of Merasheen Bank.

> *. . . head in a sinking condition . . . impossible to render assistance. Men clinging to wreckage . . . Also another small boat and mass of wreckage. Could not locate any names.*

"Perhaps the *Glencoe* picked up survivors," someone in Gran Kelly's kitchen says, offering a bit of hope.

"A proper Christian burial wouldn't be too much t' ask," another whispers.

But all hope soon disappears.

The *Evening Telegram*
August 27, 1927

Terrible Loss of Life in Thursday's Storm
Feared Not Less Than 33 Perished –
Many Vessels Wrecked

A schooner reported missing off Merasheen Bank
with men clinging to the wreckage has disappeared.
She probably had a crew of seven.

Ellen Kelly rattles the *Daily News* in her kitchen to hush the young ones playing out in the porch as thoughts of never seeing John again grow stronger.

Four schooners foundered in Placentia Bay have been identified, along with some bodies. Three of the boats were lost between Patrick's Cove and Point Verde Head, straight out from Placentia harbour.

Newspaper writers continue to speculate, with vague attempts at discovering the truth of the *Annie Healy*'s demise.

An unknown schooner floating bottom-up off
Merasheen would have had a crew of at least seven
men of whom nothing has been seen or heard.

Each word read by Uncle Mick ensures more fear, panic, and yells for mercy on the poor souls drifting and tumbling in the grip of the fierce tides of the bay.

The gaping holes in the hearts of those awaiting news at Fox Harbour widen. Word soon gets around that the mayday sent to the *Glencoe* to go to Merasheen Bank on Friday was in vain. The man who made the report passed the wreck about eleven o'clock Thursday morning. With communication lines still under repair along the coast, he couldn't get the message out until the next day.

More of the same finds its way onto the pages of the *Daily News*:

> *James Bruce, Long Hr., reports seeing unknown boat turning bottom-up in the centre of bay. James Harris, St. Joseph's, saw unknown boat submerged; both masts gone; . . . and two men clinging to wreckage. Made two attempts at rescue but failed.*

Speculation fills the hours spent on The Barrens picking berries and in gardens where vegetables still need tending to. Who were the men clinging to the wreckage? Jim King was definitely one of them, some say, given his known strength. But what difference does it make, others ask, when they're all gone?

Although it's part of the story, no one knows for sure if the hatch that turned up in Long Harbour belonged to the *Annie Healy*.

The days and nights following the storm are quiet ones in Fox Harbour. Folks lean on one another in a togetherness they've scarcely felt before. The young are not taunting the old nor getting into mischief for the sake of badness, offering no reasons for mothers or big sisters to scold. Teary-eyed children stay close to fathers and big brothers and uncles who are still alive while wives and mothers of the same tell their husbands and sons it could've easily been you and thank God you're all right. Pad Mullins, John's half-brother, thanks the Lord for his fall off the roof and the bad back which kept him off the *Annie Healy*. Mon McCue does the same for the terrible cold he's still not rid of.

Even though it's a Saturday night, there are no parties, no lancers trampling kitchen floors, no circles of hands joined in freedom songs of Ireland, stomping their way to daylight. Boilers of soup are plentiful, but appetites scarce. And for a people who'd never dream of seeing food wasted or spoil, there is little chastising for bowls left half-full on kitchen tables, buttered buns with small bites taken. They'll be soaked in tea and eaten the next morning.

Men who have fished with the *Annie*'s lost crew drink their St. Pierre rum and homemade moonshine. They wear bold faces, and shed tears once everyone else goes home or to bed.

Most are sick and tired of speculating, having discussed every possible scenario of how the *Annie* has met her doom. Reluctantly, they realize they know nothing, and agree it's a waste of what energy they have left trying to figure out where the men ended up in the water.

Some old men never give up, offering their opinions as fact. They say it was definitely the group of rocks off Argentia, The Mirrates, they struck while others say that's impossible because she was bottom-up long before she reached the Argentia coastline. So it had to be the Virgins. But she was nowhere near there, having come across the bay from Marticot or Merasheen Bank.

They agree to keep searching for a few more days, and also agree they'll likely never stop looking for pieces of the schooner and the bodies of the men. Most say the whole thing is too much to take and, unless something or someone turns up, it's better off, like all bad things, buried in the back of their minds.

When word of the tragedy comes to Anne Furlong at her home, 24 Barnes Road in St. John's, she faints and falls to the floor. She comes to only when her husband, Edward, holds smelling salts under her nose. The men aboard her family's boat had been her lifelong friends, and her thoughts take her through memories of her childhood in Fox Harbour: the places she played with friends; how they cherished their little bit of free time; where, unlike in the city, distractions in the way of material things didn't exist; and growing closer through constant interaction was inevitable. She remembers climbing the big rocks; the Crow Hill; The Neck; catching capelin in June month; The Isaacs; Daddy's store; trips on his schooners to Little Placentia and Jobs Premises at Placentia; The Sound; Ville Marie Station; the endless sayings and nicknames; the sense of humour. All of these things and places and people are part of her.

She sits, staring in over the rim of the burnt-black cast iron frying pan on top of the stove. The breeze rushing beneath the raised kitchen window sends the steam from the pan into a thousand wild dances before disappearing altogether. Anne watches the pile of food that was burnt to the bottom breathe inconsistent breaths atop the bubbling water. The pan, alive, steals her from her thoughts. A fountain of tiny drops of scalding water shoots in all directions.

The pain of her sore feet is relieved a little by the heat from the stove; its warmth, wrapped around the bottoms of her legs, reaches the insides of her knees.

Outside, now and then, sputtering noises from Model T's fill the air, but never long enough to break her spell of misery and the feelings of guilt she doesn't understand. The stove brings back a flood of memories. She'll never forget the day it came on the train to Ville Marie station, how she waited for Daddy's return with it in *Tojori*. The flame dies too much for her liking and she leans forward from the chair she's hauled up close, grabbing a couple of sticks of wood. The little chrome spiral handle of the front door isn't as hot as she thought it would be. With the long metal scraper, she hauls the embers into a pile and lays the two sticks on top. This time she leaves the front door open, throwing several more sticks of wood onto the burning mound. The sinking sun's glare touches one lens of her eyeglasses, the ones she hardly wears but needs when writing. Into a small bottle of ink labelled *T & M Winter* she dips a pen and attempts to console her friends, now widows, and maybe even herself.

"Dear Lize," one letter begins. "How truly sorry I am for the loss of Jack . . ."

It doesn't seem enough.

"Dear Bridge," begins another. "I can't believe what has happened. What the Lord has in mind for us, we obviously have no clue . . ."

Anne is suddenly no longer an outsider the years away from Fox Harbour have allowed. She's Annie Healy, the namesake for the boat—the boat these poor souls will be associated with forever. Somewhere in the cold, immeasurable waters of Placentia Bay lay the loves of these women she's attempting to write, to comfort, and apologize to. A sudden symphony of blowing leaves plucked early by the storm around her home sends chills over her shoulders, and she gets up to shut the window.

"Dear Liz," she begins another letter.

The clock on her mantle tells her two hours have passed since she began this one.

"Somehow, I feel a great responsibility for the loss of Pad and the others. My name engraved in the bow. And knowing you, you'll say, 'Don't be so foolish.' But I'm not sure how to feel or what to say at this awful time."

Anne's heart is heavy. Her childhood memories stand ablaze in great clarity, and a lifetime of images of the dead men flashing from every nook of her imagination. John Mullins. Poor John. And they the best of friends. How, in the name of God, will she begin or end a letter to Bridget? And poor Charlie, he so sweet . . . and he and John and Jack cousins . . .

A robin flutters its pretty wings before landing on the grass of her small front yard. Cars continue puttering up and down the road, as do young mothers and their babies in prams, just the way they had when she used to come in here, to the city, with her father so long ago. Now St. John's is no bigger to her than Fox Harbour, in a way. She knows her way around, and has long gotten over the excitement of modern amenities that have yet to reach Placentia Bay. But Fox Harbour is still home. There things are always the same, and change thinks long and hard about coming, let alone staying.

Men like Jack Foley and Charlie Sampson were people who made Fox Harbour feel like home to her—the same as it felt when she was a child, and then as a young woman. Always to the wharf, they were: waiting, smiling shyly, and eager to lend a big hand to help her from the boat. How will she ever face the place again in the absence of those men, in the presence of their wives and children?

And Mr. Watt. What's he saying about it all, she wonders. His old heart must be in a million pieces. Someone said he's been up and down the bay in his dory ever since, looking for his favourite nephew and best friend, Pad Bruce. They won't be surprised, they say, if he dies rowing.

Anne sighs, and tries once again to focus on the letters only half-written.

CHAPTER TWENTY

Sunday, August 28, 1927
Poor Hearts Broken

Lize Foley is inconsolable.

"Yer fadder's gone now. What will we do? What will we do?" she says to Bernadette. Over and over. The flannelette gown in her hands is soaked with her tears, and she's sure Healy's won't take it back.

"'Tis one thing," she says, "for the merchants to own everything ya ever had, but 'tis worse altogether now with no one to catch fish to pay back what ye owes."

She's supposed to leave this lifetime of misery in God's hands, and some good that will do her and Bernadette, with no one to catch fish, bring home wood, and tell stories around the stove on the long, bitter winter nights not far to come. She grabs hold of the drapes in the front room and hauls them to, dulling the lines of light sneaking through the closed blinds. The last thing she wants to see is the evening's bright sun, although the heat of it would be all right. With the drapes hauled to, she doesn't have to see the dust floating in the air after she's spent half the day making it spotless for the wake. If they ever find Jack, that is. And God help the priest this time if he mentions a bit of lint on his pressed black pants. She's hardly in the mood for that.

Moving back to the kitchen table, she looks out the window for something to take her mind off reality, to the shed where the sun's glare is blocked by a little droke of trees. She stares at the shed window, looking for Jack's head bent over in concentration, the way it always was when he was fixing something. Often he stayed out in the shed till all hours, picking at this and that, in the dim light of an old lantern once belonged to his grandfather and brought over during the Famine. She looks down to the worn spot of ground in front of the shed door and wonders how long it might take for the grass to grow over it if she never went near it again. She doubts it will ever grow over, unless the day comes when she doesn't have to burn wood to stay warm, to cook, to clean, to dry clothes in winter— unless they get the electricity, like her daughters have in the States. If it ever reaches Newfoundland, she wouldn't have to lug wood from the shed to the house and church anymore. In their letters her daughters speak of electric lights on the ceilings in their homes, glass bulbs not unlike the few she hangs on her tree at Christmastime, but without the colour, and switches on the walls to turn the lights on and off. And you don't even have to strike a match to see what you're doing, let alone pour oil, so they say.

Bernadette is told she's to go up in the woods first thing in the morning, rain or shine, and pick up whatever sticks and blasty boughs her arms can hold, lug them home, and go back for more. Lize doesn't bother to change her orders when Bernadette reminds her mother someone has brought slabs of wood and piled them up by the shed. And others have brought junks and they're on back of the house, near the door.

"No odds," says Lize, "we needs blasty boughs to make the fire start."

She gets up from her rocker and stands back-on to the stove, allowing a bit of heat to sink into the muscles of her aching back. Her lanky, thin arms hang loosely by her sides and the worn rosary beads in her hand rattle against her long black dress. Although she's not much more than skin and bones, Lize feels she's carrying the weight of a horse on her shoulders. She hurts all over, while a tingling in her spine keeps the chill in her muscles. The strain of it all causes great numbness down one side of her face, as her head is forced back and off to the side. Her right shoulder blade feels like it's going to detach from her body as she turns around slowly to put her hands up to her face. She rubs her temples with her bony fingers while the heat from the stove puts a bit of colour in her pale face. Tears sizzle and disappear on the stovetop. She'd like to open the windows, but won't for fear of disturbing the blinds. She tells Bernadette she's all in with the heat.

Lize looks to the table and sees Jack last week, and the week before, complaining of his own aches and pains, saying how he's never going back to sea again. She wishes she'd encouraged him to stay, but she never encouraged him to do anything in their time together and wouldn't know where to begin if she'd ever thought to. Instead, every time he opened his mouth, she drove him out of the house and to the shed on rainy days where she knew he was hove off in his cot or sitting up smoking his pipe. If she heard him singing, she knew someone was after giving him a drop and he was in his cups. She'd have a mind to go out to him, then. But she'd be too poisoned to look at him. She'd wait till he came in for that. But he was cute enough, always inviting some straggler into the house who would offer her a little nip. Soon enough the kitchen would be half-full and she'd be heaving the old Irish songs out of her, smiling away, with an arm linked into Jack's. Those were the times they lived for, and they mostly seemed to come by accident. The fish and flakes and boats could go to hell, God forgive her.

She'd give anything, if she had anything to give, to look out the side window now and see the outline of Jack's big frame in the shed window. He wouldn't be too pleased to see the window, smashed from something caught in the wind of Thursday's storm. She shakes her head in disgust at herself for thinking about the broken window with poor Jack dead and gone. Somewhere out there beyond The Isaacs, his lifeless body is floating or tumbling in the same undercurrent he always spoke of whenever someone fell overboard and was never seen again.

She sees him walking up the road, past the house, with Pad, and wonders what they were talking about that day last week, when he came home right willing to go back fishing. It was Gus, most likely, because Pad wasn't laughing and carrying on. And besides, Jack hardly spoke about anything else. How come Jack never talked like that with her? A great sense of betrayal comes over her. Why could he talk about anything with his friends, but nothing with her? Perhaps he did try speaking his mind, but she was too tired and vexed and told him to mind his prate and don't be so useless. She thinks of how good he was never to say a word back to her, and how she used to fight to keep in a little laugh when she'd see him going for his pipe and tobacco, and then feel bad the moment he was out the door.

"Put the kettle on, Bern'dette," she says, trying to get comfortable in her rocker.

With a cup of tea in her trembling hands, Lize wanders around the house. Thirty-two years of marriage to Jack and, all of sudden, little pieces of their lives that had helped them get by stand out from every crack and corner. The sores she imagines covering her heart, and those festering deep in her soul, are picked open. Her strongest, worst memories play over and over in her thoughts: her sister and closest friend, Sarah, dying of TB at twenty; her mother dying of dropsy; her father's fatal heart attack; little Lizzie dying in her arms; her daughters leaving home one by one, knowing they might never afford to come home again; poor Gus suffocating from the TB, coughing up the blood, and dying; and Jane's beautiful baby boy, Gus, named for his uncle, dying the same horrible death with the cursed TB last year, and he just two. It all killed her.

Now poor Jack.

The cast iron shoe last behind the door to the porch is likely never to stir from its place again. Rust works its way through the hard bubbles of black oil paint and will eventually own it. She can hear Jack now, taking the Lord's name in vain after banging his thumb with the hammer, holding tiny sprigs in place for the young ones' worn taps and soles, and Bernadette's winter boots that came in the barrel once the girls were settled away in New Bedford.

A horse bridle hangs in the corner of the kitchen, stiff and dry from years of heat from the stove. Lize hardly remembers the time they had a horse and wonders why the bridle is still there, serving no purpose, and the little stable, with barely enough room for the poor animal to lie down, crumbled in rot not far from the shed.

The weight scales in the porch remind her of Gus. Closing her eyes, she sees him, as a young boy, hears his laughter and excitement after making a fine haul of cod tongues at Healy's Wharf from the men cleaning their fish fresh from Golden Bay. He'd give some to old widows with no one left to get them a feed of tongues; the rest Lize rolled in flour, if they had it, and fried with a bit of animal fat in the cast iron pan. Jack's mouth watered and Gus rocked proudly by the stove in his mother's chair.

Now, here, she is a widow herself and wondering if someone else's young fellow will bother to ask her if she'd like a meal of tongues someday. And she with nothing to give him in return. She could give away the rusty scales. Perhaps the boy wouldn't have a set of his own. But never mind. She'll keep them where they are, on top of the barrel in the porch to keep the rats out of the flour.

The nail in the wall behind the stove is empty. Its nakedness drives her mad. It was where Jack hung his other shirt, or the double-knit mitts she'd made him and they frozen stiff or soaking wet and heavy as lead after a day in the woods. She lays her cup of cold tea on the table and walks back to the nail, caressing it between her thumb and forefinger, and cries.

On the stove is the flatiron Jack gave her the first year they were married, and she tries to imagine the number of times she'd dragged it in her tired hand over the pieced-together clothes of her family. The wooden-handled clamp belonged to the iron broke and is long gone, but she always manages to pick the iron up with a rag soaked in cold water, long enough to get the wrinkles out of her apron and Bernadette's dress now soaking in black die in a bowl laid on one of the kitchen chairs.

Poor Jack. The only man she'd ever kissed, and that so long ago. The only love she's ever known. Gone away forever. No habit, no coffin, nor proper Christian burial. And no grave for her, Bernadette, Laura, and Angela to visit. Nothing. That good man, her man, her Jack, never to be home again, and she says quietly how it's too much to take and what's the point of being alive. What use is there going on without him?

"They're not comin' home, now. Me poor heart is broke," she cries to Bernadette, and Angela, her daughter sixteen years Bernadette's senior, who lives up the lane, behind their house. "Yeer poor fadder's gone now. What will we do? What will we do?"

Bernadette stands against the sideboard, head down and bawling along with her mother and sister.

"Thank God yer only up over the hill," Lize cries to Angela, as the young mother leaves for home to feed her two girls. "An' tell Frank thanks for the bit of wood he brought."

Angela's not out the door five seconds when Lize starts again.

"An' poor Michael, he only seventeen," she cries. "Oh, yeer poor auld father. 'Tis just as well now if we were with 'im."

Bernadette walks to the rocker and kneels, crying into her mother's apron while Lize strokes her girl's long brown hair.

Bernadette sees only her father's gentle eyes and the slight nod of his grey head under his black knitted cap. The way he looked when she saw him last, thanking her for the tea buns she brought before the *Annie* sailed away. She was sure she'd see him again soon, and now that he's gone forever, she prays for that time back. She'd give him a hug.

Bernadette hates going outdoors, where people ask questions and she doesn't know what to say. She wishes to be like her mother, telling some people it's none of their concern and stop foraging for news. It's them ones who'll add and add onto her empty answers and rush to the nearest house to tell it. Then there are the ones who ask no questions at all, only whisper and stare. What do you do with them?

In her room upstairs, Bernadette sobs for Laura, who'll soon be home on the long train ride from Grand Falls Station.

The stench of sewer at low tide soon replaces the smell of fried salt fish cakes in the kitchen.

Peeking through the drawn blind, out her front window, Lize is momentarily distracted by the big leaves of the September mists stretching to meet the evening sky turning grey with fog. And while she's mad with God, she still gives thanks for little distractions like this—anything to keep her mind off the boat and crew. Jack.

The sound of the ocean pushing and pulling beach rocks along distant shores enters the room. It momentarily calms the nerves of mother and daughter.

When she picks up her mug from the flowery tablecloth, Lize's hands shake. She feels Jack's presence as the last drop of cold tea from her cup trickles past the lump in her throat. She tells Bernadette to bring her a cold cloth, as the lingering heat of the stovepipe gives her another hot flash. Dabbing her face and forehead with the damp cloth, Lize watches the grease trying to harden in the pan.

Though weak with hunger, neither can stomach a mouthful, and the fish cakes go cold on the plates.

The putt-putt of make-and-break engines grows louder and fades again. The remaining daylight sends men in two small boats out through the harbour for a look.

"Men on their way back to look for yer father," Lize mumbles, unaware Bernadette has left the kitchen.

From the back door Lize sees *Tojori* coming in the harbour. The men stay just long enough to refuel and head out again. They've been doing that for the past four days.

Voices calling out to Jim and Mike Healy echo across the water, asking if they've seen or heard anything of the *Big Annie* and her crew.

When *Tojori* is out past the shoals, the harbour is quiet again except for the scattered smack of heavy wooden oars on the water.

Lize grabs a few junks of wood from another pile her son-in-law has thrown by the porch door and goes back into the kitchen. She takes a sip from her new cup of tea and enjoys the strength of it in the hollow pit of her guts. Standing to the table rolling balls of dough for bread, she stops to find a clean spot on her apron and dabs her tears.

Bernadette wonders why her mother's making so much bread but won't dare ask. She wishes she had something to distract them, instead of thinking about someone coming to the door to say they've found her father, drowned, and then Mrs. Mart Mullins having to come and wash the body and prepare it for the wake in the front room—the same way she did when Gus died. She feels her father's big hand on her shoulder, as they both stare at Gus's gaunt, grey face in the coffin. She has uncles here in Fox Harbour, good and funny, and they will keep her occupied for a while, but it won't be the same, she knows, when it's her daddy there in the coffin.

The priest, Father Dee, has been making his rounds visiting the widows, and Bernadette can't stand the thought of being in the front room when he comes, having to sit up proper, coffin or no.

Peeping through the blinds of her room, Bernadette sees the clouds getting heavier. Soon raindrops will replace the whistles and conversations of robins and sparrows in her mother's rose bushes below. She goes back down to the kitchen and pours hot water from the heavy cast iron kettle over the dirty dishes in the white enamel pan, partly rusted at its edges, and wonders why her mother doesn't use the new one.

A gust of wind races over the harbour and hits the front of the house, rattling the windows Jack would have soon secured against the fall winds. The draft coming through the closed window where the caulk has withered and peeled away stirs the closed blinds. The candle on the shelf Jack built above the sideboard flickers. The shadows on the walls and low ceiling do a little dance until the wind moves on and the wick's flame settles down again.

Lize stares at the black oil lantern hanging from a hook in one of the ceiling beams. The flame on the wide wick is blue and low. There's little kerosene left, and she shakes her head, wishing she'd let Jack fill it up as he wanted to before he left. Go on, she told him, he'd be home soon enough and they'd scrape along with the little bit that's left. Only stubs are left of the holy candles from Lent, and it turns her stomach to look across the harbour and see some homes with light in other rooms besides the kitchen, all flickering the one time. Big shots, she calls them, and tells Bernadette to blow out the candle for the love of Jesus, it'll be dark again tomorrow night, and that candle's not an eternal flame. If there was a drop of oil in the house, she'd stay up longer, here in the kitchen, instead of up in the bedroom where it's black as pitch unless the fog is out and the moon's light off the water fills the room through the mirror in the dresser. Nights like that will be scarce, though, because everyone knows the fog is made in Placentia Bay and it seems to fancy Fox Harbour in particular.

"No odds, anyhow," she grumbles, "with the blinds closed."

Now that the last of the dough is kneaded and placed in pans to rise under a patched quilt of old clothes, Bernadette notices her mother looking more lost than ever.

"Jack will be good an' hungry when he comes home," Lize whispers, like it will bring him back, then looks toward the door.

Scuffing across the worn kitchen floor, she recalls the time, years ago, when Jack lugged the canvas home from a schooner wreck outside the harbour. And all the times they danced across this floor. She wonders if, one day, people will dance across the *Annie Healy*'s sails, having washed upon some not-too-distant shore, perhaps, and brought to someone's house in the same fashion.

Although Lize can't resist peering through the drawn blinds for Jack's return, she knows the worst is already upon them. She's lived long enough to know life is nothing more than one pile of misery after another, and the rare lulls in between are what the priest and the Bible really mean by miracles. There's a better chance of the Lord, Himself, walking in across the harbour than them ever laying eyes on Jack again. This is hell and heaven is yet to come, though the thought of Jack and Gus and little Lizzie together again brings some comfort.

When Lize and Bernadette have to venture outdoors, the sun will offer little reprieve. It will only highlight the growing lines of despair on their faces worn out from bawling. And at night it's too black, except for the brans people carry for fear of running into a wandering horse or sheep.

"Me poor heart is broke," Bernadette hears her mother cry again.

Lize moves slowly from the kitchen into the damp hallway. On her way upstairs, weakness overtakes her. She grabs the dark brown rail post, allowing her body to swing, almost lifelessly, in a semicircle until she's planked down on the second step of the stairs.

"Laura will be home tomorrow or the next day, Gus," she says, looking into the eyes of her dead son behind the rounded glass of the large oval frame on the wall.

For a moment she feels his hand on her shoulder; or perhaps it's Jack, really home to wake her from this. She looks to her side, but no one looks back at her. Gus's lost gaze offers no comfort. How sick he was on the last of it.

So handsome, she always thought him, imagining the lovely girl he'd marry and the beautiful grandchildren they'd give her; young ones to play with Angela's crowd; the only grandchildren she has in her life, here in Fox Harbour. The ones in the States, she'll never see or know. She cries again.

"Poor Jack."

She stares at the wall, her tired wrists hanging over the edges of her swollen knees. A cold weight fills the cradle of her arms. It's

Lizzie's body, a feeling that's come and gone for the past dozen years since the little girl died.

The next day the priest comes to Lize's door. He knocks three times and enters.

"Bern'dette!" Lize bawls out.

Bernadette says no, she's not coming down, she's sick and tired.

"Pity ya bad," Lize says, giving the priest a fake smile, and Bernadette is standing in the doorway to the hall in no time.

Lize looks up from the table, tosses her head, and nods to the daybed for Bernadette to sit.

Lize fumbles with the kettle on the stove.

"I knows why yer here, Father, an' you're welcome to a mug of tay, an' nothing else."

EPILOGUE

In the days following the storm, once word of the *Annie Healy*'s dismal fate seemed final, Father Adrian Dee spent a couple of days in Fox Harbour trying to convince the widows of the crew they were unable to properly care for their children in the absence of their fathers and to give up at least some of them.

"They'll be much better off at Mount Cashel and Belvedere," he said in relation to new homes for the children at the orphanages run by the Christian Brothers and the Sisters of Mercy in St. John's.

Most of the widows said no thank you, they'd find a way to manage on their own.

Mary Jane Sampson put her foot down when the priest suggested she let three of her boys go.

"I'll take 'em right off your hands to Mount Cashel . . ." he said reassuringly, as if he'd be doing her a great favour.

"No, sir! 'Deed ye won't! If I can rear five, I can rear eight," she affirmed.

The priest did convince one of the widows to see things the way of the Church. Bridge King, with her husband lost and a new baby to rear, decided it was best to send her two oldest sons to Mount Cashel.

With the boundless help of midwife Mart Mullins, Bridge gave birth to her last child, James (Jimmy), named for his father, on Monday, August 29, 1927.

The people of Fox Harbour built a new home for Bridge King and her family so they could be closer to the community. Bridge never remarried. She died in 1983 at the age of eighty-five. Jim King, Jr., lived in that house until his death in 2011. He was eighty-three.

Mart (Martha King) Mullins continued delivering babies until into her seventies. She died in 1951 at the age of eighty-four. Her cousin and best friend, Roselle Foley, died in 1951. She was eighty.

The rest of Mary Jane Sampson's birthdays marked the anniversary of Charlie's death. After five years of gloom, the priest finally convinced her to "get out of darkness," and to the great relief of her children, she raised the blinds in her home. Mary Jane never remarried. She died in 1960 at the age of seventy-eight. All of her children have since died.

After one year, Ellen Kelly raised her blinds. Fifteen years later, in 1942, she married former *Annie Healy* crew member Maurice "Mon" McCue, who'd been too sick to make what became the schooner's final trip. Ellen died in 1972 at the age of eighty. Mon McCue died in 1965, three weeks shy of his ninetieth birthday.

It was tradition for widows especially and also their children to dress in black to symbolize constant mourning for deceased loved ones. Young Liz Kelly, better known in later years as Mrs. Beth Maher, hated the colour black for the rest of her life. She died in 2007 at the age of ninety-two.

John Kelly's home remains standing in Fox Harbour, the only original house from the story.

Following the loss of her husband, Captain John, and her son, Michael, Bridget Mullins could no longer live in Fox Harbour. With her children she soon took the train to Corner Brook, on Newfoundland's west coast, to join another son, Peter, and his family. The Mullins family suffered further hardship some years later when their home caught fire and burned. Bridget never remarried. She died in 1959 at the age of seventy-seven.

Mary Ann Mullins, daughter of Captain John and sister to Michael, grieved especially for her lost brother and friend. Nearly nine years after the tragedy, in 1936, she moved to the United States, where she met and married Vito Valenti. Together they raised three children. Mary Ann worked as a seamstress in New York, where she and her family lived. Mary Ann carried Michael's photo in her wallet, retelling her last memory of him (singing from the deck of the *Annie Healy*) until her death in 2005. She was eighty-five.

Captain Mullins's brother, Patrick (Pad), whose life was spared due to a bad back shortly before the *Annie Healy* made her last trip, died in 1949. He was sixty-one.

Pad Bruce's wife, Liz, remarried and lived at Fox Harbour until her death in 1987. She was almost ninety. Her son, John (Johnny), married Bridget (Bride) Healey. He died in 1997 at the age of seventy-five. Pad and Liz's only daughter, Ellen, married her childhood sweetheart, Maurice Whiffen. They spent their lives in Fox Harbour, and were known and adored by many for walking countless miles every day, holding hands. Maurice died in 2007. He was eighty-

was eighty-seven. Ellen was the last living person interviewed for the *Annie Healy* story.

Liz Bruce's brothers, Benjamin and Michael Sampson, who disappeared in December 1899, were "lost in woods and never found," according to their death records. In the early 1980s, on his deathbed in the United States, a ninety-nine-year-old man, a first cousin of the missing brothers, confessed to murdering the boys for tampering with his rabbit slips. He said he buried them in the bog. He was fifteen at the time. Their bodies were never found.

Following the loss of her husband, Jack, Eliza (Lize) Foley lived in poverty beyond what they'd ever experienced. Lize never again saw her daughters, Jane, Margaret, and Helen, who lived in the United States. She died in 1944 at the age of seventy-four.

Their daughter, Laura, never returned to Grand Falls, staying at home after the loss of her father. In 1928 she married the schoolteacher, Jimmy Houlihan.

Recognizing the desperate need for professional navigational skills at sea, Houlihan studied navigation in St. John's during the summers and taught it for several years in Placentia Bay. Laura and Jim had their share of misfortune, too, having twenty children and losing twelve of them—some stillborn, others at birth or soon after, some who lived to be children, and one teenager. At this time of writing, their remaining eight children are living. Jim and Laura remained in Fox Harbour until 1966 when they moved to Placentia. She died in 1981 at the age of seventy-one. Broken-hearted, he died a year later. He was seventy-two.

Angela Foley, married to Frank Murray, remained in Fox Harbour until her death in 1989. She was eighty-nine.

Bernadette Foley married Frank's brother, Phil Murray, and remained in Fox Harbour until her death in 2004. She was eighty-seven.

Little is known about Walter (Watt) Sinnott after the tragedy. He is buried at the cemetery in Fox Harbour, where a few residents still care for his gravesite.

In 1928, a year after the loss of the *Annie Healy*, Mike and Jim Healy built a schooner, their last, and named her the *Henry H*. When the United States Naval Base began at Argentia in 1941, the Healys sold the schooner to an American serviceman and went to work on the base themselves.

Jim Healy died in 1942 at the age of seventy. Mike is buried in an unmarked grave next to Jim's, his death date unknown. Henry Healy moved to St. John's after Mike's death. He died an old man, and is buried in St. John's.

Anne Healy Furlong's sister, Mary (Minnie) Davis, died in 1965. She was eighty-eight.

Anne Healy and Edward Furlong had nine children. Throughout the years, Anne retold the tale of the *Annie Healy* to her children, who, in turn, told their children, making sure they'd never forget the sacrifice of these iron men in their wooden boats. She died on January 1, 1965, at the age of eighty-six.

Thomas Furlong, Edward and Anne's first child, kept over 600 coded postcards from his parents' early romance and compiled a book called *Sweet Nothings: Anne Healy's Postcards*, published in 1982.

The Furlong children are gone now, except Mary (Fantina), who lives in New Jersey. At this time of writing, she is ninety-two.

Mike Murphy, the last person on board the *Annie Healy* before the storm struck, was twenty-two years old at the time. He and the rest of his fellow sharemen made it safely to port at St. Bride's in their schooner. Mike died in 1999 at the age of ninety-four and a half.

The 1927 August Gale remains the worst storm on record in Canadian history.

No trace of the schooner *Annie Healy* or bodies of her crew was ever found.

ACKNOWLEDGEMENTS

If it were not for the co-operation, memories, and kindness of the following people, this story may never have seen the light of day. I carry the memories of our brief but unforgettable relationships in my heart and soul, and I hope your stories contained here within this book bring some form of closure where necessary.

Thanks go to: Bernadette Murray; Beth Maher; Nellie Barnett; Arthur Sampson; Maude (Sampson) Kelly; Maurice and Ellen Whiffen; William Murray (Billy Penny); Captain John Russell; Leo Murray; Anne King; Gerald Healey; Theresa Healey; Mary Benton; Helen Springham; Louise Butner; Becky Murray; Peggy Kromholtz; Annmarie Naimo; Eneida and Bill Valenti; Mike Kelly; Mary Murray Hawco; Susan Mandville; Bernie O'Reilly; Betty Howard; Shirley Duke; Jack Houlihan; Jim Houlihan; Joe McCue; Mary McCue; Mame Culletin; Frances Duke; Jimmy King; The Jim Spurveys; Mary P. F. Healy; Joan (Healy) Halley; The Centre for Newfoundland Studies; Tom Furlong; Wallace Furlong; Memorial University of Newfoundland's Maritime History Archive; the *Daily News*; the *Evening Telegram*; Joann Fantina; Mary Fantina; Bob Hyslop; Peter Murphy; Harry Murphy; Maggie Burns Widell; and Dorothy Sparrow.

Special thanks to Cynthia Howard of CH Permissions, Halifax, for the eighteen months she spent editing, as well as for encouraging me to do the best I can to represent the memories of my interviewees without compromise.

More special thanks to Tracey Duke for executing multiple interviews at Fox Harbour while I was living in the Middle East. It was there, in 2006, driven by her interest and encouragement for me to get this story on paper, that I began the actual putting together of what is now this book.

I would especially like to thank the staff of Flanker Press for believing in my work and for the tremendous opportunities to ensure this story reaches as many readers as possible. Many more thanks to Paul Butler for his amazing skills and insight as an editor on this book.

The Annie Healy

Composed and Arranged by
Darrell Duke

Verse

Rich - ard ___ K. Healy ___ in the year Nine - teen Hun - dred ___ Built a

fish - ing ___ ship that would soon meet its ___ fate ___ He

Christ - ened ___ her Ann - ie ___ for his daugh - ter at home ___ He

should have ___ left that wood a - lone ___

A fine schoo - ner ___ was she fif - ty

five feet in lenght And thir - ty ___ seven tons could she

- car - ry ___ Six men did - n't know when they

set sail ___ that morn They'd nev - er - a - gain see ___ the wo - men ___ they

mar - ried ___

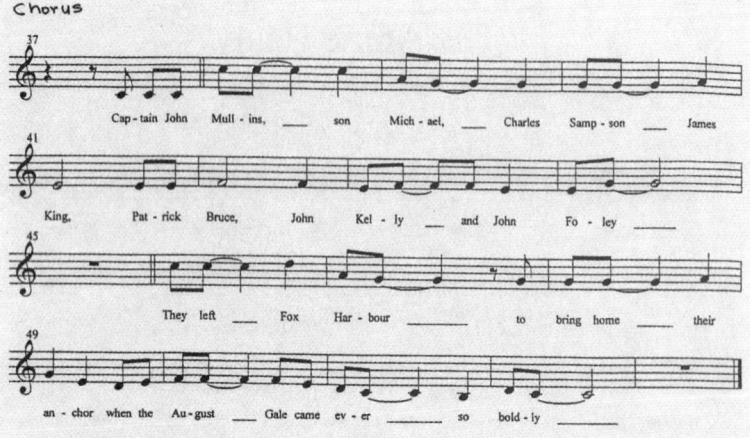

Cap-tain John Mull-ins, ___ son Mich-ael, ___ Charles Samp-son ___ James

King, Pat-rick Bruce, John Kel-ly ___ and John Fo-ley _____

They left ___ Fox Har-bour _____ to bring home ___ their

an-chor when the Au-gust ___ Gale came ev-er _____ so bold-ly _____

Year 1926, reconstructed was Annie
In an overhaul during the winter
When the summer came to be, she was ate by the sea
and found, was not even a splinter
CHORUS
She was last seen out off of Argentia
about two miles from the Isaacs, I believe
I can't imagine the fear in young Michael's eyes
when his father was drowned by the sea

She became known to be the best fishing vessel
in all of Placentia Bay
Three long days had passed with no sign of their masts
Great grandmother called out to say

Second Chorus

They're not coming home now, my poor heart is broken
for poor Michael - he's only seventeen
Your father is gone now, what will we do?
Annie Healy I want to lie down with you

The 25th of the eighth month, 19 and 27
was the year Great grandfather died
Well, I never knew him, but I feel a great sadness
when I think of how his children must've cried

So we say a long prayer for six men and a boy
and hope that they're all safe in heaven
The waters of the bay have been kind to few
Annie Healy I want to lie down with you

*Repeat second chorus

Darrell Duke is an author, singer, songwriter, performer, and photographer from Freshwater, Placentia Bay, Newfoundland. He lives in Clarenville with his wife, Lori, and daughters, Emma and Jessie. *Thursday's Storm* is Darrell's third book. His second book, *When We Worked Hard: Tickle Cove, Newfoundland*, has been in the Newfoundland and Labrador school system since 2008. Darrell is currently completing his next album, which contains his song, "The Annie Healy," and he is also writing his fourth book, a novel set primarily in Ireland in 1778 depicting his fourth great-grandfather's plight and subsequent journey to Newfoundland.